Books by Stuart Woods

SANTA FE RULES

STUART WOODS

HARPER

An Imprint of HarperCollinsPublishers

This is a work of fiction. Names, characters, places, and incidents are drawn from the author's imagination or are used fictitiously and are not to be construed as real. Any resemblance to actual events, locales, organizations, or persons, living or dead, is entirely coincidental.

HARPER

An Imprint of HarperCollins*Publishers*
10 East 53rd Street
New York, New York 10022-5299

Copyright © 1992 by Stuart Woods
ISBN 978-0-06-171163-3

First Harper Premium paperback printing: January 2009
First HarperTorch paperback printing: April 2003
First HarperPaperbacks printing: June 1993
First HarperCollins hardcover printing: June 1992

Printed in the United States of America

Visit Harper paperbacks on the World Wide Web at www.harpercollins.com

10 9 8 7 6 5 4 3 2 1

This book is for Chris Connor

SANTA FE RULES

1

Wolf Willett remembered too late that Flaps had always had a cold nose. Now it found the back of his neck, and with a girlish shriek, Wolf sat bolt upright in bed and regarded her with bleary eyes. There was only a faint glow of daylight from outside.

"Got me again, didn't you?" he said to her.

Flaps grinned. This grin had always been one of her great charms, and it did not fail to do its work now.

Wolf melted. "Time to get up, huh?"

Flaps laid her head in his lap and grinned again, looking up at him with big brown eyes.

"Right now?" he asked, teasing her.

Right now, she replied, thumping her tail against the bed for emphasis.

"All right, all right." He moaned and swung his legs over the side of the bed.

Flaps celebrated her triumph with a little golden retriever dance, throwing in a couple of squeals of happiness.

"Okay," Wolf said, standing up, "but me first." He headed for the bathroom, but somehow one leg seemed shorter than the other; he missed the bathroom door and bumped into the wall. "Whoof," he said to Flaps. "What did I have to drink last night?" He shook his head and stretched his eyes wide open, but the dizziness, not an unpleasant sensation, remained. He groped his way into the bathroom, using the walls for support, and peed, holding on to the toilet with one hand.

Flaps rewarded him with a little kiss on the ass.

"Jesus!" he screamed, jumping away and grabbing the sink for support. "You really know how to wake a guy up, don't you?"

Flaps grinned and did her little dance.

"Just a minute, all right?" He splashed some water on his face, brushed his teeth too quickly, and tossed down a couple of vitamin C's with a glass of very cold water from the tap. He grabbed a bathrobe from the hook on the door and headed back to the bedroom in search of slippers. He was navigating better now, but as he proceeded out of the bedroom and across the living room he found himself moving slightly sideways, crablike, in order to maintain his course. Light was creeping across the valley below the house, across the suburbs of Santa Fe, but the interior of the house was still dimly lit, and in the kitchen he turned on the lights, squinting against the glare.

Flaps waited impatiently for him to get coffee started, then watched, rapt, as he poured her a dish of dry dog food. She ate daintily, as befitted her gender, while he got an English muffin into the toaster and rounded up butter and jam. He drank directly from a plastic container of fresh orange juice and returned it to the refrigerator, sighing as the sweet juice made its way down.

"Want to go out now?" he asked her.

To his surprise, she trotted across the room and scratched on the door that led to the guest wing of the house.

"That's not the back door, dummy," he railed at her, shaking his head. "It's this way, remember? The way you've gone out every day of your life?"

She scratched on the guest wing door again.

Wolf kept that part of the house closed and unheated until a guest arrived. "I think you must be as hung over as I am this morning." He slapped his thigh and whistled softly.

Reluctantly, Flaps followed him to the outside kitchen door and, when he opened it, bounded outside.

Wolf left her to roam the hillside, sniffing for coyote markings among the piñons, and returned to his breakfast. He ate slowly and with a nearly blank mind. He did not think of the night before, did not try to remember what he drank, did not think of anything much until he remembered that he had to go to Los Angeles this morning. He looked at the clock on the microwave: just after seven. He calculated the time to the airport, time for the trip, time for the ride to the office. He'd be in L.A. by eleven; time for a sandwich at his desk before his meeting at two. It was Tuesday; he'd get six or seven hours of work in with the editor today and a full day tomorrow, then on Thursday he and Julia would have Thanksgiving dinner with their friends the Carmichaels.

Flaps, her ablutions completed and her survey of the property concluded, scratched on the back door.

He let her in, and she went straight to her cedar-shavings bed and settled in for her morning nap; she was as much a creature of habit as he.

Wolf shaved in the shower, using the mist-free mirror, then toweled himself dry and used the hair blower on his thick, graying hair. He still felt a light buzz, felt oddly free of worry; they were approaching completion of the new film, and he was usually nervous as hell at this point in a production, but today he couldn't think of anything to worry about. He was on automatic pilot as he dressed, doing the things he did every day. He slipped into freshly starched jeans and into the soft elkskin cowboy boots that added an inch and a half to his five-foot-nine-inch frame. He was the same height as Paul Newman, he told himself automatically, as he did every morning of his life, and, he reminded himself, the same age as Robert Redford. He wondered for a moment whether he would rather be the same height as Redford and the same age as Newman. It was a close call.

He slipped into a silk shirt and a cashmere sweater and, on his way back to the kitchen, retrieved a sheepskin coat from the hall closet. It would be a chilly morning, but he would shed both the outer garments before arriving in L.A. He took along a light blazer for the city.

As he came back into the kitchen, Flaps hopped out of her bed and went again to scratch on the guest wing door.

"What could you possibly want in there?" he demanded, and got a grin for an answer. "Listen, you," he said, shaking a finger at her, "I'm leaving Maria a note telling her you've already been fed, so don't try and get another breakfast out of her, you hear?"

Flaps looked suitably guilty, but she knew very well she'd be fed again by the housekeeper, who melted at the sight of her.

"Be good," he called out to her as he left by the kitchen door, "and don't eat the mailman." If an intruder ever actually got into the house, Wolf knew her plan would be to kiss him to death.

He opened the garage door, tossed the blazer onto the passenger seat of the Porsche Cabriolet, then eased into the car. It was like climbing into a deep freeze. He started the engine, and as he let it warm up, he thought of going back into the house and seeing what the dog wanted in the guest wing; it was unusual for her to display an interest in that part of the house when there were no guests on board. *Oh, the hell with it*, he thought. He backed out and started down the driveway, taking it slowly, since there was still snow there from the last bit of weather they'd had. The four-wheel drive of the car kept it nicely in the ruts of the driveway, and the main road out of Wilderness Gate had been plowed days before. He passed through the gate of the subdivision and headed down into the town.

There was little traffic at this hour of the morning, and Santa Fe looked beautiful with the low sunlight on the adobe houses and shops. Everything was adobe in Santa Fe—or, at least, stucco painted to look like adobe—and it reminded him a little of an English village in which all the houses were built of the same stone. The common building material gave the little city a certain visual harmony.

Wolf always felt grateful that he had chosen Santa Fe as a second home instead of Aspen or one of the other movie-colony favorites. It was harder to get to from L.A., but that kept out the riffraff, and anyway, he had his own airplane to get him there and back faster than the airlines could. Never mind that Julia didn't like the single-engine airplane and usually insisted on taking the airlines, when she couldn't hop a ride on somebody's jet; he liked flying alone. Today he would think about *L.A. Days*, the latest Wolf Willett production, written and directed, as usual, by Jack Tinney. The film wasn't right yet, and, since shooting had ended and the sets had been struck, it was going to have to be fixed in the editing, as it nearly always was with Jack's films.

As he drove, he used the car's telephone to get a weather forecast from F.A.A. Flight Services and to file an instrument flight plan from Santa Fe to Santa Monica Airport. He always flew on instrument flight plans, even in clear weather; it was like being led by the hand, especially when arriving in L.A. airspace, which was always smoggy and crowded. Santa Fe airport was virtually deserted at this hour of the morning. He drove along the ramp to his T-hangar, opened it, parked the Porsche behind the airplane, and pulled the airplane out of the hangar with a tow bar, then locked up. Normally, during business hours, he would simply call ahead and Capitol Aviation, the F.B.O. (fixed base operator—a name left over from flying's barnstorming days), would bring up the airplane for him, but today he was too early for them. Anyway, he liked the idea of the Porsche being locked in the hangar instead of being left in the airport parking lot for days on end.

The airplane was a Beechcraft Bonanza B-36TC—a six-passenger, single-engine retractable with a 300-horsepower turbocharged engine. He'd owned it for three years and had nearly six hundred hours as pilot in command. It would do two hundred knots at twenty-five thousand feet, and Wolf wore the aircraft like a glove. He gave it a quick but thorough preflight inspection, checked the fuel for water or dirt, then climbed aboard and started the engine, working his way through a printed checklist. Noting the wind direction, he taxied to runway 33, then did a run-up, checking the operation of the magnetos. He checked the sky for other aircraft that might be landing and, finding none, announced his intentions over the Common Traffic Advisory Frequency. He lined up on the runway, did a final check of everything, then took off, turning west when he reached five hundred feet.

Once airborne, he called Albuquerque Center

on the radio and received his clearance. He was cleared as filed—direct Grand Canyon, direct Santa Monica, though he knew that when he approached L.A. airspace, they'd vector him all over the place in order to sequence traffic for Santa Monica and keep it clear of LAX—Los Angeles International—the big, busy airport just next to Santa Monica. He tuned Grand Canyon Airport into the Loran navigator, set the required course, and relaxed. Then he remembered that he'd forgotten to pick up a *New York Times* from a machine on the way, and he had nothing to read aboard.

When the airplane reached its assigned altitude of twelve thousand feet and was automatically leveled off by its autopilot, he leaned the fuel mixture, ran through the cruise checklist, then relaxed, forgetting his resolution to concentrate on *L.A. Days*. Instead he switched on the CD player and punched in a Harry Connick, Jr., album. He enjoyed the singer/piano player; the young man played the music he'd always liked best—the prerock, musical theater numbers that Wolf felt were the best American music ever written—none of the electronic noise that passed for music these days. He hummed along with "It Had to Be You" and let his mind drift. He was still curiously unable—or unwilling—to recall the past evening.

The song reminded him of his childhood; it was one of the first things his mother had taught him to play on the piano. He had been born in the small Georgia town of Delano, to a music-mad piano teacher and a soldier from nearby Fort Benning. She had named him after her favorite composer: his birth certificate read Wolfgang Amadeus Mozart Willett, a name which would subject him to years of the torture of schoolmates and the amusement of others. This began to abate when he captained the high school tennis team, and because he hit the ball so hard for a smallish fellow, he earned the nickname Wham, which was almost his initials. His mother called him Wolfie (Wolfgang when she was angry with him), but when he entered the university, he was able to shorten it to Wolf, and that had stuck through law school and military service.

He'd received a Naval R.O.T.C. commission and been sent to flight school, where he'd earned his wings. Then he'd stupidly allowed himself to be hit hard in the left eye with a tennis ball during a base championship match, and the resulting injury had washed him out of flying before he'd ever had a chance to land an aircraft on a carrier. A contact lens in that eye corrected his vision, but that wasn't good enough for Navy flying.

He'd been transferred to administrative duties, and his first job, for which he had been totally unqualified, was to make a film about carrier operations for his unit. This allowed him to stay with his flight school class as they trained in the Pacific, and it had introduced him to the only man aboard the ship who knew how to operate a movie camera, one Jackson Tinney, a skinny, Tennessee-born good ol' boy who was, unaccountably, a wizard with a 16mm Arriflex.

Together, the young ensign and the even younger able seaman had put together a cinema verité account of life aboard an aircraft carrier that was still shown to Navy pilots; it had been put into general release and had won an Academy Award nomination for best short subject.

When the documentary had been completed, Jack had been transferred to a shoreside film unit and Wolf to other administrative duties aboard ship. It would be years before they saw each other again.

After being discharged from the Navy, Wolf, who had learned to love California while briefly stationed in San Diego, traveled to L.A. and began looking for a job in a law firm while studying for the state's bar examination. No L.A. law firm displayed much interest in a University of Georgia Law School graduate who had not risen to the top of his class, but Wolf had been invited by an old Navy buddy to play tennis at a Jewish country club, and there he had met and begun playing twice a week with a top agent and senior vice president of the William Morris Agency. Shortly, he had a job as a legal assistant at the agency and, when he had passed the bar exam, was promoted to staff lawyer.

Some years later, after Wolf had risen to head the William Morris legal department, Able Seaman Jack Tinney had appeared in his office with four cans of film under his arm. Using Navy equipment and studio space, he had shot a film of his own, and when Wolf had run it in the William Morris screening room he had thought it rough, but the funniest thing he'd seen in years.

Wolf had rented a cutting room, and together the two men had gotten it into shape. Wolf played jazz piano, and he and some musician friends, with whom he jammed once a week at a Santa Monica bar, had recorded a sound track, and after months of work they had found themselves with a completed feature film.

Wolf had then taken the biggest risk of his life. He went to his patron, the senior vice president, and resigned from his job; then he hired the man as his and Jack's agent and dragged him down to the screening room to see *Rough Water*, as they had named the film. Their new agent had loved it. Within a week, they had nailed down a distribution deal at Centurion, one of the big studios, and within a year, Wolf and Jack had each earned better than half a million dollars. The film was still making money on late-night television and video rentals.

Twenty-five years and eighteen films later, Wolf Willett and Jack Tinney were still in business together. Jack wrote and directed the movies, and Wolf, their agent having died fifteen years before, produced, negotiated contracts, and oversaw every aspect of production. They had an in-house production deal with Centurion, and Jack had long been established as the Woody Allen of the West Coast. His films never lost money and usually did quite well, though they had never been blockbusters—not so far, anyway. They were shot on tight budgets, with big-name stars who were happy to play parts for small money just to get into a Tinney film.

All this had earned Wolf a house in Bel Air, another in Santa Fe, a nice little airplane, and the assorted cars, boats, pools, and tennis courts that went with a seven-figure income. He earned, in fact, even more than he spent, and he had even managed to put away something for his old age, which wasn't as far away as it used to be.

Wolf was brought abruptly back to the present by a red light on the instrument panel before him. Red lights were not good. This one said LOW BUS VOLTAGE. He started looking at gauges. Alternator failure. He switched on the backup generator. Nothing happened. Backup generator failure. He started turning off electrical gear and consulted his chart. He'd never make it to L.A. on battery power, and he didn't want to fly in L.A. airspace without radios. Grand Canyon Airport looked good for repairs.

Wolf switched off the autopilot and began hand-flying the airplane.

2

The eastern end of the Grand Canyon was in sight when the instrument panel went dark.

"Shit!" Wolf yelled. He tried switching things on and off, but nothing worked; the battery was too low to operate anything. He had a hand-held radio somewhere in the airplane; he didn't use it often. He began rummaging through the pile of charts, manuals, and other debris behind the passenger seat, while trying to hold the airplane straight and level with his free hand. He unearthed the small radio, found the adapter wires that allowed him to plug his headset into it, turned it on, and tuned to the Grand Canyon control tower frequency.

"Grand Canyon, November one, two, three, tango foxtrot."

"Aircraft calling Grand Canyon, please say again. Your transmission is weak."

Shit again; his hand-held's batteries were nearly dead, too.

"Grand Canyon," he said, enunciating carefully,

"November one, two, three, tango foxtrot. I am a Bonanza B-36, estimate fifteen miles east of the airport. I have electrical failure and am using a hand-held radio."

"Roger, November one, two, three, tango foxtrot; runway two-six is active; wind is two-seven-zero at eight. You're number two behind a Grand Canyon Airways twin now on final."

"Tango foxtrot." He rested the small radio on top of the instrument panel. What now? Get the landing gear down. He hoped to hell there was enough battery power left for that. He pulled out the gear lever and pushed it down. The red IN TRANSIT light came on and drag on the airplane was noticeably increased. Was it down? Two miles out he called in again. "Grand Canyon, I will fly down the runway at one hundred feet. Please tell me if my gear is locked down."

"Roger, tango foxtrot."

Wolf tried the flaps; they didn't work, either. He reduced power slowly and got the airplane down to 120 knots for his low pass down the runway.

"Tango foxtrot, Grand Canyon. Your landing gear appears to be partly down, but not locked. What are your intentions?"

"Goddamn it!" Wolf screamed, but not on the radio. "Grand Canyon, I'll try to crank it down." He had never done this before, although he had been trained to do it. The hand crank was behind the passenger seat where all his junk was. He began throwing stuff indiscriminately into the backseat. Finally the small crank was exposed. He began cranking. How many turns? Seemed he had been told fifty. On the twentieth turn, the gear-down lights came on: all three wheels down and locked. Wolf heaved a sigh of relief; he was sweating heavily from the tension and the effort of cranking the gear down. "Grand Canyon, gear down and locked," he said into the radio.

"One, two, three, tango foxtrot, cleared to land, runway two-six."

With no flaps to slow him, Wolf had to make a fast approach, but there was plenty of runway length, and he got the airplane down smoothly. He cleared the runway and taxied to the maintenance hangar.

"Well," said the shop foreman, wiping his brow, "you got a dead alternator there, all right. Dead standby, too. I haven't got either in my stock."

"How soon can you get replacements?"

"Day after tomorrow," the man replied.

"Can't you call the manufacturer and get the parts overnighted in?"

"Tomorrow's Thanksgiving," the foreman said. "I'll call today, but Fed Ex won't deliver till Friday."

"This is Tuesday," Wolf said, relieved that the man had got his days wrong. "Thanksgiving isn't until day after tomorrow. You can have the parts here tomorrow, and I can be on my way."

The foreman turned to the mechanic waiting beside the airplane. "What's today, Charley?"

"Wednesday," the man replied.

"Thanksgiving's tomorrow," the foreman said to Wolf.

"No, no . . ." Wolf looked at the day and date displayed on his wristwatch. "It's . . ." He stopped and stared at his wristwatch. "That can't be," he said, shaking his head.

"Sure can, Mr. Willett. It's Wednesday, and tomorrow's Thanksgiving. I can have the parts here by ten-thirty Friday morning, and we'll have 'em installed by early afternoon."

Wolf rubbed his forehead. Something was terribly wrong here. "Okay, where can I get a room?"

"Try the lodge. Rent yourself a car at the terminal over there, and follow the signs. It's real nice, and they won't be full this time of year."

The lodge, a huge place, had a room for him. He explained why he didn't have any luggage, and a bellhop took him upstairs. He immediately called the Bel Air house and got a recording of his own voice. He hung up. Julia could never remember to play the messages on the machine anyway, so leaving a message would be a waste of time. He didn't have his address book with him, and the Carmichaels' number was unlisted. He telephoned his office, but got a recording saying that it was closed until Monday for the Thanksgiving holiday. He didn't remember giving everybody Wednesday, but when he hadn't shown up for work yesterday, Jack had probably given them the day off; Jack was too softhearted.

He hung up the phone and walked to the window. He had a fine view of the canyon, and it was truly grand, but he hardly noticed. Try as he might, he could not remember the past twenty-four hours. He remembered going to bed, but that must have been on Monday. He picked up the Tucson newspaper that came with the room and checked the date to be sure. Wednesday.

He had lost a day out of his life. And it wasn't the first time.

Wolf woke up the next morning feeling horny and reached for Julia. She was not there, of course; she was in L.A. At least he thought she was. He had rung the Bel Air house a dozen times and gotten only his own recording. He had rung Jack's house, too, and gotten no answer.

He and Julia had been married a year. It was a second marriage for him—he had been widowed for more than twenty years—but the first for her. She was twenty-six at the time, and an actress. Two kinds of women he'd promised himself he'd never marry—a woman in the business and somebody half his age. It had gone well, though, had exceeded his expectations. Julia was wonderful company, and she had revived his nearly dormant sex life. She made him feel eighteen again, and he would always love her for that. God knew, she was too friendly with other men, and she was making a career out of shopping, which drove him nuts, but she was beautiful and shrewd, two qualities that had always appealed to him. She would probably leave him on his sixty-fifth birthday, but if she lasted that long, it would be worth it.

He reached for his wristwatch: nearly noon. He never slept that late—what was the matter with him? He stood in the shower long enough to wake him, but when he got out, he still felt fuzzy around the edges. He shaved with the razor the hotel had lent him and got dressed, squirming in the damp underwear and socks that he had rinsed out the night before. There was still no answer at the Bel Air house.

Downstairs, he asked for a *New York Times*.

"Sorry, sir," the young thing at the desk said, "we don't get any papers at all on holidays. Will you be having Thanksgiving dinner with us?"

It was that or McDonald's in the village, he thought. "Yes, of course."

He ate hungrily, having slept through breakfast; he drank nearly a bottle of wine with lunch, feeling sorry for himself for being alone on Thanksgiving, then had a long after-lunch nap in his room. Later, he forced himself to go for a walk along the rim of the canyon, but he had seen it many times before, and it wasn't working its charm today; he was too depressed. Here he was on his favorite holiday, far from wife and friends, stuck with no way out until the new parts arrived tomorrow.

He went back to the hotel, bought a paperback novel in the shop, and tried to read it. He was asleep again by nine.

He was wakened in broad daylight by the sound of something sliding under his door. He raised a sleepy head: a *New York Times!* At least he could start the day with the news. He glanced at his watch: noon. He ordered breakfast from room service, then retrieved the newspaper, scanning the front page. He was about to open the paper and look inside when a small article in the lower right-hand corner of the front page caught his eye:

FILM DIRECTOR AND TWO OTHERS
IN TRIPLE DEATH

Oh, God, he thought, *it's going to be somebody I know.* He read on quickly. It was somebody he knew.

The film director Jack Tinney of Los Angeles has been found dead in circumstances that police sources are describing as murder.

Wolf dropped the newspaper and put his head in his hands. He took deep breaths, trying to get hold of himself. He tried not to believe it, and he tried not to think of the consequences. He picked up the paper again, read the same sentence twice, then looked at the masthead. It was truly the *New York Times*, it was not a joke newspaper; this was not some horrible gag somebody was pulling on him; this was really happening. He swallowed hard, tried to quiet the pounding in his chest, and read on. What came next nearly stopped his heart.

Tinney, 48, was found in a guest bedroom of a house in Santa Fe, New Mexico, belonging to his

longtime business partner and producer, Wolf Willett. He appeared to have been killed by a shotgun
blast.

He immediately thought of Flaps and how she
had wanted to get into the guest wing. But Jack
hadn't even been in Santa Fe, he thought desperately. He read on.

Also found in the room were the bodies of Willett, 53, and his wife Julia Camden Willett, 27, an
actress. They appeared to have been killed in the
same manner.

This got him breathing hard. He read the words
again. They still didn't make any sense. He continued.

The bodies were discovered by a housekeeper,
Maria Estavez, who had been alerted to their presence by a dog in the house. The apparent murder
weapon, an expensive twelve-gauge shotgun made
by Purdey, the famous gunmakers of London, En-
gland, was found in the room. The Santa Fe Police
Department has issued a statement saying that the
murders were committed sometime Tuesday evening and that so far they have no suspects. Obituaries on page B14.

Wolf fell back onto the bed, his head reeling.
He closed his eyes and clutched the covers, trying
to lie as still as possible, fighting nausea. Gradu-

ally he restored his breathing to something like normal. Then he tried to think.

He could come up only with this: His wife and business partner and some other unfortunate human being were dead; they had been killed in his house with his shotgun, one of a matched pair; they had been killed at a time when he was obviously present in the house. And he could remember nothing of that day or night.

It wasn't much, but it was enough to scare the shit out of him.

3

Wolf resisted the impulse to immediately bolt from the hotel, primarily because he had no place to go. He drove to the airport and paid his repair bill, then returned to the hotel and spent the afternoon fighting an overwhelming feeling of guilt—for what, he was not quite sure. By the time it got dark and dinner had arrived from room service, the guilt had become localized. He must have been responsible for what had happened. He tried to dredge up his reasons.

He had been drunk, of course—else, why would he not remember? Or were his deeds on that lost day so terrible that his mind simply could not cope with them? Sex was at the root of this, of that he was sure. Since meeting Julia he had lived with the fear that he could not satisfy her, that she would turn to another man to supplement or—God help him—replace his attentions. She had always been insatiable, but she had always had the talent of keeping him aroused. He had been keeping up with her, but just barely, and he had lived in fear of what might happen if she nudged him some night in bed and he wasn't up to it.

More disturbing of late was that Julia had begun to evince an interest in more than one sex partner. This had frightened him when she had first broached the subject, then excited him when he had realized that her interest was in having another woman in bed, a longtime fantasy of his. Twice, both times in Santa Fe, Julia had successfully propositioned another woman. They had been nights to remember. Even now, recalling it, he found himself stimulated. Both women had satisfied him beyond his fantasies, then had turned to each other, and he had been held rapt by that sight. Then he had suspected that all this was a prelude to inviting another man into their bed.

This thought seemed to point to what might have happened: He got drunk, Julia took Jack and another man to bed; he had caught them and, in a drunken fit of jealousy, used the shotgun on them. As he thought about this scenario, he realized that he had to find out exactly what had happened. First, he had to see the room where the three had died; then he had to find a way to penetrate the shield of his own memory. He had an idea of how to do that.

He waited until after dinner before leaving the hotel. Santa Fe Airport closed at ten P.M., and after that it became a ghost of a landing field. He knew, because once he had landed at a quarter past ten, his car battery had been dead, and he had nearly frozen before he had found a telephone and gotten some assistance.

It was just after nine when he took off from Grand Canyon and headed east; this would put him at Santa Fe around ten forty-five. He had filed no flight plan, and he climbed to eleven thousand five hundred feet before leveling off; this altitude would give him some westerly tail wind without requiring oxygen. He sat immobile in the airplane for nearly an hour, numb with grief, guilt, and fear. Then his eye caught something in the *New York Times* on the seat beside him: "Obituaries on page B14." His curiosity got the better of him.

There were only three obituaries on the page: his, Julia's, and Jack's. Jack's occupied the whole of the page above the fold. There was a detailed analysis of his career, his childhood in Tennessee, his four marriages, his many women, and anything else that could be found out about him by a shrewd newspaperman. It was obvious that the piece had been written well in advance.

Such care was not present in Wolf's obit. There was a brief, fairly accurate summary of his life before the William Morris Agency, then this statement:

> Wolf Willett's subsequent career was so wrapped up in Jack Tinney's as to be nearly invisible. Certainly, he devoted himself to relieving Tinney of the minutiae surrounding any filmmaker, allowing the director the time to polish his scripts and perfect his editing. Indeed, that may have been

Wolf Willett's chief, and perhaps only, contribution to American film.

"Jesus fucking Christ!" he yelled into the roar of the airplane's engine. Was that what the world thought he did? Relieve Jack Tinney of "the minutiae surrounding any filmmaker"? Did not the *New York Times*, in its artistic wisdom, know that he had browbeaten and cajoled Jack, who hated to write, into writing—then had edited, cut, compressed, and rewritten his scripts until they squeaked of economy and wit; that Jack had hardly ever entered an editing room? That he knew next to nothing about music and scoring and recording? That Wolf had paid his bills, negotiated his divorce settlements, forced him to file tax returns, cosigned his borrowings, invested his meager (and enforced) savings, paid off the paternity plaintiffs, and sobered him up a couple of times a year after Jack's monumental binges? And after that, because it worked better in the trades and newspapers and the Academy, allowed Jack to take home the credit and the Oscars? Jesus fucking Christ!

But if Jack's obituary had infuriated him, Julia's shook him to his core. It was not as brief as his own.

The woman who called herself Julia Camden before she married Wolf Willett was born Miriam Schlemmer, daughter of a German-Jewish pawnbroker, Solomon Schlemmer, in Cleveland, Ohio, some seven years before her claimed birth date. During her high school years, she was arrested on numerous occasions, usually for shoplifting or joyriding in stolen cars with boyfriends. After moving to New York in the late 1970s, she served two brief terms in the Women's Detention Center on Riker's Island for prostitution, extortion, and trafficking in cocaine. In 1985, she turned up in Los Angeles with her new name and an apparently faked resume as an actress in off-Broadway productions and soon found work in the film business, at least once in a pornographic movie. It was when she appeared in Jack Tinney's film *Broken Charms*—ironically, playing a streetwalker—that she met the man who would become her third husband. Previously, she had been married to a New York taxi driver who dabbled in procurement of women and drugs and to a man described by police as a minor Harlem drug kingpin.

In her new existence as Mrs. Wolf Willett, she became active in film charities, and in Santa Fe became a follower of psychiatrist and "wholistic psychotherapist" Mark Shea, who had previously been arrested in New York for practicing medicine without a license.

Mrs. Willett is survived by a younger sister who is serving a five- to eight-year sentence for the involuntary manslaughter of her husband, a diamond dealer in the New York jewelry district whom she had attempted, with an accomplice, to rob.

It was a good thing the Bonanza had a working autopilot, because for some minutes Wolf was incapable of flying the airplane.

4

Wolf found Santa Fe Airport as deserted as he had hoped. He taxied past Capitol Aviation down to the T-hangars, put away the airplane, drove the Porsche out of the hangar, and locked up.

He took Rodeo Road and Old Pecos Trail, avoiding as much of the downtown as possible, and it was just past eleven when he reached the entrance to Wilderness Gate. The subdivision was on the outskirts of the city, in the low mountains to the south. The area was zoned for lots of a minimum of five acres, and the houses built there were expensive. Three years earlier, Wolf had bought a mountainside lot so steep that his building costs had run an additional twenty percent just to hang the house on it. The drive came in from a point nearly level with the house and made a complete circle around it.

He drove past the drive, looking for any sign of life—a police car, maybe—then turned around and came back. He stopped at the entrance to the short drive and looked at the house. It hung there, its angular shape standing out in the moonlight against large areas of pristine snow. No light was showing. When he rolled down the window and listened, no sound came from the house, only the yip and howl of a coyote somewhere up the mountain.

Wolf slowly accelerated, then switched off the engine and let the car coast down the slight incline to the small, concealed service parking area behind the house. He left the car where it stopped of its own accord, taking a flashlight from the glove compartment. He did not use the light yet.

He was surprised to learn that a hook had been driven into the jamb of the kitchen door, a wire run from it through the door handle, then fastened with a lead seal. A sign was posted on the door, which he could just read in the moonlight:

CRIME SCENE. NO ENTRY WITHOUT PERMISSION OF THE DISTRICT ATTORNEY OF SANTA FE COUNTY.

No doubt the front door would be similarly posted and fastened. He was sealed out of his own house. Well, nearly, anyway. He fumbled along the wall on the dark side of the house and came to a window. Thank God Maria, the housekeeper, was always concerned about getting enough fresh air; the window was open a good four inches. That explained a lot about his recent heating bills, but he silently thanked her.

Wolf hoped to God the police had not left a guard. He pushed up the window and climbed silently through into the utility room, catching a whiff of laundry detergent and starch.

He switched on the little flashlight and found his way into the kitchen, half expecting to be met by Flaps. But the dog was gone. Wolf hoped someone was taking care of her, being charmed by her grins.

He turned now, reluctantly, to the guest wing. There was another seal affixed to the door. *The hell with it*, he thought, turning the doorknob. He opened the door as far as the wire would allow, then pushed his shoulder firmly against it; the wire snapped. He stopped, holding his breath. Why did he feel the need to be quiet?

He moved down the hallway, looking into doors. There were four guest rooms, and they had often been filled. On the door of the last, at the end of the broad hallway, was another seal. He paused. Did he really want to see this? He really did. He performed his seal-breaking maneuver once more, then fearfully switched on his flashlight.

The king-size bed was a horrible mess, soaked with blood, which had turned black. The headboard and the wall behind it were spattered, and there were the effects of three shotgun blasts—two in the headboard and one in the wall above it. One of the victims had apparently stood up on the bed when confronted with death. Until that moment, they had been in bed together. There was blood on the Navajo rug, too, and he remembered that he had paid $25,000 for it. The rest of the room was orderly, untouched, except for splotches of a black powder here and there. He turned the flashlight on his hands. Powder there, too. They must have been looking for fingerprints.

He had had enough of this. He left the room, closing the door behind him, and let himself out of the guest wing. He walked silently down the hall, then through the living room and into the master bedroom.

His room was neat; Maria had obviously done some of the cleaning before discovering the gory contents of the guest wing. He sat on the bed and thought for a minute. He longed to climb between the freshly starched linen sheets and go to sleep, but he could not let himself spend a night in this house. Who knew who might arrive in the morning? He had seen what he had come for . . . but there was something else. What was it?

Clothes. Of course. He went into his dressing room, closed the door, and turned on the light in the windowless room. He changed his clothes, dropping the dirty things into a hamper, then chose a large leather zippered bag from the matched set of Italian luggage and began putting things into it, including his travel toilet kit. When he had enough for a week, he switched off the light and went back into the bedroom. What else did he need? His laptop computer, maybe? He wouldn't be getting any work done for a while. Money: He would need that.

He left the bedroom, carrying his bag, started toward his study, then stopped. There had been a noise: papers being shuffled. More noise, then a light came on in the study. Wolf felt the thrill of fear associated with disturbing a burglar, only this could be anybody—policeman or thief.

Wolf moved as quietly as he possibly could until he was at the wall between the living room and the study. Consumed with curiosity, he overcame his fear and inched along the wall until he was at the door. Around the corner, not six feet away, was . . . somebody. He wanted desperately to know who. Shifting his weight, he craned his neck and sought the crack at the door hinges; as he found it, the light went off, leaving him with no night vision. Footsteps retreated; he stepped into the room, blinking. A shadow of movement at the other door, then more footsteps down the hall. He followed as quickly as he could without making a sound. Then he heard the kitchen door open and close—the intruder must have broken the seal—and then footsteps crunching on the gravel of the drive, moving toward the back of the house.

Abandoning caution, he ran to the kitchen window and looked out. No one. An engine started behind the house, on the back of the circular drive. He'd head the car off at the pass. He ran back down the hall and through the living room, and fumbled with the catch on the sliding doors to the deck, which gave him trouble; it always had. He got the door open and stepped onto the cedar deck. Far below, the carpet of Santa Fe lights winked back at him, like a mini-L.A. viewed from Mulholland Drive.

The car was just disappearing down the drive— a four-wheeler of some kind—Jeep, Bronco, who could tell? There were thousands of the breed in the city. He lost sight of it at the end of the drive, heard it turn right, then saw its dim outline and headlights as it drove purposefully toward town.

Who was the son of a bitch?

Wolf went back into the study and played his flashlight about. Nothing much disturbed; the usual mess on his desk. What could anybody want in here?

He remembered why he had headed for the study in the first place. He walked to a wall and pressed a panel, which swung out to reveal a small safe. Cursing because he could not remember the combination, he went to the file cabinet where he had taped the piece of paper, memorized the numbers again, and returned to the safe. There was a couple of thousand in cash inside—twenties, fifties, a few hundreds—and some foreign currency he kept for travel—pounds, francs—probably a couple of thousand more. He took it all, stuffing the dollars into his pockets and the foreign stuff in the bag.

There was something else in the safe, something he'd almost forgotten about. He picked up the pistol, a small 9mm German automatic, and weighed it in his hand. Should he take it? Did he need it? He stuffed it into a hip pocket of his jeans. After all, somebody had recently made an attempt on his life. Shit, somebody had recently *killed* him.

He left through the kitchen door—the seal had been broken anyway—and drove away from the house. He waited until he was at the entrance to

Wilderness Gate before switching on his headlights.

Now he headed for his next and last stop in Santa Fe. At this one, he hoped to get some answers.

5

Wolf needed advice, and he did not have to think twice about where to get it. He drove through the center of Santa Fe, went a couple of miles north on the Taos Highway, then turned left onto Tano Road. He drove west as rapidly as the dirt road would allow, dodging icy patches and gritting his teeth when mud splashed onto the Porsche. Dirt roads were thought to be chic in Santa Fe, but he had never accustomed himself to what they did to his car.

The lights of houses became more widely spaced as the land changed from five acre zoning to twelve and a half, then most of the lights disappeared. A mile farther on, he came to the gate. It was closed. Wolf pulled up to the intercom box and pressed the buzzer.

A moment later, a voice said, "Yes?"

Wolf took a deep breath. "Mark, it's Wolf."

There was a long silence.

"Mark, it's Wolf. I'm not dead, I'm at your front gate. Let me in."

Another silence, then a loud electronic beep, and the electric gate slid open. Wolf drove quickly down the long drive. The compound was set on sixty acres, a quarter of a mile from the road; the house was dark, but a light burned in the little building next door, which Mark used as an office. As Wolf drove up to the building, an outside light came on, illuminating the Porsche. He got out, and as he reached the front door, it opened.

Mark Shea stood just inside, a tall, bearlike figure, looking warily out. Then his face collapsed in astonishment. "It *is* you, for Christ's sake." He stepped forward and gathered Wolf into his arms. The two men embraced for a longer moment than usual, then Mark held him at arm's length. Tears were streaming down his face. "And I thought I was never going to see you again."

The tears didn't surprise Wolf; Mark was an emotional man, and he had always wept when moved—happy or sad. "I'm sorry you had to go through that, Mark," he said.

Mark pulled him into the room. "I expect you need a drink," he said.

"That I do," Wolf replied, looking around. The room was paneled in oak, with bookshelves, floor to ceiling, along a long wall. The furniture was leather, masculine, welcoming.

"Can I force some bourbon on you?" Mark asked, reaching for a bottle in a concealed liquor cupboard.

"You can."

Mark handed him the drink, and his hand shook; he poured one for himself. He motioned

Wolf to a chair in front of the fire, then took the one facing him. "Now," he said, "tell me what's happened."

"Christ, Mark, *I* don't know what the hell's happened. I thought *you* might."

"Of course; stupid of me. I confess, your showing up has rattled me to the core."

"I'm sorry about that, but I guess there was no way to avoid shocking you."

Mark smiled. "Nicest shock I ever had, believe me. Do you know anything at all?"

"Only what I read in the *New York Times* this morning."

Mark nodded. "Then you know the worst. About Julia and Jack, I mean." He looked into the fire, his craggy face sad. "I'm glad, at least, that I didn't have to tell you that. I'm awfully sorry, Wolf. I know how much you loved them both."

For the first time since all this had started, Wolf lost control; he sat in the big chair and sobbed.

Mark leaned forward, slapped a big hand onto Wolf's knee, and squeezed. "Go ahead, man, you need to grieve."

Gradually, Wolf got hold of himself. "Do you know anything more about this?" he asked.

Mark fell back into his chair. "I got a call from the police a little after ten Wednesday morning, asking me to come up to your place. They wouldn't tell me what was going on, just said to get up there. When I arrived, the place was crawling with Santa Fe cops, deputy sheriffs, and the state police. They had obviously been there for a while and had been through the place thoroughly. The Santa Fe District Attorney, Martinez, took me aside and told me what had happened. Your maid had already identified the bodies, but he asked me to confirm. God, I hated doing that."

"I saw the room," Wolf said, and took a big gulp of the dark bourbon.

"You've been to the house?" Mark asked, alarmed.

"I just came from there. For that matter, so did somebody else."

"What do you mean, somebody else?"

"There was somebody in the house while I was there. I never got a look at him; he left in a hurry."

"A policeman, maybe?"

"Maybe. It didn't seem like a policeman; more like a burglar. Go on. What happened next?"

"Martinez took me into the room, shooed the photographer out, and pulled back the sheet. It was . . ." he took a swig from his glass, "indescribable."

"I can imagine. Were they naked?"

"Yes. Their clothes were scattered around the room."

"You were wrong about me; how did you identify Julia and Jack?"

"Well, of course, I had never seen any of you naked before, and the faces . . . the wounds were all to the head. Jack was wearing that enormous silver ring he bought from an old Indian on the plaza that day. We were with him, remember?"

"Yes. And Julia?"

"The tattoo."

Mark nodded. Julia had, before he had known her, had a tiny sunflower tattooed onto her right breast, high enough that it would show when she was wearing something low-cut. It had always amused him; he remembered how often he had run his tongue over it. "There's no doubt about her, then."

"I'm afraid not. I hope I can be forgiven for thinking the other man was you. He was the same size and build, and his hair, what was left of it, was thick and graying, like yours."

"A natural enough mistake," Wolf said absently.

"I told Martinez about that afternoon," Mark said.

Wolf looked up. "What about that afternoon?"

"Just that I had a drink with you over there around five, then came home. The day of the murders."

"You had a drink at my house that same afternoon?"

"Well, of course; you called me. You were there alone. Surely you remember that."

"I don't remember anything about that night, Mark, and nothing about the day before."

The two men stared at each other for a moment, and some unspoken fear seemed to pass between them.

Mark spoke first. "Tell me where you've been,"

he said, in the voice he had used when Wolf had
been his patient.

Wolf told him about waking alone in the
house, about the trip to the Grand Canyon, his
stay there, the trip back.

"Well," Mark said, when Wolf had finished.
"Who would ever have thought to look for you at
the Grand Canyon?"

"Who would have thought to look for me at
all?" Wolf said. "After all, I'm supposed to be on a
slab somewhere." He winced at the thought.
"Mark, where is Julia?"

"At the county morgue, with Jack and . . . whoever. The body won't be released until a postmor-
tem has been conducted—another day or two, I
should think." He paused. "Wolf, you said you
read the *Times*; did you read the obituaries, too?"

"Yes."

"Then you know about Julia's . . . background."

"Yes. How the hell did they find out about
that? I never knew about it. Why would they put
a thing like that in an obituary, for Christ's
sake?"

"I called a friend at the *Times* and checked that
out," Mark replied. "A *Times* reporter had interviewed Julia's sister in prison a couple of times.
She was apparently trying to interest him in a
book about her case. She told him about Julia's
background when he called to tell her about the
murders."

"Mark, you were her analyst. Did you know
anything about that?"

Pain crossed Mark's face. "Yes. After a long time

had passed. I sensed she was holding something back, and finally she came out with it."

"The *Times* stuff was true, then?"

"All of it, I'm afraid. I hope you understand why I couldn't tell you, Wolf."

"Sure, doctor-patient confidentiality, and all that."

"Exactly. Julia would never have told me anything if she'd had the slightest notion that I might tell you. I was in something of a quandary about it; but I decided to go by the book."

"Of course." Wolf remembered something. "Mark, the *Times* said something about your having been arrested in New York for practicing medicine without a license."

Mark sighed deeply. "It was accurate, as far as it went. When I was in medical school at Columbia, I got a girl pregnant. We were at a lake house upstate for the weekend—I didn't know about her condition—when she miscarried. Our friends were out shopping in the car, and there was no phone. I helped her as best I could, then sedated her and made her comfortable. The other girl in the group, when she returned to the house, thought I'd performed an abortion, and turned me in. When the girl recovered enough to talk to the police, it was all cleared up, but charges had been filed in the meantime. The incident has haunted my medical career."

"I see," Wolf said. "I knew it had to be something like that; I knew you couldn't have done anything unethical."

"I appreciate that, Wolf," Mark said.

"Mark," Wolf said, "I want you to hypnotize me." Mark had hypnotized him half a dozen times a couple of years before, to help him stop smoking; he had been a good subject.

Mark looked down into his drink. "I don't know if that's such a good idea, Wolf."

"Mark, I've lost a whole day; I want it back. I've got to know what happened."

"Wolf, if your mind refuses to remember, it's for a reason. It's likely that you've suffered a trauma that you couldn't handle. It's a protective function of the mind, like a circuit breaker that cuts out when there's an electrical overload."

"I understand that. I still want to know. Maybe I . . . was a witness."

"If you couldn't handle it then, what makes you think you can handle it now? You could end up catatonic."

"I'm willing to take that chance. I can't stand not knowing."

"You have to understand, hypnotizing you now could put me in a very dangerous situation, legally speaking—dangerous for you, I mean. There are limits to doctor-patient confidentiality, and if I were subpoenaed—"

"I won't ask you to lie for me, Mark, but I can't go on living without knowing what happened that night."

Mark's shoulders sagged. "You're my friend, Wolf. I'll help you if I can."

When Wolf woke, Mark was gone from the room. He sat up on the leather couch and rubbed his face with his hands. He felt a little light-headed, but well rested; his exhaustion had left him. He looked at his watch: two A.M. He had been out for over two hours.

Mark entered the office with a tray of food. Right behind him came Flaps. There was the usual two minutes of pandemonium that constituted any reunion with the dog.

"I'm glad to see you, girl," Wolf whispered into her soft ear. She grinned for him.

"Maria was going to take her, but I thought she'd be happier here with some land to romp on."

"Thanks, Mark, I really appreciate that."

Mark handed him a large glass of fresh orange juice. "I had difficulty waking you, so I just let you sleep it off naturally."

"Does that happen often with subjects?"

"It's not rare; it's not common, either. You needed the rest, I think, and your unconscious knew that."

"I still don't remember anything. What did I say when I was under?"

"Wolf, you have to understand that what you said isn't necessarily what happened."

"I did it, didn't I?" Wolf sank onto the sofa again.

Mark raised a finger. "The mind is strange, Wolf. You've obviously been worrying about this since you read the story in the *Times*, and your mind may have . . . altered events, in order to expiate the guilt you were feeling—a kind of self-confession, if you see what I mean."

"So this was inconclusive?"

"Yes, I think so. Otherwise, I'd be in the position of having to wonder whether I should call the police."

"Why don't I remember what I said when I was under?"

"I instructed you not to. It would have done no earthly good for you to remember, and it may have done you a great deal of harm. You are fortunate, I think, that this hypnosis was not administered by a court-appointed psychiatrist, who might not have been quite so well acquainted with the nuances. Incidentally, should it come to that, I'd advise you not to submit. I should think your best chance in this would be to remain mute at your trial."

"My *trial*?"

"Assuming it comes to that, of course," Mark said, looking away.

Suddenly Wolf was ravenous. He tore into the scrambled eggs and ham that Mark had brought him. When he had finished, he sat back and looked at Mark, who had been regarding him quietly. "What am I going to do, Mark?"

Mark sighed. "I think your choices are very limited," he said sadly.

"You think I should turn myself in?"

"Only after talking to the best possible criminal lawyer," Mark said, raising a warning finger. "Locally, that would be Ed Eagle."

"The Indian guy?"

"He's thought to be among the best in the country. Ed plays by what he calls Santa Fe Rules, and it works for him and for his clients. I know him, and I'd be glad to call him for you."

"What are my other choices?"

Mark looked away.

"Run, huh?"

Mark looked back at him. "There's always Mexico. Nobody's looking for you; it's thought you're dead."

"A new life south of the border," Wolf mused. "I wonder what demand there is for entertainment lawyers in Puerto Vallarta?"

"Not much, I should think. Wolf, I think you should see Ed Eagle, but it's your choice; if you want to leave, even if only for a while, I'll help you in any way I can. I've got about thirty thousand in the bank, and if you need more, there are some bearer bonds in my safety deposit box—about two hundred thousand, I think."

"Thanks, Mark, but I'm okay for money at the moment."

"I wouldn't cash any checks, if I were you, or use your credit cards."

Wolf looked at the psychiatrist closely. "You're assuming I'm going to run."

Mark smiled. "You always had a fear of authority. That's why you chose your career as an independent producer—so you could be as free as possible from the talent agencies and the studios. Frankly, I can't see you placing your trust in the criminal justice system." His smile faded. "I wish you would, though."

"You know me well, Mark."

"I should, after two years of deep analysis, don't you think?"

"And you're a good friend, too."

Mark shrugged. "A psychiatrist isn't often called upon to be a friend. Lots of other things, but not a friend. To tell you the truth, there are some psychic rewards for me in helping a friend in trouble, so maybe I'm just being selfish." He rearranged himself in the chair and slipped back into his role as analyst. "Wolf, there was something that came up in your analysis that you wouldn't talk about at the time. I didn't want to ask you about it under hypnosis."

"What was that?" Wolf asked, knowing the answer.

"There was another time when you lost a day from your life."

Wolf looked into the fire. "A day and a half," he said.

"At the time of your first wife's death?"

Wolf looked up at him. "How did you know that?"

"It was obvious. I didn't want to press you at the time, but I will now. I think it's important."

"You mean you think that blackout and this more recent one may be related?"

"It's possible. If they are related, we should know. Start at the beginning."

Wolf looked back into the glowing embers. "All right," he said.

6

The fear came back. The dread that he had fought for so many years crept out of its banishment and seized him again. He did not try to fight it.

"Her name was Maggie. She worked for a casting agent Jack and I used, and she and I were in a lot of readings together. I was impressed with her judgment of actors, and she was extremely attractive, too. We began seeing a lot of each other." He paused.

"Go on," Mark said gently.

"I was just trying to remember how long we saw each other before . . . Oh, I guess it was seven or eight months, and after that long she was spending so much time at my apartment—I had a condo in Beverly Hills at the time—that we were practically living together. Pretty soon, I asked her to give up her place. We had talked about marriage, and agreed that neither of us had any business getting married. She thought that I was a workaholic, and I knew she didn't want to give up her career—she wanted her own casting agency." He shook his head. "She would have had it, too."

"What happened to stop her?"

"She got pregnant."

"And what was your reaction to that?"

"Panic. No other word for it. When she told me, I had this flash forward of the next twenty years, and I didn't like it."

"What didn't you like about it?"

"The confinement; the obligation to somebody other than myself."

"That's honest. What about the obligations you had to Maggie already?"

"Those either of us could end at any time; it was the sort of arrangement we had."

"Until she got pregnant."

"Yes. Then everything changed. I couldn't just say, 'Thanks, that's it, see you around the casting sessions.'"

"Responsibility."

"Yes. But you know I never shied away from responsibility; I craved it."

"But only to yourself. That's what you craved. We worked all this out long ago, remember?"

"Sure, I remember."

"Did you ask her to have an abortion?"

"Not in so many words. I think I was as afraid of doing that as I was afraid of having a child. She brought it up. 'That's what you want me to do, isn't it? Kill him?' She already had it in her mind that it was a boy."

"How did you make your decision?"

"She put it to me bluntly; she said she loved me, and she wanted us to be married and raise the child, and have others. But, she said, if I didn't want that, too, then it was over—she would have the child and raise it on her own, and I would never see either of them again."

"How did you feel about the prospect of not seeing her again?"

"The thought of not seeing her nearly killed me; I couldn't stand it. That surprised me; I guess you never really know how you feel about a woman until you face the prospect of losing her."

"So how did you deal with the problem?"

"I made my decision. I told her that I loved her, and I wanted to marry her, and I wanted the baby, and we would send him to Princeton, and he'd make us proud of him."

"And was all that true?"

"Not all of it. I loved her, God knows, but I didn't want a child. I was that selfish."

"But you made the sacrifice to keep her?"

"Yes. We were married, we bought a house. I refused to go to childbirth classes on the grounds that I was squeamish."

"And she accepted that?"

"Not really. Although I never admitted it to her, she knew how I felt about the baby. I think she thought that the first time I held my own child in my arms, all my reservations would vanish and everything would be all right."

"And was that true?"

"Maybe, I don't know. I do know that if she had felt I wasn't adapting, she'd have left me and brought up the child alone. She was a very determined girl, and she wanted that baby."

"Did you see the baby as driving a wedge between you and Maggie?"

Wolf leaned forward and put his face in his hands. "God help me, I did. I know now how stupid that was. I think I even knew it at the time, but there didn't seem to be anything I could do about it."

"What happened then?"

"Maggie went into labor about a month early. We weren't ready for it—I wasn't, anyway. She called me from her office—she was still working—and I raced over to get her and take her to the hospital. At least, I think that's how it happened."

"What do you mean?"

"It's how I reconstructed it later."

"You don't remember?"

"No. I never have. The car went over the center line on La Cienega and hit a truck nearly head on, on her side. The cops found me in a diner across the street, eating a cheeseburger, for Christ's sake. They told me later that when I was taken back to the wreck to identify Maggie, I passed out. I woke up in the hospital, and I didn't remember any of it. The last thing I recalled was negotiating with an agent about an actor Jack and I wanted for a picture, a day and a half before."

"Did some part of you believe that you had deliberately tried to kill the baby, so that you could have Maggie to yourself?"

"A big part of me did. But I couldn't remember any of the events leading up to the crash, so I've never known what I felt at the time."

"Did you seek any therapy after that?"

"No. I just lived with it."

"Wolf, my poor dear friend; what hell you put yourself through."

Wolf turned and looked at him. "I'm back in hell now," he said.

"We'll work it out together when this is over," Mark said.

"Over? When will that be? I'd like to make it be over."

Mark sighed. "Wolf, you must remember that, while you are dealing with your problems in analysis, you must also deal with the problems of your daily life. You have to do both."

"So I should call Ed Eagle?"

"I think you should. I can't see any other way of resolving the situation without causing the most profound damage to yourself."

"They have the death penalty in New Mexico. That's pretty profound."

"There are worse things than dying, Wolf. There are worse things than being in prison."

"Name one."

"Just one? The hell you were in after Maggie's death. The hell you say you're in again."

Wolf was quiet for a moment. "You're right about that, Mark. Tell Eagle I'll call him in a few days. Don't tell him my name; just tell him a friend of yours will call soon."

"Why not now?"

"Because there's something I have to do. And to get it done, I have to stay dead a little while longer."

7

Wolf flew into Los Angeles at dawn and landed at Santa Monica Airport, having given a false name on his flight plan. He had one of the few private T-hangars on the field, the result of years on a waiting list; he taxied there and exchanged the airplane for his Mercedes station wagon, locked the hangar, and drove away. The early-shift lineman at California Aviation waved idly, taking no special note of him. Apparently the boy either didn't know who he was or didn't read the papers.

He drove up Bundy to the freeway and headed north, exiting at Sunset Boulevard, then after a few miles turned left onto Stone Canyon, into the plush Bel Air neighborhood, and drove past the Bel Air Hotel. No more breakfast meetings there for a while, he reflected.

A couple of hundred yards past the hotel, he turned into his driveway, using the electric opener to roll back the gates, then again to open the garage door. Julia's new Mercedes 500SL convertible reminded him that she would not be driving it again. He remembered the fit of happiness she had pitched when he had given it to her. Since his initial outburst of grief in Mark's office, his emotions had been strange—dead, like Julia. He felt guilty for not being wracked with grief.

He went directly into the kitchen from the garage entrance. The first thing he saw was Julia. She was standing at the sink, wearing her green cashmere dressing gown, washing something. Hearing the door open, she turned and looked at him. Recognition and alarm widened her eyes for a moment, then she fainted.

Wolf went and stood over her, trembling with anger. The woman was Bridget, the live-in maid, and she was wearing Julia's dressing gown. *The bitch*, Wolf thought. *She couldn't wait to get into Julia's clothes*. He filled a glass of water at the sink and threw it into her face. Then, as she sputtered to consciousness, he realized that he needed her goodwill, at least for a while. He bent and helped her to her feet.

"Oh, God!" she warbled. "You're dead, and you've come for me."

He sat her down at the kitchen table. "Shut up, Bridget," he said. "I'm no deader than you are."

"Then I must be dead, too," she said, tears starting down her cheeks. "Am I in heaven or hell?"

"That's a good question, but I'm not in a position to give you an answer. Believe me, no matter what you've read in the papers, I'm not dead. Mrs. Willett is, though, and the first thing I want you to do is to get that dressing gown back into her closet, along with anything else you might have taken from there."

"I only borrowed it," she whimpered.

"And Bridget, I don't want you to leave this house for the next week, do you understand me?" He had learned long ago not to cajole the woman; she responded best to direct orders.

"Yessir, Mr. Willett," she said.

"Good. Now get yourself dressed and go about your work. If the telephone rings, you answer it and deal with whoever it is. Nobody, but nobody, in L.A. knows I'm still on this earth, and I want to keep it that way for a while, do you understand?"

"Yessir, I do," Bridget said. The woman was bright; she could handle the callers.

He had a thought. "If somebody asks for Mr. Amadeus, I'll take the call."

"Yessir," she said, then hurried herself from the kitchen.

He fixed himself a bowl of cereal and took it into his study. Everything here was much the same as in the Santa Fe house. Wolf had discovered long ago that he was incapable of owning a second home; what he had was two first homes. He sank into the Eames lounge chair, put his feet up on the ottoman, ate his cereal, and thought. When he had finished eating, he glanced at his watch—a quarter to seven—then made a telephone call.

Hal Berger, his business manager, answered the phone himself; he was a bachelor and had no servants. Wolf had always wondered if he was gay. "Hello," Hal said grumpily.

"You ought to get up earlier and get the worm, Hal."

There was a long silence, then: "I don't know who you are, *putz*, but if you call me again, I'll have the cops on you."

"I'm who I sound like," Wolf said, "and reports of my death have been greatly exaggerated."

"Why should I believe that?" Hal asked suspiciously.

"Gee, I don't know, Hal, am I supposed to tell you you've got a wart on your ass that nobody but me knows about?"

Finally, astonishment. "Wolf, it's really you, isn't it?"

"Why don't you get over to Stone Canyon and find out? I might even tell you what's going on."

"I'll be there in fifteen minutes," Hal said. He lived up in Coldwater Canyon, not far away.

"Wait a minute," Wolf said, "I want you to call some people first." He needed his editor and composer. "Get hold of Jerry Sachs and Dave Martinelli and ask them to meet you here right away. Tell them it's something about my estate. Urgent."

"Jerry left for Rome yesterday; a job."

"The sonofabitch didn't waste any time, did he?" Wolf hadn't worked with another editor for years.

"You know Jerry; he's always short of money. He didn't have the guts to call me until he was at the airport."

Wolf thought for a minute. "What's that kid's name who used to be his assistant, then went out on her own?"

"The little looker? Whats-her-name?"

"Yes, that one."

"Jesus, uh . . . Darling, or something; no, it's Dear."

"Deering, Jane Deering. Have you got her number?"

"I'll find her."

"Don't break your ass getting over here, Hal. Shave and shower, have some breakfast. I'll leave the gate open; you park around back and come in through the kitchen. Tell the others to do that, too."

Hal Berger was there in half an hour, shaved and showered. He hugged Wolf. "Man, am I glad to see you!"

"You just didn't want to lose a client," Wolf said, hugging him back.

"Yeah, yeah, sure." Hal held him at arm's length. "Is Jack alive, too? And Julia?" he added, almost as an afterthought.

Wolf shook his head. "No, just me. I'll explain when the others arrive; I don't want to go through it twice."

"Sure, I understand. Jane and Dave should be here shortly."

There was the sound of a car pulling up out back, then another.

"Go meet them," Wolf said. "Tell them I'm

alive; I don't want anybody else fainting on me. Bridget keeled right over."

Hal left, then came back a moment later with the editor and composer.

Wolf shook hands with them both, then waved them to a sofa. "I owe you both an explanation," he said. "Let's get that out of the way, then I'll tell you why I asked you here."

"What about Jack?" Dave Martinelli asked.

"Jack and Julia and another man—I don't know who—are dead. They were murdered in the Santa Fe house while I was stuck in a hotel at the Grand Canyon, waiting for my airplane to be repaired," he lied. That would be good enough for now.

"I'm awfully sorry, Wolf," Jane Deering said.

Wolf had forgotten how attractive she was—small, dark, a terrific figure in tight jeans and a T-shirt; she never seemed to wear anything else the few times he had met her. "Thank you, Jane."

Dave Martinelli spoke up. "It's bad enough losing your wife, but your partner at the same time—that's terrible. Why did they think the other guy was you?"

"They were in my house. A friend who knows us all well made the identification. The guy was apparently my size."

"There's no mistake about Julia and Jack?"

"None. One mistake is understandable; he wouldn't make three."

"When's the funeral?" Jane asked.

That gave Wolf pause. It astonished him that he hadn't thought about it. "Not for a while," he said. "There's something I haven't told you. Only five people, besides my housekeeper, know I'm alive. You're three of them."

There was a short silence.

"Why?" Jane asked finally.

"My lawyer and the Santa Fe police think it's better that way for a while. They want the killer to think I'm dead." He didn't have a lawyer yet, and the *police* thought he was dead, but what else could he tell these people—that when it became known he was alive, he would be the chief suspect?

"I see," Jane said gravely.

"How can we help?" Dave asked.

"I've got to finish *L.A. Days*, and I've got to do it fast," Wolf said. "Dave, where are you on the score?"

"I've laid down a piano track to the rough cut," the composer said, "and I've had most of the scoring done. I'll have to trim to the final cut, of course."

"Once we get a final cut, how long before you can record?"

"How pushed for time are you?"

"As pushed as I can get. I want to get an answer print to Centurion as soon as humanly possible. If I don't, they're liable to take it away from our company and cut it themselves."

"Ouch," Dave said. "They'd love to get their fat, sticky fingers on it, wouldn't they?"

"They've already been on the phone," Hal

Berger said. "I told them I didn't even know where the rough cut was, maybe in Santa Fe."

"That's good," Wolf said. "Tell them it's in the Santa Fe house, where Jack and I were working on it, and the police have sealed it for at least two weeks. Tell them you've already tried to get in there and couldn't."

"Okay."

"How much time do you need to trim to my cut and record, Dave?"

Martinelli thought for a moment. "If the final is close to your present cut, and you don't mind paying a hell of a lot of overtime to musicians, I can do it in three days."

"I think the final cut will be close, and you can have as much overtime as you want," Wolf said.

"I don't know about the overtime, Wolf," Hal piped up. "We're over budget as it is."

"Thanks for being a businessman, Hal, but I've got no choice."

Jane Deering spoke up. "What about me?" she asked. "How can I help?"

"I'd like you to cut the picture with me," Wolf replied.

"Jerry went to Rome, I heard," she said.

"Jane, if Jerry were here, he'd be cutting it; we both know that. But he's not here, and if you can work night and day for the next few days, I'll back you with the union for an equal screen credit. I'll also pay you what Jerry was getting. Hal will show you his contract."

"That's good enough for me," Jane said. "If I can get my sister to stay with my little girl."

"I'm sorry, I didn't know you were married."

"I'm not married; I just have a little girl. She's eight." She got up. "I'll call my sister; can I use the kitchen phone?"

"Sure. And Jane, I'd appreciate it if you'd move in here. You can have the guest house."

"Okay, but I'm going to need an hour or two a day with Sara—that's my daughter."

"Sure, whenever you like. The other twenty-two hours are mine, though."

"Deal," she said. "I'll call my sister."

"Jane, I know you've got an agent, and I know he'll be pissed off if you do this without your talking to him first, but I'd appreciate it very much if you'd wait until we have the cut before calling him. You can trust me about the money."

She nodded and disappeared toward the kitchen.

Wolf turned back to the composer. "Dave, I'll call you the minute we have a final cut. Why don't you go ahead and book studio time and musicians for . . ." He looked at the day on his wristwatch: Saturday. "Wednesday of next week?"

"Okay," Martinelli said. "If you need more time and have to reschedule, give me as much notice as you can. It'll save money." He got up, shook hands with Wolf and Hal, and left.

"A good man," Hal said.

"Damn right."

"You think you and Jane can pull this picture together by Wednesday?"

"We'll have to."

Hal looked at the carpet. "Wolf, there's something more at stake here than keeping Centurion from cutting the picture, isn't there?"

Wolf nodded. "There's the final payment, due on answer print. I'm going to need it."

Hal looked as if he wanted to ask why, but Jane returned to the room.

"Okay, we're on," she said. "I'll go home every night about six, make dinner for Sara, and put her to bed."

"That's fine," Wolf said, relieved.

"Where are we going to work?"

"I've got a moviola downstairs. How long since you worked on one?"

She smiled, revealing even, white teeth. "Not as long as you think," she said. "A girl can't afford all the latest stuff when she's just starting out on her own. Where's the rough cut?"

"In my film vault at the office," Wolf replied. "Hal, can you run over there and get it? You have the combination."

"Sure," Hal said.

"While he's getting the stock, I'll run home and pack a bag," Jane said.

"Good."

She left, and Hal spoke up.

"Wolf, you didn't say why you needed the money. You're in pretty good shape financially right now."

"Speaking of money, cut Jane a check for a third of her fee up front," Wolf said, ignoring the question.

"Okay," Hal replied.

"And when Jane goes home at six to feed her kid, let's you and I play some tennis, okay? You look like you could use the exercise."

Hal looked at him long and hard.

"Don't ask me too many questions right now, Hal. I don't have any answers."

"I just have one question, Wolf," Hal replied. "Am I—or Jane or Dave—going to have any problems with the law?"

Wolf mustered all his credibility for the lie. "No, Hal," he said. "I promise you."

He hoped to hell he could keep that promise.

8

"How do you want to do this?" Jane asked. "I mean, how do you like to work?"

"I'm a beginning-to-end man," Wolf replied. "The only way I can keep the whole thing in my head is to do it in sequence. Jack wanted to start the titles after the first setup of the first scene, then intersperse between each of the other setups." The first scene was already on the moviola, an editing machine with two reels—one for the picture and one for the sound track—and a small viewing screen. He handed her another reel labeled TITLES.

They both sat on stools, Wolf behind Jane and to her right, so they could both see the screen. There was a light scent from her—not perfume, but something, maybe shampoo. He liked it. They began work.

Promptly at six, they stopped. They had about four minutes of film done, Wolf thought, and that wasn't much. Still, they were getting used to each other. He and Jerry Sachs had worked together for so long that they had communicated in a kind of verbal shorthand of grunts, sighs, and monosyllables. Jane liked more detailed instructions, and Wolf was having trouble expressing himself in complete sentences. Still, he was getting used to her ways, and he found that articulating what he wanted helped to define it more sharply for himself.

Jane stretched and rubbed her neck. "You know what you're doing, Wolf."

"Thanks," Wolf replied, warming to the praise. He switched on the overhead lights in the small room.

"You ever think of directing?" she asked, pulling on a cotton sweater.

He caught a glimpse of flat, bare midriff as she lifted her arms. "You know that T-shirt around town—'*What I really want to do is direct*'?"

She laughed a deeper laugh than he would have expected from such a small woman. "You and everybody else, huh?"

"I've always been happy producing," Wolf said. "I guess I sort of made a career out of keeping Jack in line."

"Folks ought to make careers out of themselves," Jane said.

Something in her voice reminded Wolf of something. "You a southerner?" he asked.

"Magnolia Springs, Alabama," she said.

"Where's that?"

"Up a little river off Mobile Bay; almost in the

Gulf. You're from someplace in Georgia, I've heard."

"Little town called Delano; in Meriwether County, about eighty miles south of Atlanta."

"Not as little as Magnolia Springs," she said.

"What's the nearest bigger town?"

"Fairhope, but that's probably not as big as Delano, either. Mobile was the big city to us."

He walked her upstairs and to her car. "You've been out here long enough to lose most of your accent. I didn't catch it at first."

She stretched again. ' "Bout nine years, now. It comes back when I'm tired, or drunk, or when I'm talking to my mother on the phone. Your accent is gone, too."

"I've been out here a lot longer than you. L.A. has a way of making Californians out of everybody."

"Not me," she said. "If I didn't love this work so much, I'd be somewhere else. Not much work for film editors in Magnolia Springs, Alabama, or Butte, Montana."

"Not much work for producers in Delano, Georgia, or Santa Fe, New Mexico, either." He opened the car door for her.

"I'll be back at eight," she said. "Don't wear yourself out on the tennis court." She drove away.

Wolf walked down the path and through a hedge to the court. Hal was waiting for him, stretched out on a bench. "Be right with you," Wolf called out. He went into the little dressing house and changed.

"The bank's been on the phone today," Hal said when Wolf joined him. "They've frozen your and Julia's accounts, of course; that's usual in a death. They want to talk with your lawyer or your executor about disposition."

Wolf had been his own lawyer for his whole adult life, and Julia was his executor. "Stall them for a week or two," he said. "Now, no more business; let's play."

It took them an hour to finish a set. Hal was a rangy, powerful player, about Wolf's age, and in good shape. Wolf always relied on cunning with Hal's sort of player—chop shots and occasional hard second serves; passing shots, when he could manage them. Wolf won, 7–5.

"I don't think we've got time for another set," Wolf called over the net.

"Coward!" Hal yelled back. "Afraid I'll get even?"

"Come on, Bridget's fixing us some supper."

They dined on cold roast lamb in the small dining room. Hal seemed unusually quiet.

"I called the Santa Fe police this afternoon," he said finally.

"Why?" Wolf asked, concealing his alarm.

"I wanted to get to them before Centurion did." He sliced a piece of lamb. "They think you're dead, you know."

"I know," Wolf admitted.

"Why'd you lie to me?" he asked calmly.

"I'm sorry about that, Hal," Wolf said, contrite. "I'm trying to protect everybody else as well as myself."

"I know enough about the law to be scared about this," Hal said.

"I'm scared, too," Wolf replied. Starting at the beginning, he told Hal everything.

When he had finished, Hal was contemplative for a minute or two, then he said, "You've got to finish this film before they arrest you, isn't that it?"

"That's it, buddy."

"So, I'm sitting here in Bel Air, eating leg of lamb with a possible triple murderer," Hal mused.

"That's about the shape of it," Wolf said.

"I've known you how long?"

"Twelve, fifteen years?"

"Closer to fifteen," Hal said. "You're an honorable man, Wolf. I don't deal with many of those out here. I don't believe you did it. There's got to be another explanation."

"Thanks for that, Hal," Wolf said. "I wish I had the truth in my pocket, so you could release it to the trades."

"The downside, of course, is that you did it—whacked Jack and Julia and this other poor schmuck, whoever he is."

"That's the downside," Wolf agreed.

"Well, it surprises me a little, what I think about that."

"What do you think?"

"I think I don't much give a shit if you did whack 'em out."

Wolf turned to him in surprise. "You don't care if I'm a triple murderer?"

"I'll admit, it's not much of a character reference, but I think that if you did do it, you either had an overwhelmingly good reason, or else it was some sort of temporary aberration. I guess I could live with either of those."

"You have a forgiving nature, Hal."

"Not really. But you've been my friend almost as long as you've been my client, and I need somebody around who can take a first set from me the way you just did. Keeps me on my toes."

"Thanks, Harold."

"And since you're my friend, I'm going to give you the best advice I can muster."

"Go right ahead."

"Get a lawyer right this minute and start working on getting yourself out of this mess. I know a couple of hotshots."

"That's good advice, Hal, but no. I'm going to finish this movie first."

"You may be digging your own grave, pal."

"I may already have dug it," Wolf replied.

9

The four of them sat in Wolf's screening room and watched the cut and scored print of *L.A. Days*. Jane got up periodically and changed the reels on the big 35mm projectors, and Wolf took an occasional note. The work had taken ten days—longer than Wolf had intended, but less time than ever before, and he was pleased. In the process, he and Jane had learned to work together. They had edited four minutes of the film on their first day, and three times that on their last.

Hal, who had never seen any of the film, had laughed aloud throughout. "Jesus," he said, "it's fucking wonderful. It's Jack's best work."

Wolf and Jane exchanged an amused glance. "I'm glad you like it, Hal," Wolf said.

"I'll take it to Centurion tomorrow," Hal said.

"Hang on, we're not ready yet. I've got some notes for Dave and Jane." Wolf held up a pad. "Ready, Dave?"

"Ready," Dave replied, producing his own pad.

"In scene sixteen I'd like you to wait a couple of seconds before the strings come in—just at the point where she lifts her wineglass."

"Good idea," Dave said. "I can do that and trim without rerecording. What else?"

Wolf consulted his notes. "That's it."

"*That's it*?"the astonished composer asked.

"The score is unimprovable," Wolf said with satisfaction. "And brilliant, besides."

"Jesus, thank you, Wolf," Dave said. "I've never had an experience like this on a film. Maybe we ought to work this way all the time."

"God forbid," Jane said. "Now, what have you got for me?"

Wolf consulted the stopwatch in his hand. "I want you to take four minutes out of the film without fucking up Dave's score. We haven't got time to rerecord."

"*Four minutes*?" she wailed.

"Centurion would ask for it anyway, and they'd be right. It moves just a hair too slowly, and four minutes will trim it to an hour and forty-five minutes exactly. The distributors and exhibitors will love us for it—they can turn over the house every two hours on the hour—I bet we'll pick up an extra fifty screens on first release."

"Okay," Jane said resignedly. "When do we start?"

"*You* can start now," he said. "I've got to be somewhere."

"*By myself*?" Jane erupted.

"You can do it," Wolf said, squeezing her hand.

He didn't let it go. "You know this movie as well as Jack or I do by now, and you've got great instincts."

"By myself," she muttered.

"When you're finished, hand-carry the print to the lab and stand over them until you've got an answer print you can live with." He turned to Hal. "*Then* you can take it to Centurion. And don't leave without their signed acceptance."

When the others had gone, Wolf sat in his study and stared at the telephone. *Last chance*, he thought. *Tell Hal to raise all the money he can, then get in the airplane and head for Mexico—no, Central America, maybe even Brazil—someplace with no extradition treaty*. Finally he heaved a deep, fearful sigh and picked up the phone.

"The Eagle Practice," a woman's voice answered.

"I'd like to speak to Mr. Eagle," Wolf said.

"Whom may I say is calling?"

"A friend of Mark Shea. I believe he's expecting my call."

There was a moment's pause and a deep, rich voice drawled, "This is Ed Eagle." The tones were the pure, oddly accentless speech of the American Indian, almost regardless of tribe.

"Mr. Eagle, I believe Mark Shea called you about me."

"He did," Eagle replied laconically. "Who are you?"

"I would prefer not to give you my name until we can meet and see if we can establish a client-attorney relationship," Wolf said.

"Well, sounds like you're a lawyer," Eagle said. "When do you want to come by here?"

"I don't think it's wise for me to come to your office at the moment. Could we meet somewhere else privately? After office hours?"

"Why don't you come out to the house this evening? Say, about seven?"

Wolf looked at his watch: a little before five, and L.A. was an hour earlier. "I'm not in Santa Fe at the moment," he said. "I don't think I could make it there much before eleven." He didn't want to reach the city until after dark.

"That'll be all right," Eagle replied. "I'm usually up late. You know where I live?"

"No."

"You know Tesuque?" He pronounced it *Teh-SOO-kee*.

"Yes."

"Drive past the Tesuque Market, and take your first right. I'm about four miles up the road in the hills. You'll see the sign on your left."

"I'll get there earlier if I can."

"See you this evening, then, Mr. Willett."

"Goodbye, Mr. Eagle." Wolf had already hung up before he realized that Ed Eagle had known his name.

10

Wolf landed at Santa Fe Airport half an hour after the field closed. Once in the Porsche he became downright paranoid, working his way to the north side of town by back roads and side streets, nearly fainting when a police car pulled up beside him at a traffic light, then ignored him.

He turned right after the Tesuque Market, as instructed, and farther up the mountain found the sign, which turned out to be a life-size bronze sculpture of an eagle, its wings spread wide, a writhing rattlesnake gripped in its claws. The drive climbed for another half mile until the road leveled out at a broad, graveled area before a sizable adobe residence. As Wolf stopped the car, floodlights illuminated the front of the house. He climbed the front steps, but before he could ring the bell, the large carved door made a clicking sound and swung open.

"In here!" a deep voice called from Wolf's right. He closed the door and walked down the wide central hallway. A round table sat at its center, a big arrangement of desert flowers upon it, and doors opened to the left and right of it.

"Come in," the voice called, and Wolf turned right into a large study, lit only by a fire in the wide hearth. Ed Eagle rose from one of a pair of huge wing chairs arranged before the fireplace. He was slender, dressed in faded jeans, a chambray shirt, and expensive boots—lizard. He extended a hand. "May I call you Wolf?" He towered over his guest.

Wolf allowed his hand to be enveloped. "Sure." *The guy must be six-five or six-six*, he thought.

"I'm Ed. I'm six-foot-seven, plus another couple of inches for the boots. Everybody always wonders." He waved Wolf to the other chair, smiling a little. "I expect you can use a drink. I'm having a very nice single-malt Scotch whisky."

"I'll have the American equivalent," Wolf said, sinking gratefully into the comfortable leather chair.

"One Wild Turkey coming up. Rocks?"

"Please. Nothing else."

Eagle went to a serious bar tucked into a corner and came back with the drink, handed it to Wolf, and sat down. "Good flight?"

"Very nice."

"Sun at your back. The light must have been marvelous this evening."

"It was. How did you know I flew in?"

"You came from L.A. You own an airplane—a Bonanza, I believe."

"A B-36."

"Ah, the turbocharged version. I've got a Malibu Mirage out at Capitol Aviation."

"How did you know I was in L.A.?"

"When a man runs, he usually goes someplace he knows."

"Why do you think I was running?"

"Why do you need a criminal lawyer?"

"I'm not sure I do."

"Sure, you're sure. Let's not tap-dance, Wolf; it's tiring." He took a sip of his whisky and waited. "Well," he said finally, "why don't you tell me about it? And you may consider this conversation privileged."

"I hardly know where to start."

"At the beginning, please."

"I don't really know where the beginning is," Wolf said, sagging into his chair. He didn't, Christ knew. At the beginning of his life? When he met Jack? When he met Julia?

"Start the night of the killings."

"I have no memory of that night; none whatever."

"Is that what you're going to say to a jury?"

"You've already decided to put me on the stand?" Wolf asked, incredulous.

"I don't defend against murder charges unless my client will testify. I reckon it's more in his interests for him to lie to a jury, if he feels he has to, than to refuse to talk to them. In my experience, juries think that's kind of standoffish."

"I see."

"You will, as we get further along with this.

And you'll agree. What's the first thing you remember after the killings?"

Wolf started with waking up that morning, told Eagle about the dog, about the flight to the Grand Canyon, about the newspaper, about the day missing from his life.

Eagle listened in silence, sipping his Scotch, nodding encouragement now and then. When Wolf had finished, he was quiet for a time. "Tell me something," he said at last. "How well did you know your wife?"

Wolf laughed ruefully. "Not as well as I thought I did."

"I read the *Times* piece; did you know about any of that?"

"None of it. I met Julia in a casting session. We were married four months later. Apparently everything she told me about herself was a lie."

"Well, you probably had no reason to doubt her. Most people believe what they're told, if it's at all credible, until they have some reason to think they're being lied to. I take it she was credible."

Wolf nodded. "She was. Julia always seemed such an open person. I never caught her in a lie—not even a little one. If anything, she seemed obsessive about *not* lying. I remember once, some people asked us to dinner—some people she didn't like much—and she could have said 'We already have plans,' that sort of thing, but she said to the woman—I was sitting right there by the phone—'I think it would be a waste of time for both of us, don't you?' And she said it kindly, sympathetically, as if she were doing the people a favor. When she hung up she saw me looking at her, and she said, 'Life is too short to tell anything but the truth.'"

"An admirable attitude," Eagle said. "One adopted by every con man worth his weight in suckers: get to be known for telling the truth, and the lies will go down like honey."

"Maybe so, but I never found Julia to be anything but an admirable woman. She was good-natured, considerate, do anything for a friend, do anything for *me*." Wolf rubbed his temples. "I feel terrible that, since I read the *Times* piece, I haven't let myself think about her for more than a few seconds, and when I do, I don't seem to feel much."

"The first stage of grief is denial."

"But I don't *feel* any grief," Wolf said, shaking his head. "I just feel numb—dead at the center. Since the day after I learned about the shootings, I've been cutting a film—completely wrapped up in it—and feeling a lot of affection for a woman I hardly knew a couple of weeks ago. I think I must be insane, or something."

"That's always a possibility," Eagle said. "And it's not necessarily an inconvenient one."

"You think I should plead insanity?"

"I think you should see a shrink; then we can talk about it. Were you ever a patient of Mark Shea?"

"Yes, Julia and I both were—me, for a couple of years."

"Good, that'll shorten the process; we'll have an eminent psychiatrist who knows your background and can testify to your state of mind over a long period; Julia's, too. That could be invaluable."

"What's this going to cost me, Ed?"

"A quarter of a million dollars, if we go to trial, and that's up front. I'll take a mortgage on something, if you've got an unencumbered asset."

"What about appeals?"

"I've never had to appeal a capital case, so if it comes to that, it's on the house."

"What's your opinion of my chances so far? Could I beat a murder charge?"

"Wolf, this is Santa Fe, and everything is done a little differently here. We're playing by Santa Fe Rules, and that dictates that the first thing I should do is to see if I can work my way through the system to keep you from even being charged. Then we won't have to beat it. If I can manage that, it'll only cost you a hundred thousand. I'll want that tomorrow."

"Okay, but you didn't answer my question."

Eagle shrugged. "She was in bed with two other men," he said. "That's a hell of a motive. Looks like you were in the house, too—that's plenty of opportunity. As for means—well, it was your shotgun, wasn't it?"

"Yes, one of a pair of Purdeys. What about the unwritten law?"

"The unwritten law doesn't exist . . ." he managed a small smile, "except in the minds of a jury—and at least some of them would think that *two* lovers, present and active, would draw a thick line under the unwritten law."

"So I'd have at least a chance, you think?"

"Well, let me put it this way," Ed Eagle said. "If it's me against the State of New Mexico, it'll be a fair fight."

11

Wolf woke in a pleasant guest room of Ed Eagle's house. He found his watch—just after seven A.M.—and struggled through a shave and a shower. Feeling better, he found his way downstairs.

Ed Eagle was reading the *Wall Street Journal*, surrounded by the debris of a finished breakfast and a stack of other newspapers. He looked up. "Morning," he said. "You feeling better?"

"Rested," Wolf replied.

"I hope you didn't mind staying over, but I don't think it's a good idea to go back to your house just yet."

"I understand. It hadn't occurred to me that I'd have to sleep somewhere in Santa Fe. I didn't want to expose Mark Shea, and I couldn't have gone to a hotel."

"Exactly." An Indian woman came into the room and waited expectantly. "How about some breakfast?" Eagle asked. "Anything you'd like."

"Bacon and eggs, orange juice, toast, and coffee, please."

Eagle nodded at the woman, and she disappeared into the kitchen. When the eggs came, Eagle put down his newspaper. "Eat hearty," he said. "At nine o'clock we find out whether you're going to be arrested."

"How do we do that?"

"We visit the district attorney."

Wolf had trouble swallowing the first bite of his breakfast.

"Something I need to ask you," Eagle said. "Didn't think of it last night, and I don't want you to be offended."

"Shoot."

"Did you and your wife ever go to bed with anybody else? Together, I mean."

Wolf nodded. "We had a couple of threesomes. Julia always arranged it."

"With another man or another woman?"

"Always with another woman, although I think Julia was angling for two men."

"How did you feel about that idea?"

"Uncomfortable."

"Would it have made you wildly jealous?"

"I'm not a jealous person."

Eagle nodded. "So you wouldn't have exploded on finding Julia in bed with Jack?"

"I don't explode much. Anyway, I think that if I had found Julia and Jack and this other guy, whoever he was, in bed together, I would have thought it was bad manners on Julia's part, but I wouldn't have reacted by using a shotgun on the three of them." He managed a short laugh. "Certainly not one of my Purdeys."

Eagle laughed, too. "I appreciate your delicacy; I hope the D.A. will, as well. One more thing, and I wouldn't ask if it weren't important."

"Shoot."

"On the occasion of your pair of threesomes, were the third partners different?"

"No, it was the same woman both times."

"Who was she?"

"Her name is Monica Collins."

"That rings a bell, but I can't place her," Eagle said.

"She lives in Santa Fe; divorced from a big-time independent movie producer named Franklin J. Collins."

"I've got her now: blond, fortyish, Beverly Hills dental work."

"That's Monica."

"Tell me about her."

"We knew them a little as a couple in L.A., had dinner once at their house. It was shortly after that when the divorce happened. Story was, Monica got their Santa Fe house and a few million—opinions vary on that—and Frank got the L.A. property and the debts."

"And how did your . . . encounter with Ms. Collins occur?"

"Julia invited her to dinner; the two of them cooked. We had a good deal to drink, ended up in the hot tub. One thing led to another."

"Who did the leading?"

"At the time, I think I'd had enough to drink to believe I was just irresistible to both of them. But with hindsight, Julia."

"Did you continue this out of the hot tub?"

"We moved to a bed."

"Which bedroom?"

"One in the guest wing; the one where . . ."

"I see. And who chose that room?"

"Julia. She said something about the sheets not being fresh in our bedroom."

"What about the second encounter?"

"It was pretty much like the first, except on that occasion, I think everybody knew ahead of time where the evening was heading."

"Have you seen Monica Collins since then?"

"A couple of times, at other people's houses."

"What sort of terms are you on with her?"

"Good, I think; she was always cordial, seemed glad to see me, as well as Julia."

"Did she ever make any reference to your earlier encounters?"

"No, but then she wouldn't have had the opportunity on those occasions."

"One more thing: Would you say that, during your sexual encounters, Ms. Collins exhibited an equal interest in you and Julia?"

"No. I mean, she certainly seemed excited with me, but once I was done in, she and Julia turned to each other, and I'd say it was pretty clear that she was a lot more excited by Julia than by me."

"On both occasions?"

"Yes. It was pretty much the same both times."

"How do you think Ms. Collins would feel about testifying about these encounters?"

"Well, I . . . my impression of Monica is that she's a good deal more uptight when sober than after a few drinks—perhaps even a bit prudish. My guess is that she would be horrified at the thought of testifying."

"If I subpoenaed her, do you think she'd tell the truth under oath?"

"Hard to say, but at the time of her divorce from Frank Collins there was a lot of talk around that during the trial, which was acrimonious, she lied repeatedly on the stand."

"Oh," Eagle said.

They arrived at the state court building precisely at nine o'clock, in two cars. As they walked to the entrance, Eagle spoke only once. "Don't say anything unless I tell you to," he said. "And if I tell you to, tell the truth, but don't be verbose."

Eagle gave his name to the district attorney's secretary, and they were shown in immediately.

"Hello, Bob," Eagle said, shaking the man's hand.

"Hello, Ed," the man replied.

"This is Bob Martinez, the district attorney," Eagle said to Wolf. "Bob, this is my client, Wolf Willett."

"Hello," Wolf said.

"How do you—" Martinez stopped talking and looked at Eagle. *"Who?"*

"That's right, Bob. Mr. Willett is alive and well. May we sit down?"

The amazed Martinez nodded and sat down

himself, rather heavily. "Well, you're quite a surprise, Mr. Willett."

Wolf managed a smile, but said nothing.

"Bob," Eagle said, "Wolf came to see me last night, referred by a mutual acquaintance. Wolf expressed his desire to offer the authorities any assistance possible in the investigation of the murders at his house, and, being a lawyer himself, naturally he thought he should have counsel. He is, of course, aware of his constitutional rights, and I would like to point out for the record, before we begin, that he is here voluntarily to be of help."

"I take your point, Ed," Martinez said. "Mr. Willett, do you have any objections to answering some questions?"

"None at all, Bob," Eagle said. "Wolf has nothing to hide."

Martinez picked up the telephone. "Virginia, come in here with a tape recorder and your pad, please."

When the stenographer was ready, Martinez began.

After an hour of intense questioning, Martinez sat back in his chair. "Just one final question, Mr. Willett," he said. "Why have you waited so long to report to the authorities that you are still alive?"

Wolf leaned forward earnestly. "Mr. Martinez, I run a film production company that employs some twelve people on a full-time basis and many others part-time. Before his death, my partner,

Jack Tinney, had completed shooting on a film for which we both, had high hopes. When I learned of the killings, I had no idea what my . . . involvement with the authorities might entail, whether I would be able to work. It was vital to the health of my company and the continued employment of my people that the film be completed and submitted to the studio for which it was made. I went to Los Angeles for that reason only, and as soon as work on the film was complete, I returned to Santa Fe.

"I know very well that you would have liked to hear from me sooner, and I hope I have not impeded your investigation in any way. If I have, I apologize. I assure you that was not my intention. I am most anxious to learn who murdered my wife and my partner, and I want that person brought to justice."

Ed Eagle spoke up. "I think you can see, Bob, that Wolf really has no information relevant to your investigation, since he has no memory of the night of the killings. It's my belief that he may have been drugged."

"Of course, it's too late to learn that for sure," Martinez said accusingly. "Too much time has passed."

"Too much time had already passed when Wolf learned of the killings, what—forty-eight or more hours later? And that doesn't include the time it would have taken him to return to Santa Fe from the Grand Canyon. My sources tell me that a drug test would have been negative at that time."

"Mmm," Martinez muttered. "Maybe so. Well, it's a remarkable story your client tells, Ed."

"I don't believe there's any evidence whatever to contradict his account," Eagle said blandly.

Fishing expedition, Wolf thought.

"Not so far," Martinez said, biting. "The shotgun had been wiped clean."

Eagle nodded as if he had known this all along. "Of course, Wolf will be very willing to assist in any way he can at any time, with a view toward developing further evidence." He leaned back in his chair. "In the meantime, there doesn't seem to be any reason to detain Wolf further, and he hopes it will be possible for you to release his house from evidence now."

"Already been done," Martinez said. "The cleaning lady barged in and cleaned up everything anyway, but we had already finished with it, so no harm done."

Bless Maria, Wolf thought. Her entry would account for the broken seal on the door.

"Do you have any plans to leave Santa Fe, Mr. Willett?" Martinez asked.

"None," Eagle replied before Wolf could speak. "Wolf will be available to you at all times until your investigation is complete." He stood up and stuck out his hand to Martinez. "Will you let me know when that is, Bob?"

"All right," Martinez said. "I'll want Mr. Willett to formally identify the bodies, of course. The Santa Fe Police Department will be in touch about that."

"Of course." Eagle herded Wolf toward the

door. "Of course, I'd like the courtesy of being present if you should have more questions," he said over his shoulder.

"Sure, Ed," Martinez said. "I'll be in touch."

Eagle took Wolf by the elbow and steered him out of the building.

"That's it?" Wolf asked, a little dazed.

"Not on your life," Eagle said "When Martinez has recovered from the shock of finding out you're alive, he'll be all over you, and so will the Santa Fe cops and the state police. But at least we've bluffed him into not arresting you."

"Thank God for that," Wolf said. "I wasn't looking forward to the prospect of jail."

"Of course, if they come up with anything even remotely incriminating, they'll lock you up in a hurry, but we might be able to make bail even then."

Wolf produced his checkbook and wrote Eagle a check for a hundred thousand dollars, grateful that he had the money. "My bank still thinks I'm dead," he said, handing over the check. "Give me a couple of days to get my account working again before you deposit that."

"Sure," Eagle replied, pocketing the check.

"What do I do now?" he asked.

"Go home, live your life as normally as possible. Go grocery shopping, go out to dinner, be seen around. But wait until tomorrow; it won't hit the *New Mexican* until then, and we don't want acquaintances screaming at the sight of you. The TV stations will get it from the wire services, if not sooner, and they'll be on your doorstep quick. Say you can't talk about it until the investigation has been completed, and refer them to the district attorney's office. Be regretful; don't appear to be ducking them. Do you have an unlisted phone?"

"One of my two lines is unlisted."

"Good. Don't answer the other one for a while; that'll slow them down." Eagle stuck out his hand. "Call me, night or day, if you need anything, and especially when you hear from Martinez or the police."

Wolf gave him the unlisted number, then shook his hand. "Thanks, Ed."

The two men parted. Wolf got into the Porsche and headed for the house in Wilderness Gate. The car seemed to know the way; it was just as well, because Wolf was somewhat disoriented to be in Santa Fe and still a free man.

12

A van from an Albuquerque television station was waiting behind the house when he got home. The Albuquerque stations kept units in Santa Fe to cover the statehouse. Still, Wolf was astonished; no more than fifteen minutes had passed since he had left the district attorney's office. Somebody there must have a direct line to the press, he reckoned.

An incredibly young girl got out of the van with a microphone as soon as she saw him. A cameraman followed, buckling on a battery pack.

Wolf held up a hand. "Hang on," he said to the breathless young woman.

"Just a few questions, Mr. Willett," she puffed, sticking a microphone into his face and glaring at the cameraman, who seemed to be having trouble with his equipment.

"There are two ways we can do this," Wolf said in a reasonable tone.

"How's that?" she asked.

"My way, or not at all," Wolf said.

"What's your way?"

"I'll make a brief statement on camera, and I won't answer any questions. And if you try to ask me any, I won't talk to you again—ever."

"We'll do it your way." She sighed, turning her attention to the cameraman. "Have you got the fucking thing going yet?"

"Up and running," the man said.

"Shut it off," Wolf said to him.

The man looked at the reporter. She nodded. He switched it off.

"Now, I'll stand here, with my back to the tree, and I'll say my piece. When I say 'That's all,' you cut. Understood?"

"Okay, okay," the girl replied.

Wolf positioned himself and nodded to the cameraman, who gave him a thumbs-up. "I just want to say," he began, directing his gaze to the reporter off camera, "that I have just left District Attorney Bob Martinez's office, where he and I have discussed at length the murders of my wife and my business partner. I've told him I have no idea who the other victim was, and that, of course, I will do everything in my power to cooperate with him and the police in their investigation. Mr. Martinez and I both want the murderer brought to justice at the earliest possible moment." He took a deep breath. "Mr. Martinez and I agree that it will be most helpful to the investigation if I do not speak to the press about recent events or answer any questions relating to the investigation until it is complete. Therefore, this will be my only statement on the matter until that time. Thank you very much. That's all." He waited for a beat, then looked at the cameraman and drew a finger across his throat.

"We're off," the cameraman said.

Wolf spoke to the reporter before she could speak to him. "What's your name?"

"Sheila Jackson."

"Miss Jackson, I'd like you to go now and spread it among your colleagues that you have an exclusive and that I am not going to talk to anybody else. If you do that, and not bother me again, then when this business is over, I'll give you an interview. If I hear from you before that time, I'll give it to your rival station. Understood?"

Her shoulders sagged. "Understood." She and the cameraman piled into the van and left.

Wolf was unlocking the door when a plain sedan pulled up and two men got out.

"Mr. Willett," a trim-looking Latino said, producing a badge. "I'm Captain Joe Carreras, of the Violent Crimes Section of the Investigations Bureau of the Santa Fe Police Department." He indicated his colleague, a tall, weathered Anglo. "This is Major Sam Warren of the New Mexico State Police Special Investigations Unit. We'd like to speak with you, please."

"Of course. Come into the house." Wolf led them into the living room and seated them on a sofa. "Gentlemen, I'm happy to cooperate with you in any way I can, but I'd like my attorney to be present. Will you excuse me while I call him?"

"Yessir," Carreras said.

"Can I get you something to drink? Coffee, a soft drink?"

"No, sir. We'll wait while you call Ed Eagle."

Eagle was there in ten minutes. "Did you say anything at all to them?"

"I offered them coffee; they declined." He told Eagle about his television statement.

"That was the way to handle it," Eagle said. "Now let's go talk to the cops. I'll stay out of it, unless you start getting yourself into trouble."

It was clear to Wolf that any astonishment at his being alive had passed and that he was now a prime suspect in a murder investigation. Carreras and Warren bored into him for over an hour, covering every step of his movements since the murders and looking very doubtful when he told them of his memory loss.

"Who was the other victim, Mr. Willett?" Warren asked, as if he expected an answer.

"I have no idea," Wolf said.

"We'd like you to try to make an identification of him," Carreras said.

"Gentlemen," Ed Eagle interrupted. "Dr. Mark Shea, who knows Mr. Willett very well, was unable to give you an accurate identification of the body. I understand most of the face is missing. Were there any sort of marks or tattoos that might mean something to Mr. Willett?"

"None," Carreras said.

"Then I fail to see how putting Mr. Willett through this could help you."

"I'm afraid I'll have to insist," Carreras said.

Wolf spoke up. "It's not an unreasonable request," he said.

"When would you like to do this?" Eagle asked.

"How about right now?" Carreras said.

"Where are the bodies?" Eagle asked.

"Well," Carreras said, "normally we would have moved them to the morgue at the office of the state medical examiner in Albuquerque, but because the M.E. has been ill, the autopsies were performed in Santa Fe, at St. Vincent's Hospital, and the bodies are still there. If we wait until tomorrow, you'll have to come to Albuquerque for the identification."

"Let's get it over with," Wolf said.

At the St. Vincent's morgue, Ed Eagle took charge. "You wait here," he said, pointing at a chair in the waiting room. He turned to the policemen. "I want to see them first," he said.

Carreras shrugged and led Eagle out of the room. They returned a couple of minutes later.

"All right, Wolf," Eagle said.

Wolf was suddenly afraid. His mouth went dry and he had trouble swallowing; his knees felt watery. He followed the three men into a room lined with tile on three walls and three rows of stainless steel drawers on the other. Three of the drawers stood open, and sheets covered the three bodies.

"Over here first," Carreras said, motioning to the drawer farthest to the right. He took hold of the sheet and pulled it off, exposing the entire naked body of a man. A towel had been draped across the face; Carreras did not remove this.

"I had them cover the faces," Eagle explained. "It wouldn't have helped you to see them."

Wolf stepped up to the table and looked at the body. At first his attention was fixed to the stitching that had followed the autopsy; then he forced himself to consider the body. It was about his size and build, he thought. The hair on the chest was graying, like his, the feet larger than his. He could see, though, how Mark might have mistaken the man for him, under the circumstances.

"There's a significant scar on the inside of the left wrist," Carreras said, picking up the corpse's hand and exposing the wrist. An ugly scar about three inches long was exhibited.

"Suicide attempt?" Eagle asked.

"Probably not," Carreras replied. "It's too jagged. When people slash their wrists, they usually do it with a razor blade or something else sharp, so they won't cause themselves too much pain. They usually do both wrists, too."

"I've never seen the scar," Wolf said. "I don't know the man."

"You're sure?" Warren asked.

"As sure as I can be under the circumstances," Wolf said. "Without seeing a face."

"There is no face," Warren said. "Is there anything else about him that looks familiar?"

Wolf shook his head. "Nothing."

Carreras led him to the next table and removed the sheet. Jack's body lay before him; there was no doubt. "It's Jack," Wolf said.

"How can you be so immediately sure?" Warren asked.

"I knew him for a long time," Wolf replied. "We've shared hotel rooms, houses; I've seen him naked dozens of times. When he came to my house to swim, he would never wear a suit. It's Jack's body."

"One more," Carreras said, stepping to the other drawer and removing the sheet.

Wolf had not been prepared for this. The sutures seemed a horrible violation of her body. The corpse was so white, when Julia had always been so tan. It might have been made of marble, yet it seemed shrunken, diminished. The large breasts had settled, like puddles of plaster. Two things heightened the familiarity: the brightly painted fingernails—Julia had always been careful with her nails—and the tattoo of the flower on her right breast, the bright colors of which stood out against the skin, now alabaster in death.

He wanted to pull the towel off her head and look at her face, but he reminded himself that there was no face. A strand of hair spilled from under the towel; it was clotted with something black.

Wolf nodded. "It's my wife," he said.

"You're positive?" Warren asked.

His shoulders sagged. "It's Julia."

Carreras paused on the sidewalk in front of the hospital. "I've asked you this before, Mr. Willett, but I want to ask you again. Can you think of any reason why anybody would want to kill you, your wife, or Jack Tinney?"

"No, none," Wolf said. "It just doesn't make any sense. It must have been an intruder, somebody who was trying to rob the house or something. Several of the houses at Wilderness Gate are unoccupied a lot of the time—weekend or summer places. There have been break-ins before."

"We know about that," Carreras said. "It's a possibility. Still, I've dispatched an officer to your place. We'll keep a watch for a while."

"Do you think that's really necessary?" Wolf asked. He didn't want to be watched, himself.

"Somebody has already attempted to kill you," Carreras said.

Ed Eagle spoke up. "He has a point, Wolf."

"Anybody who knew me would know it wasn't me he was killing," Wolf said.

"Not if he was a contract killer," Carreras replied. "After all, the dead man generally matched your description."

This was a possibility Wolf hadn't considered. "All right, if you think it's advisable to have a man up there," he said.

"Will you ask him to keep the press out?" Eagle asked. "A television crew has already been there, and when it becomes public that Mr. Willett is alive, a lot more are going to show up."

"Okay," Carreras said. "I'll tell my man no press." He turned back to Wolf. "You understand, Mr. Willett, we don't want you leaving Santa Fe."

"I understand," Wolf replied. "I have no plans to leave." He thought of something, was ashamed he hadn't thought of it sooner. "When can I have my wife's and Jack's bodies?" he asked Carreras.

"Did Mr. Tinney have any family?"

"No one, just some ex-wives. I'm his executor."

"I'll have the bodies released immediately," Carreras said. "There are the personal effects, too."

The two policemen shook hands with them and left Wolf and Ed Eagle standing on the sidewalk.

"I'll make the arrangements with a funeral parlor, if you like," Eagle said. "They'll deliver the effects later."

"Thank you," Wolf replied.

"Do you have someplace to bury them?"

Wolf shook his head. "No. I think cremation is best. I'll figure out what to do with the ashes later."

"Wolf," Eagle said, "it's important that if you even consider leaving Santa Fe, you talk with me first."

"Of course, Ed."

"There's something else I wanted to mention to you," the lawyer said.

"What's that?"

"I want to go to New York and interview Julia's sister, the one in prison."

"If you think it'll help."

"I don't know. I just wanted to clear it with you before I travel at your expense. You've paid for my time, but there'll be airline, hotel, all that."

"Sure, go ahead."

"It'll be sometime next week before I can get away. Call me if you need me in the meantime."

"Sure, Ed. Thanks for coming today."

"Don't mention it."

"Ed, there's something I don't understand."

"What's that?"

"Why haven't they arrested me for the murders? It seems to me I'm the only logical suspect."

"Santa Fe Rules, Wolf. They haven't arrested you because they're scared shitless of me. I've tried more than a dozen capital cases in Santa Fe County over the past twenty-odd years, and they haven't gotten a conviction yet. They don't have any hard evidence against you, only supposition, but the minute they think they have a real case, they'll come for you."

"I see," Wolf muttered.

"Don't worry. If it happens, we'll be ready for them."

They shook hands and went to their respective cars.

Back at Wilderness Gate, there were two television vans and two other cars parked in the road near his gate. Several people, some with cameras, were talking to a uniformed policeman. Wolf pulled up to the gate and produced his driver's license. "I'm Willett," he said to the cop.

The policeman inspected the license and

moved between Wolf and a television cameraman. People were shouting questions from behind the cop. "Go on in, Mr. Willett," he said.
"I'll get rid of these people."

Wolf hurried down the drive, thinking not
about the reporters at his gate, but about Julia's
sister, in prison. He wanted to know what she
knew.

13

Maria arrived as Wolf was finishing breakfast, and tears began to flow the moment she saw him.

"Oh, Mr. Wolf," she blubbered. "When I saw you on the TV I was so happy."

He calmed her and listened to her story of finding the bodies. It told him nothing he didn't already know. "Was there a policeman at the gate when you arrived today?" he asked.

"Yessir."

"Please take him a Thermos of coffee." That would get her busy and out of his hair. Maria had brought the morning mail. He didn't get much mail in Santa Fe, but this morning there were two invitations, both for dinner. The first was from neighbors he didn't particularly like—he would beg off. The second interested him more. It was from the Duke and Duchess of Kensington, English nobility who lived for part of the year on a large estate out on Tano Road, near Mark Shea. He had met them once at a dinner party at an actor's house two years before, and had not heard from them since. Now he was desirable company, it seemed. Well, what the hell, Ed Eagle had told him to go out. He phoned the R.S.V.P. number and left an acceptance on an answering machine. As soon as he hung up, the phone rang. Wolf let his answering machine pick up, then he heard Hal Berger's voice.

He picked up the phone. "Hello, Hal."

"Wolf, you okay?"

"Yes, I'm fine."

"You square with the cops?"

"For the moment. Listen, will you call my bank and let them know I'm alive? I've written a check for a hundred thousand dollars, and I don't want it to bounce."

"Sure."

"What's happening there?"

"The office is on an even keel. The L.A. stations picked up the report from Santa Fe in time for the eleven o'clock news last night, so the employees know you're alive and kicking. It gave them a lift, I think; things had been pretty uncertain around here. Anything you want me to tell them?"

"Tell them it's business as usual. Give Jack's new script to Bob in production and tell him to start costing it. It's not ready for that, really, but it'll give him something to do."

"Okay. The Academy has been on the phone wanting to do a memorial service for Jack. They had been thinking of a service for the two of you, but the TV report fixed that."

"Hold them off for a while, will you? I can't leave Santa Fe right now, and I want to participate in the service when it happens." He had a thought. "Hal, will you look in the safe—top shelf, right-hand side, I think? Jack's and my wills are in there. I'm his executor, so I guess I should do something about it."

"Want me to do it now?"

"Yes, I'll hold on." He would be handling Jack's affairs in death, as in life, and he wasn't looking forward to it.

Hal came back on the line. "Got it. Want me to break the seal?"

"Yes, go ahead."

"Okay, it's dated last month."

"Last month? I wrote a will for him a couple of years ago; I didn't know he'd done another one. Give me the highlights."

"Let's see. A few small bequests—the Academy, U.C.L.A. film school, some others."

"Nothing much has changed, then."

"Who got the bulk of his estate in the last will?" Hal asked.

"He divided it equally among the ex-wives—four of them."

"Not anymore," Hal said. "Everything goes to you."

"To *me*?" Wolf was stunned.

"Everything. His half of the business, his house, cars, furnishings, savings, everything."

"Jesus Christ," Wolf said. "I wonder why he did that."

"It says here, 'In gratitude for his friendship,

professional partnership, and wise management of my affairs.' "

"I'm floored," Wolf said, and he was.

"At least you won't have to struggle with the ex-wives to run the company."

"That's true. I'm grateful to him for that."

"You want to enter this for probate?"

"There's no reason to delay, I guess; go ahead. And fax me the will, Hal. I want to read it."

"Sure. Anything else?"

"Have you got an answer print from Jane Deering yet?"

"Oh, I forgot. She called yesterday and wanted to talk to you. Shall I give her the Santa Fe number?"

"That's fine."

"I think she's having some last-minute nerves about the final cut."

"I'll talk to her. Anything else?"

"That's it. Keep in touch, you hear?"

"I will." He hung up and tried to grapple with the idea of being Jack Tinney's heir. The fax machine rang; the will was coming through.

He heard voices from the kitchen, and a moment later, Flaps burst into the room and was all over him. Mark Shea followed her in.

"Caught you on TV," he said, smiling broadly. "Thought you'd like to see the pup."

Wolf stroked and calmed the dog. Then the sound from the kitchen of dry dog food hitting a plastic bowl lured her away.

"How are you?" Mark asked.

"Okay, I guess."

"Had a chat with the police yet?"

"Yeah, last evening. Ed Eagle is holding them at bay for the moment. Thanks for recommending him. How about some coffee?"

Mark glanced at his watch. "Wish I could. I've got a patient in twenty minutes. I just wanted to bring Flaps home and make sure you were all right."

"I saw the bodies yesterday. I can see how you might have thought it was me."

"Thanks. I've been feeling badly about it."

"Don't. Anybody could have made the same mistake."

"What are you going to do about a funeral?"

"Nothing at the moment. The Academy wants to hold a memorial service for Jack later. I haven't decided what to do about Julia."

"I see."

"Mark, Ed Eagle is going to want to talk to you about me; he's looking ahead to the possibility of a trial. I told him it was fine with me. I hope it's okay with you."

Mark started to speak, then stopped. "I'll do whatever you want, Wolf," he said after a moment.

"I think he's most concerned with my psychiatric history, and since you've been my analyst, you could testify about that. Julia's, too. Tell him whatever he wants to know."

The psychiatrist made no reply.

"I don't think you need to go into the hypnosis—unless he brings up the idea."

Mark nodded. "Want to have dinner one night soon?"

"Sure. Ed says I should be seen around town. Speaking of that, the D & D have asked me over."

"Tomorrow night? I'll be there, too." He waved from the door. "See you there."

The phone rang, and Wolf picked it up without thinking. "Hello," he said, annoyed with himself for answering.

"It's Jane. Hal said I could call. Is this a bad time?"

"No, no, it's fine; I'm glad to hear from you. What's up?"

"I've got a final cut, but I want you to see it before I give an answer print to Hal."

"I trust your judgment, Jane."

"Thanks, but it's too important for me to approve on my own; you might think it's sort of . . . radical. I want to Fed Ex you a videotape."

He had a thought. "I've got a better idea; bring it."

"To Santa Fe?"

"There's a noon flight from LAX. I'll meet you at the Albuquerque airport."

"I'll have to see if my sister can stay with my daughter."

"Do it. I'll be glad to see you. And bring a hot dress; there's a dinner party tomorrow night."

"I'll call you back."

He hung up, and for some reason, he felt a lot better. There was another incoming call, and he picked that up without thinking, too.

"Good morning, Mr. Willett. This is John Harvey at Harvey and Sons Funeral Directors."

"Hello, Mr. Harvey."

"The county released the bodies of Mrs. Willett and Mr. Tinney to us this morning. Mr. Eagle said you were interested in cremation."

"That's right. I'd like both bodies cremated as soon as possible, quietly and without ceremony."

"I can arrange that for tomorrow in Albuquerque," Harvey said. "Would you like to be present?"

"No," Wolf replied. "You may deliver the ashes to my home when it's done."

"Would you like to choose the urns?"

"Do it for me, please. Something simple. Bring me a bill for your services with the ashes."

"Would five o'clock tomorrow afternoon be convenient for delivery?"

"That will be fine." He gave the man his address and hung up, feeling like a shit for ducking the occasion.

Jane called back. "You're on. How long will I be there?"

"Allow a couple of days, in case we have to make changes."

"Okay."

"I'll meet the plane this afternoon."

"See you then."

"I'll look forward to it."

14

Jane arrived in the terminal smiling, carrying all her luggage. Wolf bundled her into the Porsche with her bags and headed north on the interstate.

"So, what have you done with my movie?"

She took a deep breath. "I took your four minutes out of the middle third."

He looked at her, surprised. "I would have chopped little stuff throughout."

"I know you would have, but I got this idea, and I want to see if you think it works."

"Tell me about it."

"I'd rather show you."

Jane pointed the remote control at the VCR and stopped the tape. "That's it. The rest is the same as before."

"I'm amazed," he said. "I wouldn't have thought it possible."

"I figured that by quick-cutting from Helen's to Joe's plot lines in the middle I could cut more than a minute out of each of the three long scenes."

"It worked. Call the lab and tell them to print it."

With a triumphant laugh, she leapt up and hugged him. "I *knew* you'd let me do it."

He liked the hug. "Then why didn't you go ahead and make the answer print?"

"Well," she said, "there was always a chance you'd be in a bad mood and not spot my brilliance."

"I spotted your brilliance." He pointed at a phone across the room. "Phone the lab; use line two."

She went to the phone, and Wolf looked idly around for something to interest him while she talked. His eye fell on the fax machine; he hadn't read Jack's will. Leafing through the pages, he found it simple and straightforward. Jack had gone to another lawyer to have the will drawn. Wolf knew Bob Marx well enough—they had played tennis in the old days, and Marx had a successful entertainment practice. He punched the other line and dialed Marx's office.

"Wolf, is it really you?" Marx sounded truly uncertain.

"It is, Bob. I'm still around."

"I heard about your television interview," Marx said.

"Bob, Hal Berger just faxed me Jack Tinney's will, which was in our office safe."

"You knew his intentions, of course."

"No, I had no idea. I drew a will for him a couple of years ago that left everything to the four ex-wives. As far as I knew, that one was still in force."

There was a brief silence before Marx spoke again. "That was not my information," he said.

"What do you mean?"

"I mean that Jack told me he was going to tell you about it."

"Well, he didn't. Why did he change his will? Did he tell you that?"

"He stated his reasons in the text."

"I read that, but it sounded like boilerplate."

"Well, Wolf, I'm sorry you disapprove of my writing style, but Jack liked it. That was what he wanted to say."

Wolf looked at the document again. "I'm still his executor," he said.

"That's right. He didn't see any reason to change that."

"Well, there might be some reason to change it now."

Marx didn't respond.

"I mean, this might not look good to some people—Jack's being murdered in my house, and my being his beneficiary."

"I take your point," Marx said blandly. "How can I help?"

"I think, under the circumstances, I'd like to assign my executor's powers to you, since you drew the will."

"I'll be glad to handle that as a courtesy."

"Thank you, Bob. I'll draw up an assignment of powers and get it to you in a day or two."

"All right. Wolf, is there anything else I can

help with? I mean, are you in need of any other legal help at the moment?" The question was heavy with meaning.

"No, Bob, but thanks for the thought."

"Call me if you need anything."

Wolf thanked him and hung up.

Jane was hanging up the other line. "Okay, they'll deliver to Hal on Monday."

"Great. And thank you for doing such a terrific job."

"It was my pleasure."

"Well, let's find you a room, shall we?" He grabbed her bags and led her to the guest wing, choosing the room farthest from the murder scene. "I hope you'll be comfortable here," he said, placing her bags on the bed. "The heat will be a little slow taking hold; it comes from pipes under the floor, and it has to heat the stones."

"I'll be fine," she said. "I'd like to have a shower. That'll warm me up."

"Go ahead. I'll book us a table for dinner somewhere."

"Fine."

"Dress casually; Santa Fe is like that."

"Okay. What's the hot dress for?"

"Oh, that's tomorrow night; dinner with the D & D."

"Who?"

"The Duke and Duchess of Kensington."

"Whatever you say," she said, shaking her head.

He left her and went back to his study. Another reading of Jack's will provided no clues to the director's state of mind. Jack had never mentioned the new will to him, but he had always been embarrassed about discussing personal matters.

He rang Santacafé, his favorite restaurant, and booked a table for two.

The owner, Jim Arno, greeted Wolf warmly at the door, and on the way to their table they passed three groups of people Wolf knew. Some greeted him; others waved halfheartedly. He didn't introduce Jane to any of them.

"Friends?" Jane asked archly as they sat down at their table and picked up menus.

"That remains to be seen," Wolf said.

"They looked surprised to see me with you," she said.

"Fuck 'em," Wolf said lightly. "I can recommend the smoked pheasant spring rolls or the Chinese dumplings to start; the fish is always good, and I'm fond of the duck."

"Surprise me," she said.

"Seems only fair," he replied. "You've been surprising me for the past two weeks."

"Oh? How?"

"Well, you were always just the editor's assistant before; I had no idea you were so good."

"Why did you ask for me, then?"

"I wanted a cutter—a technician; I didn't expect more than that."

"I like to give people more than they expect," she said.

"A good policy," he replied. "Tell me, how did you become a single mother?"

"The usual way," she said dryly.

He laughed. "That wasn't what I meant. Why didn't you marry the guy?"

"And compound my error? He was an out-of-work actor—still is—and it was just a roll in the hay. I was on the pill, but I guess it didn't work."

"Was having the baby a tough decision?"

"Not really. I had two strong feelings: one, I didn't want to have an abortion, and two, I wanted a baby. No conflict."

"Has it been tough?"

"Not as tough as you might think. My sister, who's single too, has been great. She lived with me until Sara was old enough for school; otherwise, it would have been *really* tough."

"No disadvantages to being a single mother?"

Jane shrugged. "Not many. Not much time for things other than work and Sara, I guess."

"So you've been a social recluse for the past eight or nine years?"

"Well, not entirely; but I found myself turning down invitations that were just dates. There didn't seem to be time for anything that didn't have more meaning."

"Does her father see anything of Sara?"

She shook her head. "She gets a birthday card from him most years; sometimes it comes with twenty bucks inside. He's in New York—was on a soap for a couple of years, but now he's at liberty again." She looked down at the tablecloth.

"Actually, I prefer having him in New York; I wouldn't want to share Sara with him. I'm too selfish. You were married once before, weren't you?"

He nodded and told her about the accident, skipping his blackout.

"That must have been tough."

He nodded again. "You get over these things," he said. "In fact, I think I'm getting better at getting over them."

She looked at him oddly but didn't question him further.

When they got back to the house in Wilderness Gate, he said goodnight at the door to the guest wing. They didn't touch.

15

Ed Eagle drove through the open gate and down the drive toward Mark Shea's house. As directed, he turned off to the little building where Shea received patients.

As he parked the car, the door to the office opened and Shea made his goodbyes to a tall, very beautiful woman Eagle recognized immediately. He had, in fact, seen her latest film the week before and had thought her brilliant. He was struck with an unexpected reluctance to make eye contact with her, and he waited until her car drove away before he got out of his. On his way to Shea's front door he analyzed his reaction. Was it timidity? Probably not; hardly anybody made him feel timid anymore. Tact, that's what it was, he decided. She wouldn't want to be seen leaving her psychiatrist's office, so he hadn't seen her.

"Morning, Ed; come in," Mark Shea said, smiling and shaking his hand. "Can I get you a cup of coffee?"

"If you'll join me, Mark." Eagle had known Shea since the psychiatrist had come to Santa Fe some years before, but they were not close friends. Still, he was grateful for the occasional referral of a client—especially one like Wolf Willett—and he liked the man. He'd heard that Shea had become a cult figure in the community, drawing wealthy patients from all over the country, some of whom had taken up residence in Santa Fe to be near him. Given Shea's charm and intelligence, this did not surprise the lawyer.

Shea poured their coffee and settled into a chair opposite Eagle.

It was much like the arrangement in his own study, Eagle reflected: cozy, friendly, and designed to draw out the visitor. "I want to talk with you about Wolf Willett, Mark," he said. "I have his permission to do so; you can call him, if you like."

"That won't be necessary, Ed. Wolf has already spoken to me about it."

"A little background: When did you first meet Wolf?"

"About three years ago, shortly after he built his house here."

"Did he come to you at that time for treatment?"

"No. We first met at a dinner party, and he called me some weeks later."

"What did he feel his problems were at the time?"

"He initially came to me for help in stopping smoking, and we fixed that, but Wolf felt he had difficulty forming close relationships with other people—both men and women—although he seemed to be better with women than with men. He was also going through a midlife reassessment of his existence: Did his work mean anything? Did he deserve his success? Was there any reason why anyone should love him? His concerns were typical of an intelligent, reflective, rather decent middle-aged man, and lacking a full relationship with a woman, he was without the support that a good marriage can bring. He needed some reinforcement."

"Is that what a psychiatrist does? Reinforce?"

Shea smiled. "There are nearly as many opinions about what a therapist's role is as there are psychiatrists. Many regard themselves as objective observers who, merely by listening to their patients, offer them a means of sorting themselves out. I do that with some patients, but on the whole, I lean toward a more activist view."

"What role did you take with Wolf?"

"I'm beginning to think this is more an examination of my technique than a conversation about Wolf."

"I'm sorry, but it's important for me to know his mind as well as a lawyer can, and it would be helpful if I understood how you worked with him."

"Wolf came to me a very self-sufficient man who had the dual burden of running a business and propping up a rather . . . ah, undisciplined partner. There were times when he felt inadequate to the job—especially the second role—and one of the things he needed from me was someone to tell him that he was all right, that he was doing a good job. I offered him that support. He deserved it."

"What other sorts of support did you offer him?"

"Mainly someone to talk with openly. I regarded Wolf then as a stable, self-aware human being who was coping well. He just didn't seem to be enjoying his life enough. I found him relatively free of neurosis, and—"

"Relatively?"

"None of us is free of neurosis; we all have our quirks."

"What were Wolf's quirks?"

"He was having some moderate difficulties with impotence; he wasn't enjoying sex much."

"How did you treat his impotence?"

"I prescribed a drug which is gaining a reputation for effectiveness. It's based on an old herbal remedy, and it seems to dilate the blood vessels that carry blood to the penis and cause an erection."

"What do you mean, 'seems'?"

"The effect may be that of a placebo—who knows? As far as I'm concerned, an effective placebo is as good as a cure."

"Did it work for Wolf?"

"Hard to say. He met Julia about that time, and she may have had a greater effect than the drug. He was capable again, anyway, and enjoying himself."

"What other quirks did he have?"

"The only thing of any importance was something he wouldn't talk about for a long time, something he really would talk about only after the murders."

"What was that?"

"His first wife, who was pregnant, was killed in an automobile accident while Wolf was driving her to the hospital for delivery."

"Did he have guilt feelings about that?"

"Of course; who wouldn't?"

"What effect did this guilt have on him?"

"Depression, of course, for quite a long time. And—" Shea suddenly looked grave—"something else."

Eagle leaned forward. "What else?"

"He blacked out. He told me that after the accident the police found him in a restaurant across the street, eating a cheeseburger as if nothing had happened. He had obviously suffered an enormous emotional trauma."

"How much time did he lose?"

"A day and a half, he says."

"Sounds familiar, doesn't it?"

"Yes."

"Have you talked with him about what happened the night of the murders?"

"Yes."

"What do you think happened?"

"I don't know enough to draw any conclusions."

"Come on, Mark, you're not on the stand here. Help me out."

"I think he may have discovered the bodies. Or . . ." Shea stopped.

"Go on."

"Or, it's possible he may have . . . been present at the time of the murders."

Eagle sat back in his chair. "Mark, you choose your words carefully; have you ever testified at a trial—as an expert witness?"

"No."

"All right, let's have a little psychodrama here. You're on the stand. The defense has already questioned you and elicited that Wolf is a normal person with few neuroses. You've conveyed to the jury that you have a high opinion of him. Now, I'm the prosecutor. Remember, you're under oath; you have to tell the truth. But be brief; I'm a sonofabitch of a prosecutor, and since you're a witness for the defense, you don't want to give me any gratuitous information."

"All right," Shea said. He shifted his position and crossed his legs.

"Don't cross your legs; don't do anything that might lead the jury to feel that you're defensive or contemptuous of the prosecutor. Don't give smart-ass answers. You're trying to be helpful, even if this guy is attempting to nail your patient with the death penalty."

Shea uncrossed his legs. "All right, I'm ready."

"Dr. Shea, is Wolf Willett a sane person?"

"Sane is a legal term, not a medical one."

"Don't get defensive; answer the man's question."

"I believe Mr. Willett to be in full possession of his faculties."

"So if Mr. Willett murdered his wife and his partner and another person, he knew exactly what he was doing?"

Shea froze.

"Answer the question."

"It's possible for a normal human being to have a moment when he doesn't know what he's doing."

"You mean temporary insanity?"

"Yes, you could call it that."

"Mr. Willett isn't pleading temporary insanity; he's pleading just plain not guilty. You're his psychiatrist. Is Wolf Willett capable of murder?"

"Only to the extent that anyone is capable of murder, that you yourself might be capable of murder."

"Is it psychologically possible that Wolf Willett committed three murders?"

"It is unlikely in the extreme."

"But is it possible?"

"Sir, it is *possible* that the *judge* committed these murders, but that is also unlikely in the extreme."

Eagle laughed. "Very good. You'll be hard to corner."

"Thank you. Is Wolf going to be tried for these murders?"

"I hope not. I'm doing everything in my power to prevent it, but if he is tried, we have to be ready. I take it you'll testify?"

"Of course."

"Mark, if we call you as an expert witness, the state will be entitled to have a psychiatrist of their choosing examine Wolf, too. Do you think another man might be able to find something in an examination that would reflect badly on Wolf?"

"Another psychiatrist, on hearing that Wolf can't remember the night of the murders, would immediately ask if he had ever had another such episode. He might try to make something of Wolf's previous experience."

"I think I could handle that," Eagle said.

Shea smiled. "I'm sure you could."

Ed Eagle left Mark Shea's place feeling that Shea knew more than he was telling about Wolf Willett, but he wasn't terribly bothered by that. If the psychiatrist was trying to protect Wolf, he would protect him from a prosecutor, too. And he was smart; he wouldn't be lured into damaging his friend. Eagle felt a little better about his case. He would feel even better, he thought, when he knew more about Julia Willett's background.

16

A dark lump swam up on the horizon. Wolf pointed. "See that? The big rock in the distance?"

"What rock?"

"There."

"Oh, yes. It doesn't look so big."

"That's because we're forty miles away from it. Wait a few minutes."

They had been flying for three-quarters of an hour, northwest from Santa Fe toward the Four Corners, where New Mexico, Arizona, Colorado, and Utah meet. Chaco Canyon was behind them, its ancient ruins snowy and still in the winter sun.

"That's Ship Rock," Wolf said. "So called because the settlers on the wagon trains thought it looked like a big sailing ship from a distance."

"Now it looks impressive," Jane said, squinting. "How tall is it?"

Wolf glanced at the aeronautical chart in his lap. "About two thousand feet above the surrounding terrain."

"It just gets bigger and bigger as we get closer."

They passed the big rock and flew on west, over a high ridge etched with little canyons, then over a broad plain.

"What's that in the distance?" Jane asked, pointing ahead.

"In a few minutes you'll know," Wolf replied. He pointed below at a circular structure. "Look down there; that's a hogan, a Navajo dwelling."

"They still live in those?"

"There's a more modern house just next to it, but the hogans are still used."

Wolf reset the altitude selector on the autopilot and the airplane began to descend.

"Are we landing?"

"Not quite. We're just going to fly low for a while." Another ten minutes passed.

Jane peered at the formation before them. "I know what it is!" she exclaimed delightedly. "I've seen it so many times—in a hundred movies, I'll bet, and in most of John Ford's!"

Monument Valley loomed ahead. Soon they were five hundred feet above the valley floor, flying among the ancient towers of red sandstone.

Jane was busy with her camera. "This is fantastic! What a sight!"

Patchy snow covered the ground for as far as the eye could see, and crowned the monuments with dashes of white. "I often wonder what the first settlers who saw this place must have felt," Wolf said.

"It has an almost religious quality, like a cathedral," Jane replied. "I've never seen anything so beautiful."

Wolf threaded the airplane among the monuments for another quarter of an hour, then turned toward the southwest and climbed to ten thousand five hundred feet.

"Wow! Where to now?"

"Someplace else you'll recognize."

Half an hour later Wolf pointed ahead to a large lake and, leading from it, a narrow cut in the stone. "Recognize that?"

"No. What is it?"

"Wait and see." He turned south over the narrow gorge, which began to widen out.

"I think I can guess," Jane said. "It's starting to look familiar, but it's still too small."

The Grand Canyon widened before them, and as the airplane flew over the north rim, it seemed that the bottom had fallen out of the world. The late afternoon sun struck the mesas and valleys of the enormous gulley, casting long shadows and turning the earth red.

"I thought airplanes couldn't fly over the Grand Canyon," Jane said, snapping pictures furiously.

"Only in certain zones; that's where we are. You used to be able to fly *in* the Canyon, until a helicopter and a sightseeing airplane collided. Then the rules were changed."

They reached the south rim, and Wolf turned east again, glancing at the airport, remembering his last visit there.

Jane read his mind. "That's where you were when . . ." Her voice trailed off.

"Not exactly," Wolf said. "I was in the house. At least, I think I was." He began to tell the story again. He was becoming practiced now, and telling it hurt less than it had before.

When he had finished, Jane was quiet for a while. "Well," she said finally, "it sounds as though you're telling me you may have killed Jack and your wife."

"I don't know," he said truthfully.

"I know that anybody is supposed to be capable of murder," she said, "but I can't bring myself to believe that you had anything to do with it."

"I'm glad you feel that way," he sighed.

"There's got to be some other explanation."

"I hope so."

They flew east toward Santa Fe in silence.

17

An off-duty policeman glanced at their invitation, then allowed them through the high gates of the Kensington estate.

"Exactly who are these people?" Jane asked.

"He is said to be one of the richest of the English dukes," Wolf replied, "and that's rich. The current duchess is his fourth wife, and I hear they are socially jealous of our other D & D, the Bedfords, who have a place in Tesuque. That's all I know about them."

Jane looked around at the lighted grounds as they drove down the drive. "I wouldn't want their electricity bill," she said.

"Or any of their other bills." Wolf laughed. He looked around, too. "They seem to have about five acres walled in. Apparently the Duchess has spent a fortune planting and watering an English garden. Pity it's cold weather and we'll miss the blooms."

"Pity."

Their car was taken away, and they were met

at the front door by a uniformed butler, who asked for their invitation. Wolf could see the Duke and Duchess waiting farther down the entrance hall.

The butler braced up and announced loudly in a broad Scottish accent, "Mr. and Mrs. Wolf Willett!"

"Oh, Christ," Wolf muttered, then he corrected the man.

"Mr. Wolf Willett and Miz Jane Deering!" the butler yelled, unabashed.

The D & D stood waiting, smiles frozen onto their faces. Wolf looked farther down the hall and saw a flash of blond hair and a face he would rather not have seen disappearing into the living room.

"Mr. Willett, how very nice to see you," the Duchess said, extending a tiny hand.

"Yes, yes," the Duke echoed, offering a hand nearly as small. "Jolly nice."

"May I present Ms. Jane Deering?" Wolf said.

"So very nice," the Duchess said to Jane.

"Jolly nice," the Duke said.

"Please do go through and have a drink," the Duchess said, dismissing them and turning toward her next arriving guests.

Wolf took Jane by the elbow and steered her toward the living room.

"I thought he was rather sweet," she said.

"No one knows for sure," Wolf said. "She does all the talking for both of them."

They paused at the entrance to the enormous living room to peer inside, and as they did so, they stepped into a spotlight that had been trained onto the broad doorway. A hundred and fifty heads turned, and the room went suddenly quiet.

Wolf stood there, momentarily stunned, then recovered himself and led Jane down the short steps into the room. Conversation in the room continued; Wolf knew exactly what the topic was.

"That was very weird," Jane said.

Wolf nodded. "Once, I was in a London restaurant not long after the Manson family murders in L.A., and Roman Polanski walked into the room. Exactly the same thing happened."

Mark Shea was making his way toward them. "Wolf, good to see you out," Mark said, shaking his hand warmly and looking at Jane. "And who's this?"

"This is Jane Deering, the editor of our new film," Wolf said, feeling suddenly defensive.

Mark turned his attention to Jane. "Jane, welcome to Santa Fe. Is this your first visit?"

"Yes," she said, immediately warming to Mark, "and I think it's wonderful."

"I can see this won't be your last trip," Mark said, smiling. "And how is work going on *L.A. Days*?"

"Work was completed just yesterday," Jane replied.

"Congratulations to you both. You must feel an enormous sense of relief, having it in the can."

"I certainly do," Wolf said.

"Got something new to move to the front burner?"

"It's being costed right now," Wolf replied. He glanced across the room and saw Ed Eagle, head and shoulders above the crowd, making his way toward them.

A waiter appeared with tall flutes of champagne on a tray. Wolf snagged two, passed one to Jane, and managed to get a long swallow down before Ed Eagle arrived.

"Evening, Wolf," Eagle said, smiling slightly.

"Evening, Ed. Let me introduce you to Jane Deering, who is the editor of our new film."

"Miss Deering, it's a great pleasure to meet you," Eagle said, enveloping her small hand in his giant one. He turned back to Wolf. "Could I have a brief word with you?"

"Sure. Mark, would you take care of Jane for a moment?"

"Of course."

Eagle steered Wolf toward a sliding glass door and ushered him out into the frigid night air. He turned to face his client. "Are you out of your fucking mind?" he asked pleasantly.

Wolf was baffled. "What? I thought you said for me to go out, to be seen."

"I didn't tell you to be seen with a beautiful woman in a killer dress, two weeks after your wife was murdered," Eagle said. His voice was perfectly modulated and friendly. There was, if anything, a note of regret.

"Oh," Wolf said helplessly. "I see your point."

"I wish you had seen it a couple of days earlier," Eagle said. "The first bit of gossip I heard when I arrived here was that you were at Santacafé last night with a woman, and now you turn up here with her. I suppose you went to meet her in Albuquerque."

"Yes."

"You're not supposed to leave town; that's a violation of what I promised the D.A."

"I'm sorry about that," Wolf replied. It didn't seem like the best moment to mention the airplane trip with Jane to Monument Valley and the Grand Canyon.

"Martinez is going to know about this evening before he even has his coffee tomorrow morning, and it's just feasible, should you, God forbid, come to trial, that one or more of the people here tonight might be on your jury. I don't suppose you considered that."

"Not for a moment, I'm afraid," Wolf said sheepishly.

"All right. It's done," Eagle said. "Now I want you to go back into that room, take that girl by the hand, and introduce her to every single person you know here. There's nothing to do but brazen it out. Be sure to be among the last to leave." He opened the sliding door and waved Wolf back into the room.

Wolf, feeling abashed, had hardly stepped into the warmth again when he saw a blur of blond hair and gold dress, and Monica Collins stood before him trembling with anger.

"Good evening, Monica," Wolf said uncertainly.

"You bastard," Monica said, winding up to deliver a blow across his face.

Mark Shea's hand snaked between them and caught the slap before it could land. In one swift motion, he swung the woman around and swept her from the room. "Now, Monica," he was saying, "you must behave yourself."

Wolf stood transfixed, trying to keep an expressionless face. Everyone seemed to have noticed what had happened. He forced himself to move toward Eagle and Jane.

"You all right?" Jane asked, peering closely at him.

Ed Eagle spoke up. "I take it that was Monica Collins."

"Yes," Wolf said.

"I don't think we'll seek her testimony," Eagle replied.

"I guess not." Wolf sighed. "Come on, Jane, I want you to meet some people."

"Who the hell was *that*?" Jane asked under her breath as they moved into the crowd.

"A friend of Julia's."

"Such nice friends."

On the way home, Jane shook off her shoes and braced her feet against the dashboard. "Whew," she said. "I never knew you were such a social lion. Was there anybody we didn't talk to?"

"I hope not," Wolf replied wearily.

"Who was the tall Indian again?" she asked.

"His name is Ed Eagle."

"The hotshot lawyer?"

"You've heard of him?"

"Yeah, he got that actor, what's-his-name, off a rape charge in L.A. last year, remember?"

"Right."

"Is he *your* lawyer?"

"Yes."

"And he wasn't very pleased to see me with you tonight, was he?"

"No, but that's not your fault; it's mine. I've been behaving as if nothing has happened, when one hell of a lot *has* happened. I think it's just hit me for the first time."

"Julia's death?"

"No. I've been dealing with that. I've just realized that, no matter what happens now, nothing is ever going to be the same again—not my social life, not my work, not the way people look at me or think of me. Nothing."

"I think maybe you'd better put me on the first plane to L.A. tomorrow morning."

"You're right," he said. "It's not what I want, but it's the only thing, under the circumstances."

"It's not what I want, either, if that helps." She put her hand on his.

"It helps," he said.

18

Ed Eagle drove north from New York to Pough-keepsie and turned off at the sign for the correctional facility for women. The road was slushy from a snowfall the night before, and light flakes were still coming down. Eagle had visited a lot of such places in his time, and this one was no different from the dozens of other low-security prisons around the country; the only difference was that it held what the courts regarded as hard cases. Apparently the state felt that hard-case women didn't need high walls, guard towers, and vicious dogs to keep them inside.

He presented his card to the man at the gate, who checked his appointment on a list, then waved him to a parking area. He walked through another gate and to the administrative office.

"I'm here to see Hannah Schlemmer," he said to a uniformed female clerk.

"Take a seat," the woman said, then made a phone call.

Eagle sat on a hard chair and waited ten minutes, his overcoat in his lap. Finally another woman in uniform appeared and ushered him to a small, nicely furnished sitting room, with a window overlooking a wooded area at the rear of the prison. The room had obviously been arranged to make visitors feel at ease. A moment later, a strikingly beautiful woman walked into the room. She was tall—five-ten or -eleven, he reckoned— something that had always appealed to him. She was dressed in tight designer jeans and a blue work shirt that had been knotted at the waist, covering ample breasts but revealing a couple of inches of flat belly. Her hair was cut short—dark with highlights of red; her nose was long and straight, her lips full, her eyes large, under lush eyebrows; the lashes were incredibly long. Her skin was perfect, and she wore little makeup.

"Mr. Eagle, I'm Barbara Kennerly," she said, sticking out a hand. Her grip was firm and frank.

His own hand did not swallow hers, the way it did with most women. "What happened to Hannah Schlemmer?" he asked.

"I've just had it changed; the system here hasn't quite caught up with the courts. Won't you sit down?" She might have been an elegant housewife entertaining a guest in her home, instead of a convicted felon.

Eagle took a comfortable chair; Barbara took the sofa.

"Would you like a cigarette?" she asked.

"Thank you, I don't smoke."

She smiled a little. "I've given it up, myself, but

cigarettes are legal tender here, so I always keep a pack in my pocket."

Eagle couldn't imagine how she could squeeze a nickel into one of her pockets, let alone a pack of cigarettes.

"How can I help you?" she asked.

"I'm a lawyer, Miss . . . Kennerly, and—"

"I know who you are, Mr. Eagle; I read the papers."

"I'm representing Mr. Wolf Willett—your sister, Miriam's, husband. I'm trying to get to the bottom of what happened to her."

She laughed again, something she seemed to do easily. "You mean Julia. She changed her name long before I did."

"Yes, Julia."

"Has Mr. Willett been charged with anything in connection with Julia's death?"

"No. As I say, I'm just trying to get to the bottom of the murders."

"You're not exactly a private detective, Mr. Eagle. If Mr. Willett has hired you, it must be for a defense."

"There is no charge to answer at the moment."

"You're just being prepared, in case there is?"

"I don't anticipate a charge." He was not exactly controlling this conversation.

"I'm impressed that you came all this way yourself, when you could have sent somebody," she said, looking him in the eye. "Frankly, if I'm going to talk with you, I want to know what you're up to."

Eagle sighed. "All right, I'll be frank with you. Wolf Willett had nothing to do with the murders—I feel certain of that—but it's possible that the New Mexico authorities might, if they can't solve the case, try to make a victim of him."

"That's close enough to the truth, I guess," Barbara said. "You're here to protect your client, and you hope I can somehow help you."

"I'm here to find out the truth, because I believe the truth will vindicate my client," Eagle said.

"Forgive me if I sound cynical, Mr. Eagle; prison does that to you. You're always looking for people's hidden motives, especially lawyers'." She shrugged. "All right, I'll tell you whatever I can. The truth can't harm me."

"Were you and Julia close?"

"I hadn't seen her for a couple of years when she was killed."

"What were the circumstances the last time you saw her?"

"She was in jail, at Riker's Island. She wanted money for a lawyer."

"Did you give it to her?"

"I managed to scrape up a couple of thousand. I didn't want my husband to know."

"Had you been close before that?"

Barbara Kennerly looked out the window. "I don't know," she said. "There were times when I thought we were close, but I learned that you could never tell what Julia was thinking. She was like that from childhood."

"Was Julia older than you?"

"Yes, by two years."

"And you grew up in Cleveland?"

"Yes. Daddy had a pawnshop on the wrong side of the tracks. Tough neighborhood. He tried to protect us from it, but Julia didn't want protecting; she was always fascinated by the slick guys and fast talkers. I was the straight arrow—good grades in school, all that. It's ironic that I ended up in prison, just like Julia."

"Did Julia have anything to do with that?"

"No. I was married to a man who had a diamond distribution business on West Forty-seventh Street in New York. I fell in love with another man—*really* in love, head over heels—and he convinced me that the only way we were ever going to be together was to rob my husband and get out. I got him into Murray's office—there was quite an elaborate security system—and the minute he got his hands on the diamonds, he shot Murray. I was stunned. He forced me to go with him. They caught up with us in Florida, just as I was about to try to sneak out and turn myself in."

"What happened then?"

"I turned state's evidence, pled to involuntary manslaughter. I got five to eight; I'm up for parole next year."

"And the man?"

"He got life. Broke out of prison last year; they still haven't caught him. That's partly why I changed my name; I don't want him *ever* to find me."

"After you saw Julia at Riker's Island, did you ever hear from her again?"

"Yes. She'd write a postcard now and then. When she got married to Wolf Willett, she sent me a phone number, and I called her a couple of times. She was going to help me when I got out." She laughed. "That's funny. Julia was always in trouble, always came to me for money. Now the tables were going to be turned. I, the conventional married Jewish lady, stable home and all that, needing the help of my sister with the criminal past."

"Did you ever get the feeling that Julia was working some sort of con with Willett?"

"No. If anything, she seemed to have changed. Whenever I talked to her, she always seemed happy as a clam. I guess she got the things honestly—more or less—that she had been trying to get dishonestly for all those years."

" 'More or less'?"

"Oh, I think Julia would always have conned people to get what she wanted. But lots of women do that to marry the right man."

"Did she love him, do you think?"

Barbara frowned. "That might be stretching things a little far. Julia mostly loved herself, but she seemed to be working at being a wife when I talked to her. I think she was trying to live some sort of normal life." She laughed again. "Mind you, it was normal life with houses in Bel Air and Santa Fe—hot and cold running Mercedes, that sort of thing. Julia could get used to that— for a while, anyway. Nothing and nobody ever lasted very long with Julia. She always had ants in her pants."

"Do you think that Julia had any friends in L.A. from her old life?"

Barbara shook her head. "I think she made the break. The last thing she would have wanted was somebody from her past turning up."

"From what I read in the *New York Times*, she didn't break from her past right away when she moved to Los Angeles. There was mention of her making a porno movie."

"She was flat broke. She told me about it."

"That would open her up to blackmail, wouldn't it?"

"It never did. She would have told me. She used yet another name, of course."

"Barbara, something I don't understand."

"What's that?"

"When the *Times* reporter was up here to see you, you told him about Julia's past. Why would you do that, when it might threaten her new position in life at a time when she was going to help you?"

Barbara sighed. "He'd reported on my case when I was convicted, and he said he wanted to do a book about me, something that might be made into a movie. He'd made a couple of trips up here, and he was coming again. I heard about Julia on the news the night before, and, well, I thought it couldn't hurt her for me to tell him, and it might help me by keeping him interested. I certainly didn't expect it to turn up in the paper the next day. I guess I was naive."

"Is he going ahead with the book?"

"Well, as I figured, when he heard who Julia

was married to, he got all excited. He's taking it to publishers now, he says. Thing is, I don't think I want the book anymore, what with my parole coming up. I think I'd rather just fade into the sunset, get a job somewhere."

"Do you have any skills?"

"I was a secretary before I married, and during the first couple of years I helped Murray with the business. I know how to run an office—word processing, bookkeeping, all that. And I worked in a restaurant when I was single."

"Is there anything else you can think of that might shed any light on Julia's murder? Was there anybody who might want to kill her? Some enemy from the old days, maybe?"

Barbara looked thoughtful. "I didn't know a lot of the details of Julia's life, but I can't think anybody would want to kill her. She had a way of making people like her—even when she'd done them wrong. Daddy helped her until the day he died—even left her some money—and God knows, she'd made his life hell since she was twelve."

Eagle stood up. "Well, I'd better be going." He produced a card. "If you think of anything else, I'd appreciate a call—collect, of course." He felt sorry for the woman, and he was attracted to her. "And if I can help, let me know."

She accepted the card. "Thanks, but I don't know if I'll get that far west."

"I know a few people in the East, too."

"I'll keep that in mind."

Eagle shook her hand again. "Thank you, Barbara, for your help."

"Not at all. If I ever need a lawyer, I'll call you."

He was at the point of telling her to call him anyway, but he stopped himself. Now that he was middle-aged, he was trying not to follow his cock around quite so much. "Goodbye, then, and good luck."

"Thanks." She gave him her large, strong hand again.

Driving back to New York, he tried to forget how she had looked in those jeans, about the full breasts under the work shirt. It wasn't easy.

He'd asked her every question he could think of, but the answers hadn't helped much. He wondered for a moment if there was something she hadn't told him, but he discounted that. He was a damned good reader of people, and he reckoned she had been open with him.

19

When Ed Eagle awoke the following morning in his room at the Pierre, he found that his mind had been at work during the night, something that often happened, and he felt uneasy about his interview with Barbara Kennerly, née Hannah Schlemmer. He picked up the phone and dialed a friend in the office of the district attorney of New York County.

"Brian, this is Ed Eagle. How are you?"

"I'm good, Ed. You in town?"

"Yeah. I'm flying back this afternoon, and I need some information from your office."

"What sort of information?"

"I'd like to see the prosecutor's notes on a case your office tried."

"How long ago?"

"A couple of years."

"Those files would be stored in County Records. We only keep that stuff until there's a disposition of the case. You're talking about a week or ten days to unearth it; they're always backed up over there."

"I see. Maybe I could talk to the prosecutor."

"What was the case?"

"A diamond merchant named Murray Rifkind murdered by his wife's lover during a robbery attempt."

"Hang on a minute. I'll ask around."

Eagle toyed with a piece of toast from the remnants of his breakfast while he waited.

"Okay, the case was tried by a guy named Herbert Stein, a senior prosecutor. I'll transfer you. You still leading the bachelor life out West?"

"You bet."

"Lucky bastard. Hang on."

There was a series of clicks on the line, followed by a ringing.

"This is Herbert Stein."

"Mr. Stein, this is Ed Eagle."

"Hi. What can I do for you?"

"You tried the Murray Rifkind case?"

"That's right."

"Can you tell me in general about it?"

"Rifkind's wife had a lover with an armed robbery record. He got her to let him into Rifkind's office, where he blew the guy away. The two of them decamped with a couple of pounds of diamonds. They were arrested in Miami, but the guy had already fenced the goods."

"What was the disposition?"

"The killer—his name was, let me see—Grafton, James Grafton—got life; Rifkind's wife cooperated, copped to involuntary manslaughter, got a five-to-eight."

"You remember the woman?"

"Do I! She was a knockout!"

"How much help was she?"

"Gave me everything I asked for. Got up and said her piece in court. A stand-up lady. Grafton was a nasty piece of work, too, a slick guy, con man, but with a violent streak."

"He's out, I hear."

"Out? No way. He'll do twenty years before he comes up for parole, and since we never recovered the diamonds or any money, he's not likely to get it."

"I saw . . . Mrs. Rifkind yesterday. She says he broke jail."

"News to me. I wouldn't put it past him, though; he was a piece of work, that guy."

"Do you remember a sister of Mrs. Rifkind being around the case at all?"

"Nah. She didn't seem to have anybody. A public defender, some kid, handled her plea."

"Do you remember what Grafton looked like?"

"Yeah. Medium height, slim, late forties, dark hair going gray, good dresser."

"Thanks very much, Mr. Stein, I appreciate your help."

"Anytime."

Eagle hung up, then dialed the district attorney's office in Santa Fe.

"This is Martinez."

"Bob, it's Ed Eagle. How are you?"

"Okay, Ed."

"Bob, did you run the prints on the John Doe you thought was Wolf Willett?"

"Sure, Ed. You think we're slack around here?"

"Yes. You didn't bother until Wolf turned up alive. Did you make him?"

"Maybe."

"Don't be coy, Bob. Who was the guy?" He could hear Martinez shuffling papers.

"I don't know that I'm required to give you that information, Ed."

"Mind if I take a wild guess?"

"Suit yourself."

"Grafton, James. A record of armed robbery. Escaped from a New York state prison."

There was a stunned silence. "How the fuck did you know that?"

"I don't know that I'm required to give you that information, Bob."

Eagle was laughing as he hung up the phone.

20

Wolf sat and stared at the two containers on the kitchen table—all that remained of the two people he had loved most. Or had he? He thought about it.

Jack was easiest. He'd loved Jack. Nobody could have put up with what he had endured from the man without loving him; Jack had been like an alternately errant and repentant child. The money they'd made together wouldn't have been enough to hold together the relationship. Wolf knew that his partner hadn't had an evil bone in his body, and if he'd needed proof, then Jack's will was the final evidence. Wolf missed him.

Julia was another matter. He thought about what she had given him for the past year, and he knew it wouldn't seem like much to an objective observer; it boiled down to sex, one way or another. Certainly Julia had been a responsive and inventive lover, but there was more to it than that. She had come into his life when it was gray and empty, except for his work, at a time when he thought he would never sleep with another woman. She'd made him love sex again, and crave it, and he'd loved taking her places where other men could envy him. But love? Too strong a word.

The personal effects were spare—of Julia's, only her wedding and engagement rings; of Jack's, some money, a wristwatch, a wallet, keys, a large silver ring.

He made himself move. He got into a coat, gathered up the two urns, and put them into the Porsche. He drove aimlessly for a while, then started up the mountain road to the Santa Fe Ski Basin, tall evergreens rising around him. He stopped at an overlook and got out of the car. The ground fell away sharply into a forest of winter-bare, silver-skinned aspens; beyond lay Santa Fe to the northwest, and far to the north, visible in the clear mountain air, a peak he had been told was in Colorado, more than a hundred miles away. The wind gusted, tearing at his coat. He buttoned it and shoved his hands into its pockets to protect them.

Finally he took an urn—he didn't know if it was Julia's or Jack's—unscrewed the top, and when another gust came, tossed the ashes into the air. He repeated the task with the other urn and watched the remains lift and spread, disappear into the trees. Then, with all his strength, he threw the urns after them. He got back into the car with a feeling of completion, as if an era of his life had ended.

On the way back down the mountain, he thought about Jane Deering, now back in L.A. That wasn't over, not by a long shot—not if he could stay out of prison.

There was a car—a four-wheeler of some sort—in the rearview mirror. It had been there on the way up the mountain, too, he thought. He put it out of his mind.

Wolf took the slow way home, turning toward the plaza at the heart of Santa Fe. The streets were crowded with Christmas shoppers, the Indians selling silver jewelry on the sidewalk in front of the eighteenth-century Palace of the Governors huddled down into their blankets to defeat the gusty wind. If Julia were alive, they'd be there shopping; she had a gift for picking out the best stuff from among the run-of-the-mill pieces the Indians brought to town. He missed Christmas shopping. He had no one to shop for.

The short day was ending when he got back to the house. Ed Eagle was standing on the back steps writing a note.

"Hello, Ed," he called, getting out of the car.

"Hello, Wolf. I thought I had missed you."

"Come on in." Wolf led him into the study, took his coat, and offered him a drink. "You like single-malt Scotches, as I recall. I've got some Laphroaig."

"That would be very good."

Wolf poured them both a drink, lit the fire, and sat down.

"I'm just back from New York," Eagle said.

"Did you see Julia's sister?"

Eagle took a sip and nodded. "Quite a striking girl."

"Well, she's Julia's sister," Wolf said. "Did she help out at all?"

"She was very cooperative, but I'm not sure how much she helped. Do you know somebody named Grafton? James Grafton?"

Wolf put down his drink. His hand was trembling.

Eagle leaned forward. "Wolf, are you all right?"

"Yes, I think so," he replied. "It's just . . ." he stopped.

"You do know Grafton, then?"

"No. At least, I don't think so. But the name just did something to me. It was like being kicked in the stomach."

"Can you remember him at all?"

Wolf calmed himself and tried to remember. "No, I can't. I'm sure I don't know anybody by that name." Sweat was leaking from his armpits now. "I don't understand this. Who is James Grafton?"

"He's the man in the morgue; the one they thought was you."

"How did you find out?"

"Julia's sister told me, sort of; at least, she gave me enough to go on, and I figured it out." He explained the relationship between the sister and Grafton.

"And he came here after breaking out of jail? Why?"

"I don't know exactly, but I think Julia's sister must have told him about Julia's marrying you.

He might have thought Julia was a good target for blackmail."

"But how would he have ended up in bed with Julia and Jack? This doesn't make any sense at all."

"No, it doesn't. We'll have to know a lot more before it does."

"Do the police know about this guy?"

"They know who he is; they don't know about the connection to Julia. I'll have to tell them, though. I don't want Bob Martinez yelling about obstruction of justice; it's better to be aboveboard with them. The relationship between Julia's sister and Grafton can't reflect on you, since you didn't know either of them existed."

"I can't prove that, though."

"They can't prove otherwise. That's what's important."

Wolf stood up. "I need another drink; let me get you one."

Eagle handed him the glass and waited for him to return. "When was the last time you saw Julia? Alive, I mean."

Wolf thought back. "In L.A. The editing on the new film wasn't going all that well, and I wanted a break—a few days in Santa Fe. Julia didn't want to come with me; she didn't like the airplane much. I was supposed to be back there for Thanksgiving dinner with some friends, the Carmichaels."

"Did you see Jack around the same time?"

"No. Jack had a way of disappearing right after shooting on a picture was completed, while I worked with the editor."

"You have no idea where Jack went after shooting was completed?"

"Mexico, probably. He had a place in Puerto Vallarta; he could go down there and drink and screw without my being on his back about it. He'd come back sober, though—usually, anyway."

They drank in silence for a few minutes.

"Christ, I don't know," Eagle said finally. "I've never had anything like this to deal with."

Wolf made them both another drink. When he came back he asked, "Is it unusual for you to go to interview somebody like Julia's sister?"

"Not really. I often interview potential witnesses myself. I don't have that big a staff—just two associates and some office workers. It is unusual for me to go as far as New York, but I had an idea that the sister might have some answers. Turns out she didn't even know she had the one answer she had—the one about Grafton."

"You think she told you the truth?"

Eagle sipped his Scotch and nodded. "She seems to be a truthful person; the prosecutor who handled her case thought so, anyway."

"I'm going to fix myself a steak. Will you join me?"

"Sure, why not?"

Wolf got up. "Let's move into the kitchen."

"Sure." Eagle got up.

"You know," Wolf said, "Julia seemed to be a truthful person, too."

21

They were in the living room now, each stretched out on one of the facing sofas before the fire, a bottle of cognac on the coffee table between them.

"That was a very fine burgundy," Ed Eagle said. His speech was even slower and more deliberate than usual.

"I'm glad you enjoyed it," Wolf said, trying hard to pronounce the words clearly. They had drunk two bottles of it with their steaks.

"What was it again?" Eagle asked.

"Uh . . . La Tache, Domaine de la Romanée Conti, '78."

"Right. La Tache."

"Right."

Wolf reached for the brandy bottle and nearly fell off his sofa. "I think we have to keep the cognac just a little bit closer to me than to you," he puffed, rearranging himself on the sofa. "You have a great advantage in reach."

"Right."

Long pause while both men sipped.

"You ever play any basketball, Ed?"

"Yup. Arizona State, four years. On a scholarship."

"Were you any good?"

"Good enough to keep the scholarship. I never made All-American or anything, and I wasn't good enough for the pros. I was better on defense than offense." He chortled to himself. "Harbinger of things to come."

Wolf found this wildly funny. "Jesus," he said when he had brought his laughter under control, "you're a sketch, Ed."

"I am," Eagle solemnly agreed.

"I always thought of Indians as being a little short on humor. What tribe are you from?"

"Ashkenazi," Eagle said.

"You mean Anasazie." The Anasazies—which meant "the old people"—had occupied the area a thousand years before, leaving hundreds of elaborate ruins before they inexplicably died out.

"Nope, I mean Ashkenazi."

"They're not from around here, are they?"

"Promise to keep this to yourself, Wolf?"

"Keep what to myself?"

"This."

"Oh. Sure."

"Scout's honor?"

"And cross my heart."

"I'm from the Ashkenazi tribe."

"What the hell are you talking about?"

"It's one of the twelve tribes of Israel. Ashkenazi."

"You're drunker than I thought."

"That's true, but I'm still Ashkenazi."

"You're not making any sense."

"I'm making perfectly good sense."

"But that would make you Jewish."

"Right."

"A *Jewish* Indian?"

"Nope. Just Jewish."

"What are you talking about, Ed?"

Eagle reached for the brandy bottle and poured himself a generous slug. "Let me see if I can clear this up for you, Wolf. I'm not an Indian. I'm a Jew."

"What the living *fuck* are you talking about?"

"I think I'd better start at the beginning."

"I don't see how that could possibly help, but go ahead."

"Okay, I'll start at the *very* beginning. I was born in the Williamsburg section of Brooklyn, New York."

"What the hell kind of Indian is born in Brooklyn?"

"Well, there were some Mohawks, but I wasn't one of them."

Wolf sighed. "This isn't making any sense, but go on."

"My parents were Hassidim—that's a very strictly orthodox Jewish sect."

"I know what Hassidim are, for Christ's sake."

"Well, I was one—at least until I was fourteen."

"Then you changed into an Indian?"

"No, not yet. I started to play basketball."

"Wait a minute, I'm getting a déjà vu here. Isn't this a Chaim Potok novel?"

"That was softball or something; I played basketball."

"Why?"

"Because I loved doing it. It drove my parents nuts, though, because there weren't any Hassidic kids good enough to play with me. I wanted to go to public high-school and play basketball."

"So you went to an Indian high school?"

"There aren't any Indian high schools in Brooklyn."

"So, anyway, what happened then?"

"Big family crisis. I moved in with my Uncle Harry and Aunt Nellie, who had also left the Hassidim, and I went to public high school and played basketball."

"What does all this have to do with Indians?"

"There was a Mohawk kid on the team, name of Marty. There's this Mohawk settlement in Brooklyn—they're all steelworkers on buildings—up high, you know?"

"I think I read something about it once."

"Anyway, Marty and I were the best players on the team, and people got to calling us Big Chief and Little Chief. I wasn't an Indian, of course, but nobody knew that. My name sounded Indian, and in this particular school, which had a lot of Irish and Italian kids, tough customers, it seemed like a better idea to be an Indian than to be a Hassidic Jew. So I kept my mouth shut and became an Indian. I had a prominent nose and sort of dark skin, but I never actually *claimed* to be an Indian; the other kids did that for me. Marty thought it was funny as hell, so he kept his mouth shut, too."

"Ed, you're drunk."

"Sure. Well, four years of high school went pretty well; Marty and I made All-City, and the colleges started sniffing around. Marty was too short, but I got some offers—N.Y.U. wanted me— even Fordham. Then along came Arizona State, and I saw an opportunity to get out of New York for good, so I accepted."

"Were you an Indian at Arizona State, too?"

"It was effortless. There were a bunch of Indians in the school, but I ran around with basketball players, mostly, who thought I was pretty exotic. I refused to talk about my background, and that made me mysterious, started a lot of rumors. The consensus was, I think, that I was a Mohawk who had gotten too tall to work on high buildings."

"So how did that get you into practicing law in Santa Fe?"

"It didn't, exactly. I came up to Santa Fe with a girlfriend a few times when I was at Arizona State, and I liked it; the Indian thing seemed to work very well here. I got into Yale Law School, and Uncle Harry put me through. When I graduated, the best offers were in New York, but I didn't want to go back there, so I came to Santa Fe, put out my shingle, and hung around the courthouse looking for work. The rest, as they say, is history."

"And everybody thinks you're an Indian?"

"Right. Remember, though, I never *said* I was an Indian."

"What about the Indians? They buy it?"

"Seem to. I haven't met many, really; only had one for a client. Their crimes aren't usually big enough for my kind of help, and anyway, they can't afford me."

"So you're not an Indian."

"No, Wolf. I'm a Jew."

There was a long silence while Wolf considered this. "Ed, what are you talking about?"

22

Ed Eagle waited a week before he told the district attorney how he had known who James Grafton was. A few days passed, then Martinez called him back.

"Ed, are you trying to fuck with me, or what?"

"What are you talking about, Bob?" Eagle asked, genuinely puzzled.

"I'm talking about the Schlemmer woman."

"What about her?"

"I sent a man to New York to interview her, Ed." Martinez sounded thoroughly exasperated.

"Good move, Bob," Eagle replied sarcastically. "And I'll be willing to bet you he didn't get any more than I did."

"You know damn good and well he didn't get *anything*."

"I'm only guessing, Bob; you make it sound like I queered your man's interview."

"*What* interview?"

"Bob, you're not making any sense."

"She wasn't there, Ed."

"Schlemmer?"

"Right. She was paroled last week."

"Oh. I didn't know that. She said she was coming up for parole soon, but she didn't say *that* soon."

"Ed, do you swear to me you didn't know she had been paroled?"

"I swear I didn't. And anyway, I didn't know you were sending a man east."

"You're sure."

"Bob, I promise you. Listen, if she was paroled, she must have had an address. Didn't they give him her address?"

"Sure they did. Turned out to be her old house, where she lived with her husband. His mother was there, said she hadn't heard a word from Schlemmer."

"Well, I'm sorry you had to go to all that trouble, but I really told you everything she had to say."

"All right, then, tell me if she was in something with Grafton."

"Bob, they were convicted at the same time; they were in different prisons. It would have been pretty tough for her to be in something with him, wouldn't it?"

"I don't like coincidences."

"Who does? I told you, my theory is that somehow—from Schlemmer or the papers, or something—he found out that Julia Willett was Schlemmer's sister, operating under a new name. Grafton was just the kind of slime who would try for a blackmail score on Julia. Doesn't that make some kind of sense?"

"Maybe."

"Well, it's all I've got to offer. If I think of something new, I'll call you. I'm not obstructing your investigation, Bob, I really want to help. So does Wolf Willett, but he's in the same box you and I are in: He read about the sister in the newspaper. That was the first he knew of her, and he never heard of Grafton. That's what he told me, and I believe him."

"All right, Ed, we'll leave it at that. But if you hear from the Schlemmer woman, I want to know about it, you understand?"

"Bob, I haven't the slightest reason to think that she will ever cross my path again, but if she turns up, you'll be the first to know, I promise."

Martinez hung up, and Eagle sighed. That was that, and he was pleased that the district attorney had never gotten to the woman; it would have been embarrassing if he had turned up something that Eagle had missed.

His secretary stuck her head in the door. "Excuse me, Ed, but there's a Barbara Kennerly in reception. She says you know her."

Eagle put his face in his hands and whimpered. "Christ, Martinez is never going to believe this." He sat back and sighed. "Send her in."

Barbara Kennerly walked into the room wearing a Chanel suit and looking like a million dollars. "Good afternoon, Mr. Eagle," she said.

Eagle stood up. "Good afternoon, Ms. Kennerly. Have a seat, and call me Ed, please."

"Call me Barbara," she said, sitting down and crossing her long, beautiful legs.

"You're out on parole, Barbara?"

"That's right, Ed."

"Then I think we have a little problem, here."

"What's that?" she asked, looking surprised.

"It's customary when a prisoner is released on parole for him—or her—to report regularly to a parole officer, to have a fixed address, and, most important, to remain in the jurisdiction."

She smiled broadly, revealing perfect teeth. "Oh, that. I was unconditionally released."

"Now, why would the State of New York do that?" Eagle asked skeptically.

"I got lucky. Shortly after your visit, a federal judge ruled that several state prisons were overcrowded and that the populations had to be reduced immediately. I was only a few months away from my parole hearing, and I was a model prisoner, so they brought it forward."

"But why was your release unconditional?"

"Half a dozen other prisons had to release prisoners early, too, and the numbers apparently placed a heavy strain on the parole system. The parole board gave unconditional release to those it felt were unlikely to be repeat offenders. Since I had no previous record and had cooperated at my trial, I was one of them." She spread her hands. "I'm a free woman."

"Congratulations," he said. "Now—"

"Why have I come to see you?" she interrupted. "Well, in all the time I was in prison, you were the only visitor I had, apart from the *Times* reporter, and I have kissed him off, refused to cooperate further on the book. The only people I knew in New York were friends and relatives of my late husband, and they would not have been pleased to see me. I wanted a new start in a new place, and you did, after all, say to call you if you could be of any help."

Eagle laughed. "That's right, I did say that. All right, Barbara, how can I help?"

"I need a job," she said. "As I told you, I've had experience at running an office, with bookkeeping and computers; I'm smart, pretty, and I'd be an asset to any office."

"I believe you would."

"How about your office? You need somebody?"

Eagle shook his head. "No, we're training somebody new right now, and she's working out well. I'm afraid we're fully staffed." *I'm also afraid*, he thought, *that if you came to work here, I'd soon find myself banging you on my desk.*

"Oh," she said, crestfallen.

"Do you have any other work experience?"

"Well, before I was married, I worked in a restaurant as a hostess."

"I know a few restaurateurs around town," Eagle said. "Let me make some calls."

She rewarded him with another dazzling smile. "Thank you," she said.

"There's something I want to ask you first," he said.

"Shoot."

"When was the last time you communicated with James Grafton?"

She looked surprised. "How did you know his name? I never mentioned it, did I?"

"No. I did my homework."

"Communicated," she said, looking at the ceiling. "I suppose we communicated at the trial; he stared daggers at me through the whole thing."

"Did you speak to him or write to him or send him any messages while you were both in prison?"

"Certainly not." She snorted. "I don't think he would have been glad to hear from me, after I testified against him, and I wanted to forget the bastard existed. To answer your original question, the last time I communicated with Jimmy was in the moment before the police burst through the door of our hotel room in Miami. I was telling him that I was going to turn myself in, and he was telling me that he'd kill me before he'd let that happen."

"Did Grafton know Julia?"

"I think you asked me that when you visited me in Poughkeepsie. No."

"Did he know *about* Julia?"

She looked thoughtful. "He knew she existed. Once, he saw some photographs I had of Julia and me together."

"When Julia got married to Wolf Willett, were there pictures in the papers?"

"I saw it mentioned in some gossip column in the *New York Post*, but there was no picture. Listen, why all this sudden interest in Jimmy

Grafton?" She suddenly looked alarmed. "He hasn't turned up in Santa Fe, has he?"

"You might say that. He turned up at Wolf Willett's house and got himself shotgunned for his trouble. He's on a slab in Albuquerque right now, missing most of his head."

"*What*?"

"At first they thought he was Wolf. They eventually identified him by his fingerprints."

"My God." She sighed, shaking her head. "This is bizarre."

"It is."

"Do you think he saw Julia's picture in the papers and . . ." she paused for a moment. "I'll bet he tried to blackmail her about her record."

"That's my best guess."

"He'd do that. The man would stop at nothing to get money."

"Speaking of money, the diamonds he stole from your husband were never recovered. What happened to them?"

"Jimmy got rid of them before we even left New York."

"And what happened to the money he got for them?"

"I don't know, but I never saw any of it. The police said he only had a few thousand dollars when we were arrested, but what he took was worth more than a million wholesale."

"So Grafton had the money stashed somewhere?"

"He must have. He didn't have time to spend it, and he didn't give it to the United Way."

"If he was flush when he got out, why would he rush off to blackmail Julia?"

"Money didn't last long with Jimmy; he was a big-time gambler."

"I'm sorry to be grilling you like this, but it'll be good practice for you. The local district attorney is very anxious to talk to you about Grafton."

She looked alarmed. "Does he know my new name?"

"I don't think so."

"Well, that's a relief. If I'm going to start some sort of new life here, I don't want the local law breathing down my neck all the time. Do I have to see him?"

Eagle shook his head. "No, but I'll have to tell him I've talked with you. I said I would."

"Oh." She looked depressed.

"Tell you what. Call him, say you talked to me and that you want to help if you can. Tell him the truth, and tell him if he needs to get in touch with you he can call me."

She brightened. "All right."

He dialed the number for her and listened while she talked at length with Martinez. Finally she wound up the conversation. "If you need to reach me, call Mr. Eagle, and I'll get back to you as soon as I can." She hung up. "God, I hope that's the end of that."

"So do I," Eagle said. "Where are you staying?"

"I found a nice bed and breakfast off Canyon Road."

Eagle thought fast. This woman was not his

client, she was not a suspect in the murders, she was square with the D.A. No problems here. "Would you like to have dinner one night soon?" he asked.

She flashed her smile. "I'd love it."

23

The week before Christmas, the weather did the right thing. In the middle of the night snow began to fall in Santa Fe, and by the time Wolf woke up there was a soft coat of white on the mountainside at Wilderness Gate. When he saw it, he remembered Christmas.

Wolf had been working nonstop on Jack's last screenplay—editing, rewriting, tightening. He'd gotten it down to a hundred and ten pages, then sent it to Hal Berger in L.A. for revised costing. In the normal course of events; he'd have been in preproduction in a week, ready for casting by the new year and shooting in February, but not now. All he could do was get the script right and wait.

Wolf had spent the last Christmas in Santa Fe with Julia, who hadn't liked Christmas much, except for the gifts he gave her. She wouldn't have a tree in the house—claimed she was allergic to them, so they had just gone to a few parties and had slept late on Christmas morning. Thinking back, he realized he hadn't had a proper

Christmas since the death of his first wife, and he had always loved the holiday.

Glancing at his watch, he picked up the phone and called Jane Deering.

"Hello," the sleepy voice said.

"Come on, it's eight o'clock. How come you're still in bed?"

"Oh, hi. Sara's out of school for the holidays, and we're both sleeping in."

"What are your plans for the holidays?"

"Oh, not much. We're sticking close to home."

"I've got a better idea. Why don't you pack a bag for yourself and Sara, get on a plane this afternoon, and come to Santa Fe for the holidays?"

There was a long silence at the other end.

"I know what you're thinking," he said. "How's it going to look? Well, I know I screwed it up when you were here before, but this time we'll lie low, take drives in the desert, stay home a lot."

"Wolf, I don't know."

"Sara will love it here. It's snowing; we're going to have a white Christmas."

"Kids are funny about Christmas. I don't want to upset her by yanking her away from home."

"Talk to her about it, see what she says, and call me back."

"Okay, give me an hour."

Wolf hung up, went to the kitchen, and made himself some breakfast, nervous about what her answer would be. If she couldn't come, then he'd be stuck in the house by himself. He'd been turning down invitations to parties, even one for Christmas dinner with friends, and now he realized, too late, that he didn't want to be alone. The phone rang; he grabbed the kitchen extension.

"Okay, you're on. We're arriving in Albuquerque at four o'clock."

"That's terrific! I'll meet you." The hell with not leaving Santa Fe.

"I assume I don't need any hot dresses this time?"

"All you need is jeans and a warm coat. It's cold here."

"See you at four."

Wolf hung up the phone, elated. He had one hell of a lot to do before his guests arrived.

By lunchtime, he had filled the Porsche with presents and Christmas tree decorations. The plaza was alive with shoppers, and he had exchanged greetings with a dozen friends and acquaintances. Every shop and house was decorated for the season; he had forgotten how lovely Santa Fe could be at Christmas.

By one o'clock, he was shopped out and starving. He pointed the car toward Santacafé, and miraculously found a space in the parking lot. The place was jammed, and as he squeezed through the front door, he was greeted with a sight that struck him like a blow: standing at the reservations booth, talking on the telephone, was a woman who looked so much like Julia that he at first thought he was hallucinating. True, her hair was dark, where Julia's had been sandy blond, but everything else—her gestures, movements, and above all her smile—were Julia's.

From behind, a large hand took his elbow and steered him into the bar alcove to his left.

"Hello, Ed," Wolf said, looking up at the lawyer.

"Hello, Wolf," Eagle replied, grabbing a barstool and shoving it under his client's backside. "I'm glad I ran into you. I've got something to tell you."

Wolf was barely paying attention, craning his neck to catch sight of the front door. "There's a woman out there who looks enough like Julia to be her twin," he said.

"Wolf, it's Julia's sister."

Now Wolf gave him his whole attention. "I thought she was in prison."

"She was unconditionally released last week. She turned up in Santa Fe and came to see me—I had offered to help her, never believing she would turn up here. I gave her a few names, and she got a job here; she's keeping the books for the restaurant and working the lunch shift at the desk."

"Jesus Christ, she gave me a start," Wolf said. His pulse was starting to go down.

"I'm sorry about that. I was going to call you about her. I really had no idea the resemblance was so strong."

"It's uncanny," Wolf said.

"I'd never even seen a photograph of Julia, so I didn't know. I'm sorry if it upset you."

"It didn't exactly upset me; it was more of a disorientation, like going back in time—Julia here, in this restaurant, where she had been so many times."

"I understand. Again, I apologize for not letting you know about her sooner. I don't really have a good excuse."

"It's okay, Ed. I'm fine."

"I was on my way back from the men's room when I saw you. I'd better get back to my lunch group."

"Sure, go ahead."

Eagle stopped. "Wolf, would you like to meet her?"

Wolf considered that for a moment. "I don't think this is a good time, Ed. After all, she's working." In fact, he was terrified of meeting her, of being anywhere near her.

"Sure, I understand. Another time."

"Sure. What's her name?"

"She's known as Barbara Kennerly. She seems like a decent person, in spite of her past." Eagle explained the circumstances of her imprisonment. "I think she was just caught up in something she couldn't control. She had some therapy in prison; she's all right now, I think."

Wolf nodded. "I hope so, for her sake."

"In my experience, the most ordinary people can get caught up in something extraordinary. Half the people I defend are just folks."

"Like me," Wolf said.

Eagle smiled. "Like you. And like her, too. Try not to hold her past against her." Eagle excused himself and went to join his party.

Resisting the urge to leave, Wolf forced himself to order some lunch at the bar and tried to keep his mind on it. He was still disturbed, though, and when he left the restaurant, he was glad she wasn't at the desk.

24

Ed Eagle checked the contents of the refrigerator, then spent a couple of minutes arranging things. He took a head of romaine lettuce from the icebox, rinsed it, and set it aside to drain. He got down a wooden salad bowl from a cupboard, separated two egg yolks from the whites, and opened a can of anchovies. He looked around; everything else was at hand.

The headlights of a car flashed briefly by the kitchen window. Eagle rinsed his hands and walked to the front door. Barbara Kennerly was just getting out of what looked like a brand-new Jeep Cherokee.

"Hello," he called.

"Hello, yourself," she replied, reaching back into the car for something and coming out with a large bunch of flowers.

"Come into the house before you freeze."

"I like the cold weather."

"Then you've come to the right place." He laughed, closing the door and helping her off with her coat. She was dressed in flannel slacks and a heavy, long-sleeved silk blouse. She was not wearing a bra, he noted. "It's supposed to go down to ten degrees tonight."

"Fine with me," she said. "Have you got something I can put these in?"

He led her into the kitchen and found a vase, then watched as she expertly arranged the flowers. "They're beautiful," he said. "Thank you for bringing them."

"Well, if you're cooking, it was the least I could do. I would have brought some wine, but it probably would have been the wrong thing."

"Don't worry, we're well fixed for wine. Would you like a drink, or can I force some champagne on you?"

"Oh, yes, please, force me."

He got out two crystal flutes and opened a bottle of Schramsberg *blanc de noirs*.

She raised her glass. "To freedom," she said.

He clinked his glass against hers. "I'll drink to that."

"Mmmm," she said, savoring the wine. "It's delicious. French?"

"Californian. The best, I think; equal to a lot of the French stuff."

"And the glasses—they're Baccarat, aren't they?"

"You have a good eye."

"You have good taste, sir."

"Thank you, ma'am."

"I'm not old enough to be called 'ma'am,'" she said solemnly.

"You're right. How old are you, anyway?"

"I'm thirty-two. Do you always ask women their age?"

"Always. It's an important question."

"Why is it important that you know a woman's age?"

"Knowing her age is not important. What's important is if she will *tell* you her age. You passed the test."

She laughed. "I'm glad."

"So, no more ma'ams; I'll call you Barbara."

"I'd like that better. I'm still getting used to it, you know. There's a girl at work named Hannah, and I have a tendency to turn whenever somebody speaks to her."

"Why did you change your name?"

"I would have thought that was obvious," she said. "But it wasn't just to get away from the ex-convict label. I simply didn't want to be Hannah Schlemmer anymore. I didn't like what she had become, and while I was inside I made a point of becoming somebody I liked better."

"So how do you feel about Barbara Kennerly these days?"

"By the time I got out, I was liking her a lot. She's changing, though. She's reinventing herself, now that she has her freedom."

Eagle took some beef tenderloin from the refrigerator and began expertly trimming and slicing it. "Something I don't understand," he said.

"What's that? Barbara Kennerly is an open book; she'll answer any question."

"You just arrived in a new car."

"And I found an apartment today, too. It's been a big day for Barbara."

"How does Barbara afford all this?"

"Ever the inquisitor. I don't mind telling you. I didn't get anything from my husband's estate—under the circumstances—but Murray was a generous man, in some ways. He was in the jewelry business, and he gave me a lot of jewelry. When I got out, I went to New York and sold some of it." She pulled back her hair to reveal a very nice diamond earring. "Not all of it, but some. I'd been around the diamond business enough to know how to go about selling it without getting scalped, so I have enough of a nest egg to get me going again."

"Now, that's very interesting," Eagle said. "But you had a public defender at your trial. If you'd sold the jewelry then and used the money to hire a good lawyer, I don't think you'd have done any time at all."

"You know a lot about my case, don't you?"

"Do you mind that I know?"

"No, I don't. Like I said, Barbara is an open book. I'll tell you straight, I didn't do that because I was stupid. It wasn't until I was in prison that I learned from my . . . new colleagues what the score was, and by that time it was too late. And I'll tell you something: I don't regret what I did."

"You don't regret going to prison?"

She sipped her champagne and shook her head. "I don't know what I would have done if I'd walked after the trial. I needed to get my head on straight again, and prison did that for me, gave me a chance to think about what I'd done wrong and what I was going to do to fix myself."

"That's what prison is supposed to be for, I guess."

"Well, it worked with me. I'm never again going to break any law—I'm not going to speed, I'm not going to get a parking ticket, I'm not going to jaywalk."

"That's a good resolution."

"And I'm keeping it forever."

Eagle dropped the sliced meat into some clarified butter and sautéed it. While that was happening, he took the salad bowl, crushed some garlic in it, added a few anchovies, pureed them with a fork, added the egg yolks, and began dripping oil into the bowl as he whipped the combination into a froth. He seasoned it with salt and pepper, added a spoonful of coarse Dijon mustard, then grated fresh Parmesan cheese into the mixture, whipping it up with a fork.

"What is it?" Barbara asked.

He dipped a finger into the bowl and offered it to be tasted. She sucked the dressing from his finger, and he liked the way she did it.

"Mmmm," she said. "I hate anchovies, and I got worried when I saw them go in, but this is terrific!"

He tore the romaine lettuce into bite-sized pieces and dropped them into the salad bowl, tossing them until they were lightly coated with the dressing.

"Caesar salad!" she said. "I've never seen it made before, just ordered it in restaurants."

He sprinkled some croutons on the salad and served it. They ate at the counter, while he kept an eye on the cooking.

"And what's that going to be?"

"Beef Stroganoff," he replied.

"God, I haven't had that in years!"

He moved them to the small dining table in the kitchen and served the food. A bottle of red wine stood open and waiting.

"This is wonderful," she said, sipping the wine and looking at the label. "Clos du Bois Merlot," she recited.

"One of my favorites, and not very expensive."

"Murray liked sweet wines," she said. "He was very Jewish."

"But you're Jewish, too."

"Yeah, but I'm sort of a civilian. Not that Murray was religious, but he was culturally more Jewish than I was. He liked to eat and drink the traditional things his mother had brought him up on."

"And did you learn to make matzoh ball soup and gefilte fish?"

"Not on your life. We had a cook who did all that. Murray knew from the beginning I was never going to be any good at cooking."

"What sort of life did you have with him?"

"Confined. We never saw anybody socially but his family, who hated me because I wasn't Jewish enough, or his clients, who always wanted to grope me."

"I can see how you might have wanted out."

"I didn't, consciously, until I met Jimmy. Then I began to see another world."

"What sort of world?"

"Oh, Jimmy was very smooth. He told me he'd made money in the stock market, and I believed him. He loved the best restaurants, the best seats at shows, expensive cars, the hundred-dollar window at the track. For a naive kid like me, it was like being in a movie, instead of real life. It was a while before I began noticing that everybody he knew seemed to have an angle. We'd bump into people at the track that I couldn't believe he was friendly with." She stopped talking for a moment. "Listen, I hope you don't mind, but this is starting to get to me. I'd rather not talk about that life anymore; I want to put it behind me."

"Of course, I understand. I shouldn't have pried."

"I'll still tell you anything you want to know." She put her hand on his.

"I know enough," Eagle said, leaning over and kissing her lightly.

She kissed him back. "I think it's time I did a little questioning myself," she said.

"Okay, shoot."

"How old are you?"

"Well, uh . . ."

"Your age isn't important, but it's important that you're willing to tell me."

He laughed aloud. "Forty-eight."

"Ever married?"

"Nope."

"Why not?"

"Just lucky, I guess."

She burst out laughing. "What do you have against marriage?"

"Not much. I just think marriage is something you should do when it's the only alternative, when you can't stand it if you're not married. That never happened to me. Not at the same time it happened to the girl, anyway."

"You never found the perfect woman?"

"Once, I think."

"What happened?"

"She was looking for the perfect man."

She laughed again. "That's a very old joke."

"It's an old question."

They finished dinner and moved into the study, settled on the big leather sofa. The fire was their only light. She kissed him.

Things moved quickly after that.

In the middle of the night, Eagle got up to go to the bathroom. When he came back, he stopped and looked at Barbara. In the moonlight she seemed startlingly pale, sprawled across the bed, her hair in her face, her arms thrown out, her breasts free and beautiful.

Eagle bent over to kiss her and was stopped by an oddly familiar sight. Tattooed onto the inside of her right breast was the shape of a flower—he didn't know which one; he was lousy at flowers. The colors were bright, and even the moonlight failed to wash them out.

25

They came back from Albuquerque crammed into the Porsche, the three of them and a lot of Christmas presents. Wolf had watched the rearview mirror all the way, but the police didn't seem to be on his tail. He relaxed when they crossed the county line.

Sara, tucked into one of the tiny rear seats and walled in by packages, pointed at everything, asked about everything.

"You're talking too much," her mother said to her.

"I know, but I can't help it," Sara said. "I like it here."

"You're going to like it even more in Santa Fe," Wolf said. "It's like something out of a picture book." He avoided the strip-city called Cerillos Road and detoured through the East Side Historic District.

"It looks real old," Sara said, pressing her nose to the car window and taking in the adobe houses.

"It is," Wolf replied. "There was an Indian settlement here for centuries before the Spanish founded the town in 1610. Santa Fe is the oldest state capital in the United States."

"What's the Santa Fe Trail?" Sara asked. "There was a movie on television called that, with Ronald Reagan, but they didn't say much about the trail."

Wolf laughed. "The Santa Fe Trail was one of the main routes west for the settlers," he replied. "It started in St. Louis, Missouri, and ended right here, at the plaza. There's a hotel right at the end of it." He turned a corner. "In fact, we're on the Old Santa Fe Trail right now."

Sara looked around at the restaurants and shops. "It doesn't look much like a trail to me."

"I guess it doesn't now, but it was once filled with covered wagons and trail herders, all making their way here. In some parts of it, east of here, you can still see the ruts the wagons made, and there are rocks with the settlers' names carved on them." He pointed at a small adobe house. "Look, see the sign? That's the oldest building in the United States, put up about the year 1200."

Sara did a quick calculation. "That's almost eight hundred years old."

"That's right."

"Why are all the buildings made out of mud?" she asked.

"People made their houses of mud because there were too few trees for building, and mud was the most available and cheapest material. Nowadays, houses are made of stucco, then painted to look like mud. A real adobe house has to have a new coat of mud every year, and that's too much maintenance for most families."

"Don't you get dirty living in a mud house?" Sara asked.

Wolf and Jane laughed aloud. "Nope," he replied. "It has a regular inside, just like a house in Los Angeles."

They were climbing up to Wilderness Gate now, and Sara took in the view. "You sure can see a long way," she said. "Why don't you get to have any smog?"

"Well, there aren't as many people and cars here as in L.A., and we're also about seven thousand feet up in the Sangre de Cristo Mountains," Wolf explained. "The mountain air is so clear that on some days you can see over a hundred miles."

When Wolf opened the door to the house, Flaps was all over them. At the sight of a child, the dog went berserk. The feeling, apparently, was mutual; the eight-year-old burst in; hugged the dog, and the two of them ran from room to room, Sara asking questions about everything, while Jane tried to quiet her and Wolf laughed at her questions.

She found the Christmas tree immediately. "But it's not decorated," she complained.

"That's your job," Wolf said. "Yours and your mother's. The decorations are in those boxes."

By dinnertime the tree was magnificent, and all the presents were tucked under it. Jane fed Sara early and put her to bed, protesting; Flaps wouldn't leave the child's room. Wolf made pasta and a salad, and they sat at the kitchen table and ate slowly.

"I've missed you," Wolf said.

"I've missed being here," Jane replied. "Life has seemed dull."

"Have you been working?"

"Not on a feature. I cut two commercials that a friend shot. That pays the bills while I build a career."

"You're not going to have to worry about a career when *L.A. Days* is released. The phone is going to be ringing off the hook."

She grinned. "That would be nice."

"How do you feel about your agent?"

"Not so hot. I seem to get all the work myself; he just negotiates the contracts."

"Do you have an out in your contract with him?"

"Thirty days notice."

"Call him tomorrow and fire him."

"But then I won't have an agent at all."

"You'll have an agent by the middle of January, I promise you. There's a young woman at the Creative Artists Agency who's doing great things for people on the production side; I'll call her. She'd be perfect for you."

"It's scary being without an agent, even for a month."

"You've got to get that thirty days out of the way; you don't want him suing you for breach of contract later."

"All right, I'll do it."

"I like it that you trust me so much," he said.

"I owe you a lot."

"You don't owe me anything. I owe *you* for the way you came through on *L.A. Days*."

"It was the kind of break everybody in this business dreams of."

"It was a break for me, too," he said honestly.

"I'm glad you think so."

"Sara is an amazing child."

Jane laughed. "She's a handful, she really is."

"She's extraordinarily bright."

"She is that. She drove her teachers crazy for a while because she learns so fast; she's in a special class for bright kids now."

"She also has the good fortune of looking like her mother."

Jane laughed. "When she's eighteen, I plan to start passing her off as my sister."

"Good plan; it'll work."

"So how's work on Jack's script coming along?" she asked.

"It's finished. Oh, there'll be the inevitable changes as we get closer to production, but I've taken it as far as I can, for the moment. It's lean now, and that'll give us a little room to get creative during shooting."

"What are you going to do for a director?"

"I haven't figured that out yet. I can't go into production until this mess is behind me, anyway, so there's nothing pressing about figuring that out."

"Why don't you direct?" she asked.

"Oh, no," he said, throwing up his hands as if to ward off an attack. "That's not for me; I'd rather stay above it all and complain about the director."

"You'd be a terrific director. I know; I worked on *L.A. Days* with you, remember? You were always improving Jack's work. You knew when the camera should have been placed better. You were right on target in your comments on the performances."

"That's kind, my dear, but I don't even know if I could get the film financed if I directed."

"You've got a deal with Centurion, haven't you?"

"Sure, but that was with Jack directing."

"Listen, Centurion is yanking teenagers out of UCLA film school and throwing money at them. Why do you think they wouldn't go with somebody as experienced as you are?"

"With Jack, we had the final cut; they'd never give me that."

"They might. And even if they won't, they'll have to after your first feature."

"You've got a lot of confidence in me," Wolf said.

"No more than you've got in me."

Wolf took a deep breath. "This is scary," he said. "I mean, I've thought about this, sure, but not seriously."

"Who were you thinking about to direct the new project?"

"Nobody, really. I didn't have a name in mind."

"You were thinking about you, that's what you were doing. You just wouldn't admit it to yourself."

"I'll think about it," Wolf said. "But I don't think I'll do it. It's too much responsibility, producing *and* directing."

"No, it's not. Dozens have done it, and most of them weren't any smarter than you."

"Well, I—" The doorbell rang, causing Wolf to jump a foot. "Excuse me." He got up and walked to the back door, a few yards away. When he opened it, he recognized the two men immediately—Carreras of the Santa Fe Police Department and Warren of the state police; they had interviewed him at the beginning. He felt sick to his stomach.

"Mr. Willett," the Latino officer said, showing a badge, "you're under arrest on a charge of triple first-degree homicide. I'll have to ask you to come with us, please."

Wolf tried to speak and failed, then tried again. His bowels felt loose. "I'd like to call my attorney," he finally managed to croak.

"You can do that from the police station," the officer said. "Get your coat."

The two officers stood and watched as he went to a closet and got a coat. He came back to the table, where Jane sat, looking frightened. "Jane," he said, "I have to go down to the police station for a while. Please call Ed Eagle for me and tell him where I am. The number is in my address book in the study."

"Let's go, Mr. Willett," the officer said.

Wolf stood his ground. "If for any reason I can't get back tonight, I'll have Ed call you and explain." He put his car keys on the table. "Use the house as your own, and the car. Show Sara some of the town; there are some guidebooks in the study."

"Mr. Willett?" the officer said.

"Jane, don't worry about this. It's going to be all right. Just call Ed Eagle, all right?"

She squeezed his hand. "Of course, Wolf. Don't worry about us. We'll be all right."

He smiled at her and left the house with the two officers. He heard a clink of metal, and handcuffs were produced. "You won't need those," he said.

"Sorry, Mr. Willett, it's policy."

His hands were drawn behind his back, and he felt cold steel encircle his wrists. As they walked toward the police car, Carreras began reading Wolf his rights.

26

The two policemen drove Wolf to the Santa Fe County Detention Center, a low adobe structure on Airport Road. Wolf had passed it dozens of times on the way to and from his airplane, never thinking that he might one day end up there.

A sergeant booked him. He was told to empty his pockets, and his wristwatch and belt were taken away; he was allowed to keep a quarter, then everything else was sealed in an envelope and he was given a receipt. During this process he stood between a very dirty drunk who could hardly stay on his feet and a short, wiry Latino who, although bleeding copiously from an apparent knife wound to his arm, remained handcuffed, while cursing all those around him, including Wolf, who tried to meet all this new experience with numbness.

Carreras led him down a hallway and stopped before a pay phone. "Okay," the officer said, "you can call your lawyer—or whoever you like."

Wolf thought for a minute. Jane would already have called Ed Eagle; he put the quarter in the phone and dialed his own number.

"Hello?" Jane said, sounding anxious.

"Hi, it's me. Did you get hold of Ed?"

"He was out. I left a message on his answering machine, and I called his office and left a message on the machine there, too."

"He's probably at dinner. We'll hear from him soon. Are you all right?"

"Of course, but what about you?"

"I'm fine. Don't worry about me."

Carreras broke in. "Okay, that's it. You'll have to hang up now."

"I'm being paged," Wolf said. "Talk to you soon."

"I'll keep trying Eagle," she said.

He hung up the telephone. "All right, now what?" He did his best to sound calm, but he was seething with fear inside. His attempt at numbness wasn't working.

"Follow me," Carreras said. He led the way, while the silent Warren followed Wolf. They entered a small, windowless room that stank of stale tobacco smoke; a steel table and four matching chairs were the only furniture, and a tape recorder was on the table. "Have a seat."

Wolf sat down.

Carreras produced a pack of cigarettes. "Care for one?"

"No, thanks."

"Mind if I smoke?"

"I'd appreciate it if you didn't."

This brought Carreras up short. He thought about it, then put away the cigarettes. "Sure," he said. "Look, Wolf—can I call you Wolf?"

"If you like."

"I'm Joe, and this is Sam. I want to keep this on a friendly basis."

"Okay with me, Joe, Sam."

"You mind if I tape-record our conversation?"

"I thought this was going to be friendly."

"It's for your protection. That way we can't claim you said something you didn't."

"Okay, turn it on."

Carreras turned on the machine and spoke into one of the microphones. "Questioning of Wolf Willett conducted by Captain Joe Carreras and Major Sam Warren at the Santa Fe City Jail." He added the date and time, then read Wolf his rights again. "Do you understand these rights?"

"Yes," Wolf said.

"Have you been given an opportunity to call your lawyer?"

"Yes."

"Are you willing to answer our questions at this time?"

Wolf was starting to feel better now, more confident. "All right. I'll let you know if I change my mind."

"You do that. State your name and address for the record."

"Wolf Willett, Wilderness Gate, Santa Fe."

Carreras loosened his tie. "Okay, Wolf, what we want to do is clear this thing up once and for all."

"I'd be very happy if we could do that," Wolf said sincerely.

"During the time since Sam and I talked with you the last time, a lot has come out."

"I'd be interested to hear about it," Wolf said, leaning forward.

"Well, let's just say that what's come out hasn't backed up your story. In fact, everything we've learned has contradicted what you've told us."

Wolf felt a sting of alarm. They obviously knew something he didn't. "I don't see how that's possible," he said. "I've told you the truth right down the line." The truth as he knew it, he reminded himself. What truth did they know?

Carreras shook his head sadly. "You told us you didn't know one James Grafton."

"I don't. I'd never heard the name until Ed Eagle mentioned it to me."

"Come on, Wolf, we're wasting time here. We've got witnesses who can put you in a Los Angeles restaurant, having lunch with Grafton. A very friendly and intense lunch—just the two of you."

Wolf was stunned. "That's ridiculous. What restaurant? When?"

"Don't worry, it'll all come out at your trial. We've also got a witness who can put you in that bedroom that night, when your wife and Grafton and Jack Tinney died."

"What?" He was terrified now. His worst nightmare was coming true.

"And you didn't tell us that Jack Tinney made

a will a couple of months ago that leaves you everything."

"I didn't even know that the last time I saw you," Wolf said, trying not to hyperventilate.

Carreras was angry now, and his voice began to rise. "That stuff about not remembering anything just isn't going to work, Wolf. We know too much, and let me tell you, you sonofabitch, we're going to nail you for these three murders. You're going to get the needle."

Before Wolf could speak, Warren broke in. "Hold it, Joe," he said, placing a hand on the officer's shoulder. "Look, why don't you go have a smoke and let me talk to Wolf?"

Carreras glared at Wolf. "Okay, Sam, but you better talk some sense into this guy, or when I come back I'm going to take him apart." He got up and left. He pointedly lit a cigarette at the door and blew the smoke back into the room.

"Take it easy, Wolf," Warren said, leaning back in his chair. "It doesn't have to be as bad as all that. Would you like some coffee?"

Wolf's mouth was dry. "A soft drink, maybe."

"Sure." Warren got up and left the room. He came back a moment later with a diet cola. "Hope this is all right," he said. "The machine was out of everything else."

"It's fine," Wolf said gratefully, sipping the drink, thankful for the icy wetness against his parched throat.

Warren leaned forward. "Now, look. I'm afraid you're zipped up on all sides here. Let me explain something to you that your lawyer may not have told you."

"All right."

"New Mexico has the death penalty."

"I'm aware of that, but it's only if a police officer is murdered, isn't it?" That thought had given Wolf the only peace he had had with regard to what might happen to him.

"I'm afraid not," Warren said. "You can also get the death penalty for killing a witness to a murder."

"A witness?" Wolf asked weakly.

Warren nodded gravely. "You see, when you killed the first of those three people, the other two immediately became witnesses." He stopped and waited for this information to sink in.

Wolf gulped but didn't reply.

"Wolf, I want to help you if I can, and if you'll let me, I think I can save your life."

"That would be nice," Wolf said.

"This is what I think I can do—I'll have to talk to the D.A., of course, but with my experience of him, I think he'll go along. He wants to clear this up as much as anybody."

"What did you have in mind?" Wolf asked.

"Joe is right about the needle. If you go to trial on this, with what we've got, you'll be convicted of three counts of murder one, two of them of witnesses, and in New Mexico that makes the death penalty a certainty. But that doesn't have to happen. I mean, I don't think you *planned* this thing. Hell, it could happen to anybody. If I

walked into a room and found my wife in bed
with my partner and another guy, I'm not sure I
could answer for myself. I might do just what you
did. It's obvious to me that this was done while
you were in a state of sudden and intense anger,
brought on by the worst kind of provocation. And
I'm willing to stand up in a courtroom and tell a
judge just that, put my whole professional reputation on the line to back you up."

"That's good of you, Sam," Wolf said, by this
time grateful for any kind word.

"I'm willing to call up the D.A. right now and
recommend that he accept a plea of diminished
responsibility and agree to, say, twenty-five to
life—no, I'll go further than that; I'll recommend
five-to-fifteen—I mean, shit, you were out of
your mind with rage that night. That would mean
you'd be eligible for parole in two and a half
years, Wolf. That's nothing, believe me. You'd do
it standing on your head, and when you're a free
man again, you can make a movie about the experience. That'd do big business, wouldn't it?"

Suddenly two and a half years in prison looked
good to Wolf. If it would bring an end to all this, if
it would get the pressure off, it might be worth it.
He stopped himself. "This is awfully nice of you,
Sam, but I think I'd better talk to my lawyer."

"Sure, Wolf, you can do that," Warren said
reasonably, "but you're a lawyer; you're capable
of handling yourself." He paused. "I've got a serious problem here," he confided.

"What's that?"

"Well, don't tell Carreras I told you this, but

he's hot to trot. He didn't even want me to have this conversation; I had to talk him into it. If he comes back in here and we haven't come to an arrangement, I don't know if I can hold him off."

Wolf was silent.

"You're a lawyer. If you had a client in this position, what would you advise him to do?"

Wolf still didn't speak.

"I have to tell you, Wolf," Warren continued, "I can't contain Carreras. This is his case, really; I'm just a state observer, and if he won't go along with me, well, I can't go to the D.A. on my own. I've got to have something to give Carreras when he comes back in this room." He leaned forward and lowered his voice. "Come on, Wolf, what's it going to be? Two and a half years—and I think I can get you into a minimum-security joint, a country club—or a trial and a sentence of death, and a year or two down the road, you watch them slip that needle into your arm? What's it going to be?"

Wolf placed his hands on the table to keep them from trembling and looked down at them. "Sam, get Carreras back in here. I've got something to get off my chest."

Warren nearly knocked over his chair getting up. "Sure, Wolf. I'll be right back." He left the room. When he came back, Carreras was with him, looking expectant. They sat down. "All right, Wolf, tell us," Warren said.

"Have you got paper and a pen?" Wolf asked. "I want to write this down."

Carreras opened a drawer in the table and took out a legal pad, then produced a ballpoint pen.

Wolf stared at the pad for a moment, then began to write, in firm, assured strokes. When he had finished, he signed and dated what he had written, then pushed the pad across the table to Carreras. "Would you read this aloud for the tape recorder?" he asked quietly.

Carreras nodded. "Sure, Wolf." He arranged the microphone and held up the pad. "To whom it may concern," he read, enunciating distinctly, "I write this, being of sound mind, and I would like to state, unequivocally and of my own volition, that I think that Captain Joe Carreras of the Santa Fe Police Department and Major Sam Warren of the New Mexico State Police can, as far as I am concerned, go and find a quiet place and fuck themselves"—the officer's voice began to trail off—"or each other, whichever they prefer." Carreras reached over and turned off the tape recorder.

"And that, gentlemen," Wolf said, "in addition to being my fervent wish, is my full and complete statement. If you have any more questions you can put them to my lawyer. This interview is over."

Warren's jaw was working. "Lock him up, Joe," he spat.

27

The door slammed behind Wolf, and the noise echoed down the hallway. He had never known jail cells were so small.

He looked around the room. Three walls, a folding sink in the corner that emptied into a toilet—no seat—and two steel bunks attached to the wall. The cell was no more than six feet by eight and was lit only by the light of the waning moon through a steel-slatted window. He looked out the window: a view of a row of barred windows across a yard.

The top bunk had a sheet, an army blanket, and a pillow resting on it. There was movement in the lower bunk, and a pair of high boots swung over the edge and landed on the concrete floor with a slap. "Welcome to purgatory," a hoarse voice said.

"Thanks," Wolf replied.

The man stood up and stretched. Wolf made him to be at least six-four and two hundred and fifty pounds. He was dressed in his boots, greasy black jeans, and a studded leather vest. No shirt.

Biker, Wolf thought. *Oh, shit.*

"Who are you," the man said. It wasn't a question.

"My name's Wolf."

The biker burst out laughing. "I like it, I like it!" He stuck out a hand. "I'm Spider."

Wolf shook the hand and found it softer and gentler than he'd feared.

"I like it! The Spider and the Wolf!" He indicated the lower bunk. "Take a pew, Wolf. Let's talk; it's been three days since I talked to anybody but a screw."

Wolf was tired, but he didn't like the thought of sitting next to Spider on a bunk. He walked to the window and turned, leaned on the wall. "Thanks, but I've been sitting for the last hour. I need to stretch."

"Sounds like they been talking to you."

"Right."

"What you in for, Wolf?"

Wolf hesitated, then realized this might be his best card. "Triple murder," he said.

"No shit!" Spider said, awed. "Did you do it?"

"The two guys I just talked to think so."

"They offer you a deal?"

"Yeah."

"Did you take it?"

"No."

"Smart, like a wolf." Spider laughed. "Never take a deal; that's my policy. Tough it out."

"What're you in for, Spider?"

"Aw, they say I hit a guy upside the head with a bike chain a few times. It's a bullshit rap. If I'd hit the guy upside the head with a bike chain, he wouldn't *have* a head no more."

"They offer you a deal?"

"Sure, sure, second degree assault, down from assault with a deadly weapon. One to three, they said."

"What'll you get if you're convicted?"

"Two to five, since I've got no priors. Oh, I been busted, but I never done no time. Don't worry, I won't do none this time, neither."

"How come?" Wolf was interested. He'd never met anybody who was experienced with the system in this way, let alone a biker.

"Because when they talk to the guy, he's not going to point the finger at me."

"They haven't talked to him yet? I thought you said you'd been in here three days."

"Oh, yeah, but last I heard, the guy hadn't come around yet."

"Come around?" Wolf was baffled.

"Regained consciousness," Spider explained.

"Is he going to come around?"

"Oh, sure. I didn't hit him *that* hard."

"Why did you . . . ah, why did this guy get hit?"

"He was messing with my old lady, you know?"

Wolf didn't know. What kind of idiot would mess with *this* guy's girlfriend? "Oh."

"Can't let a guy get away with that, can you?"

"Let me give you some advice, Spider. Never tell anybody in jail what you've done."

Spider looked hard at Wolf. "You some kind of fink?"

"If I was, I wouldn't be giving you that kind of advice, would I?"

Spider nodded. "That makes sense, I guess. You'd be amazed how guys talk to each other in the slammer."

"You mean they confess to each other?"

"All the time, man. I guess they just need somebody to talk to. I'm glad you're here; I haven't had nobody to talk to for three days."

"You live in Santa Fe?" Wolf asked.

"At the moment. I'm a free man, you know? I go where the bike takes me."

"What kind of bike?"

"You kidding? A Hog—a Harley, you know?— that's all there is."

"Somebody taking care of the bike for you?"

"The old lady. She can't pick it up if it falls over, and she can't kick-start it, but she can ride the motherfucker!"

Wolf laughed at the thought. "She sounds like she's okay."

"Fuckin' A, man." Spider paused. "Tell me something, man, what'd those dudes say they got on you? I'd like to know."

"Oh, they said they've got a witness who saw me having lunch with somebody I never heard of; they said they've got another guy who saw me in the room where three people were killed."

"That sounds familiar," Spider mused.

"What?"

"That second witness. There's a guy in here

told me he saw something like that. Said it was going to get him on the street."

"In jail? Here?"

"Yeah. I was out in the yard this morning; there's this guy, oh, one of them spic names, you know? Makes out to be some kind of cat burglar. I bet he'd stumble over his own feet. Anyway, he was telling me this shit, says he's going to beat a burglary rap with what he saw."

"That's very interesting. I think my lawyer would like to know about that."

"Who you got for a mouthpiece?"

"A guy named Ed Eagle."

"That Indian dude? I hear he's hot shit. How'd you get him?"

"Friend of a friend."

"Well, Wolf, you got some kind of friends out there. What line are you in?"

"I make movies."

"No shit! Anything I might have seen?"

Wolf rattled off half a dozen titles.

Spider looked puzzled. "I don't know any of them ones. You made any movies with Arnold Schwarzenegger?"

"Nope."

"I like that dude! He knows how to kick ass!"

"Yeah, I guess he does, at that. He kicks some ass at the studios, too."

"Yeah, I heard he's got 'em by the balls out there in Hollywood. They have to pay him whatever he wants."

"That just about sums it up," Wolf agreed.

"Do you know any movie stars?"

"A few, I guess," Wolf replied. "Nobody as big as Schwarzenegger, though."

"You know Madonna?"

"I met her once at a party after an opening—didn't really talk to her, just shook her hand."

"No shit? You know Madonna?"

"Not really, Spider. I just shook her hand."

"I'll be fucked; my cellmate shook Madonna's hand. Christ, I'd like to stick it in her!"

"A lot of guys would, I guess."

Spider laughed. "Crystal would cut my pecker off, though, if I did that. She wouldn't care if it was Madonna or not."

"Your old lady sounds like a tough cookie."

"You better believe it! She don't take no shit from nobody, not even me! You know, when I hit that guy, I was sort of protecting him; Crystal would have cut his fucking heart out, if I'd let her at him. Oh, forget I said that."

"It's forgotten."

"Well, I'm going to get some shut-eye, I guess," Spider said, swinging his boots back onto the bunk.

"Good idea. I think I'll try it, too."

"You need any help gettin up top, Wolf?"

"I can manage, Spider. Thanks anyway."

"Sure."

Wolf spread the sheet and blanket, then hoisted himself up on the bunk. He didn't bother undressing; he was exhausted. Wolf wondered where the hell Ed Eagle was, and what he was going to do about this. But right now he didn't care; he just wanted to sleep. He was almost out when Spider spoke up again.

"Hey, Wolf?"

"Yeah, Spider?"

"You're an okay guy, for an educated dude, and all that."

"Thanks, Spider."

"You know that spic? The cat burglar?"

"Hmmm, yeah." Wolf was nearly gone.

"I think I'll have a word with him in the yard tomorrow morning."

Wolf didn't reply. He was out.

28

Wolf came awake with something heavy on his chest. He opened his eyes and saw his cellmate staring at him; Spider's huge hand was shaking him.

"Breakfast, Wolf," Spider said. "I would have woke you up earlier, but you looked like you needed the sleep."

There was an amazing amount of noise in the jail: People were yelling at each other in English and Spanish, somebody was singing, there were half a dozen radios tuned to different stations. He was surprised he'd slept through it all.

The cell door slid noisily open.

"Let's go, buddy," Spider said. "They don't let you sleep through breakfast here."

Wolf followed Spider out of the cell, and they joined a long line of prisoners shuffling down the hallway. They emerged into a large room that wasn't very different from the school cafeteria at Wolf's high school; he wasn't sure exactly on which facility that was a comment. He picked up a steel tray and followed Spider through the line, watching, appalled, as white-suited servers covered his tray with dollops of polenta, beans, a slice of half-cooked, streaky bacon, and a serving of green Jell-O. At the end of the line he was handed a paper cup of coffee and a packet of cream and two sugar cubes.

Spider picked a table, and a couple of men got up to give him room. Indicating that Wolf should sit beside him, Spider sat down and immediately began to stare fixedly toward the food line.

Wolf followed his gaze to a stocky Latino who was just picking up a tray when he realized Spider was looking at him. The man stood frozen for a moment, like a deer caught in headlights, then dropped his tray and left the room.

"What was that all about?" Wolf whispered.

"That's the dude going to testify against you at your arraignment this morning," Spider replied. "I just give 'im the look."

"Arraignment?"

"Yeah, sure; that's what they do when they charge you with murder. You gotta be arraigned."

Wolf's practice of law had not included arraignments, but he realized that Spider was right.

"You didn't know that?" Spider asked.

"I should have, but I didn't," Wolf admitted.

"You'll be okay with that Indian dude. Just keep your mouth shut and let him do the talking."

"Right. What was that about a 'look'?"

"That's the *look*. You gotta have a *look* to keep these spics in line, you know?"

"Oh." Wolf looked around the dining hall and realized that eighty or ninety percent of those present were Hispanics.

"Otherwise, a white guy has got no chance in a place like this. You gotta give 'em the look, and you better be able to back it up, too. 'Course, with me, the look is just about always enough. Cons are scared shitless of bikers; they know we don't give a shit. I don't have to do much fighting."

"I'm not surprised," Wolf said. He was thinking about the arraignment now, and what the hell he would do if Ed Eagle didn't show.

"Spider, my lawyer may not know I'm in here. What should I do if he isn't at the arraignment?"

"Well, you got three choices," Spider said, slurping up his beans. "You can ask for a postponement of the arraignment, but then they put you back in here. You can ask for a P.D.—that's a public defender—but you'll either get some kid still wet behind the ears, or some old rummy can't make a living anyways else. Or you can represent yourself."

"What do you do in those circumstances?"

"Oh, I always take the P.D. See, I know what's going on in there, and if he drops the ball, I pick it up."

Wolf picked at his food and tried to remember what went on at an arraignment. He hadn't thought about that since the second year of law school, and he was embarrassed to ask Spider.

"Ain't you hungry?" Spider asked, eyeing Wolf's tray.

"No, I'm not," Wolf said. "Do I have to eat it?"

"I'll do it for you," Spider said, stacking Wolf's tray on top of his empty one.

"Thanks."

"Don't mention it," Spider replied, tucking into the polenta.

After breakfast, they were taken back to their cell.

"Hop up on your bunk a minute, will you, Wolf?" Spider asked.

Wolf got out of his cellmate's way.

Spider spread his blanket on the floor and started doing push-ups, counting aloud.

Wolf watched, fascinated, as Spider did fifty push-ups, then as many sit-ups. He did a hundred deep knee-bends, then ran in place for ten minutes. When he finished, he was drenched in sweat.

"It's shower day for me," Spider said, "so it's okay to break a sweat."

The cell door suddenly opened, and a guard appeared. "Willett, you're up for arraignment. Let's go."

Spider offered him a hand down and a firm handshake. "Good luck, Wolf. You ever need any help, just phone me up at a bar called the Gun Club and leave a message. I'll get back to you."

"Thanks, Spider." He thought of giving the biker his own number, but shuddered at the thought of Spider coming to call. He began to regret that one of his phone numbers was in the Santa Fe directory.

"Let's *go*, Willett," the guard said, dangling a pair of handcuffs.

Wolf got into his coat and allowed himself to be cuffed with his hands behind him, then followed the guard. In a vestibule before the last barred door, he was handcuffed in tandem with seven other men, and they were marched outside and into a van. The cold air bit hard, and since both his hands were handcuffed to others, Wolf was unable to button his coat. The van pulled out onto Airport Road, then turned left on Cerrillos and headed into town. All the men were quiet. Nobody met anybody else's eye. The only view out of the van was to the rear, through a heavy steel screen. Santa Fe was going to work.

Twenty minutes later the van halted, and a police officer opened the rear doors. The eight men were hustled out and into a rear door of the Santa Fe County Courthouse. They entered a room furnished with benches, and one by one their handcuffs were unlocked, then refastened with their hands in front of them. Wolf remembered that he hadn't used the toilet that morning.

Wolf sat in the room for nearly two hours. He was taken to a men's room and allowed to urinate once, but not to linger for other business. He was hungry now.

A guard came into the room, looked at a clipboard, and shouted, "Willett!"

Wolf stood up, and his handcuffs were removed. Massaging his wrists, he followed the guard to the door and found himself in a large courtroom. He looked around for Ed Eagle, who was nowhere to be seen.

"People versus Willett, arraignment," the bailiff called. Wolf looked around and saw District Attorney Bob Martinez at a table in the well of the court.

"Is the defendant represented?" the judge asked.

"His attorney of record is not present," Martinez replied.

"Bring up Willett," the judge called.

A guard led Wolf into the well of the court, before the bench.

"Mr. Willett, you are represented by . . ." the judge consulted a paper on his desk, "ah, Ed Eagle," he said. "Where is Mr. Eagle?"

"Your honor, I was arrested last night without warning, and I have been unable to reach Mr. Eagle," Wolf said.

"Well, Mr. Martinez, you and I both know what kind of hell Ed Eagle will raise if we arraign his client in his absence. Do you have a suggestion?"

"I suggest we return Willett to the city jail, Your Honor," Martinez replied. "I tried to reach Mr. Eagle last evening and failed."

"I see," the judge said. "Well, Mr. Willett, it looks like you're going to have to be the guest of the county until Mr. Eagle turns up. Unless you'd like a public defender?"

Wolf wanted desperately not to return to that

cell, but he hung on. "I'd like to wait for Mr. Eagle, Your Honor," he said.

"Very well—"

"Your honor, Mr. Willett's counsel is present!" The voice came from the rear of the courtroom.

Wolf turned to see Ed Eagle striding down the aisle and into the well of the court.

He came and stood next to Wolf. "Your Honor, I apologize for my tardiness, but I was in Los Angeles when I received both Mr. Martinez's and Mr. Willett's messages late last night. I have only just returned. May I have a moment to consult with my client?"

"Of course, Mr. Eagle, and welcome back. Mr. Martinez, let's continue with the next case while Mr. Eagle and Mr. Willett consult."

Eagle took Wolf by the arm and led him out of the courtroom and into a small anteroom. "I am terribly sorry about this, Wolf," he said. "It was midnight when I got Ms. Deering's message and returned her call, and there was no way to get word to you."

"I'm just glad you're here, Ed," Wolf replied.

"Martinez did call, but he didn't say what it was about—just said to call him. I think he's playing games with us; he waited until he knew I was away before arresting you. Did the police pump you last night?"

"Yes." Wolf gave Eagle a complete account of his interview with the two detectives.

Eagle laughed aloud. "That's very good," he said. "I'll have to remember that one."

"It didn't seem very good at the time. I'll admit, their offer sounded pretty good for a minute or two."

"You're not going to need any deals," Eagle said. "You're in the very best of hands, believe me."

"I believe you."

"So they're claiming witnesses, now?"

"That's what they said. My cellmate last night thinks he knows one of them. The guy's in for burglary and he's been telling people he's going to get off by testifying against somebody he saw while attempting to burglarize a house."

"This sort of thing happens all the time when the police haven't got enough. Word gets around the jail about a crime, and somebody decides that being a witness will do him some good. I'm more worried about this business of your being seen with Grafton in L.A. Are you absolutely certain you didn't know him? This is important, Wolf."

"Ed, I have lunch in L.A. restaurants every day of my life, when I'm there, but I swear I didn't know Grafton."

"All right, I'll handle that. The main thing in this arraignment is to get bail. If we can get it, my guess is it's going to run high. How are you fixed for cash?"

"Pretty good. I've just been paid by the studio I release films through; I've got some investments, too. Also, I've got the Santa Fe house to put up. There's no mortgage."

"The house is good."

A guard opened the door. "The judge is ready for you, Mr. Eagle."

"We're on, Wolf," Eagle said. "Just relax and leave it to me."

"I'll leave it to you," Wolf said, "but I'm not going to relax until I'm out of here."

29

M r. Martinez," the judge said, "do you wish to address the court?"

The district attorney rose. "Your Honor, this is a preliminary hearing in the matter of the State of New Mexico versus Willett, comprised of three counts of first degree murder."

"Do you wish to call any witnesses?"

"Your honor, the state calls Captain Joe Carreras."

Carreras, whom Wolf had not noticed, rose from a spectator seat, took the witness stand, and was sworn in.

Martinez addressed Carreras. "State your name, rank, and occupation."

"Captain Joe Carreras of the Santa Fe Police Department. I command the Investigations Division."

"Captain Carreras, would you outline your career history for us briefly, please?"

"I have served in the Santa Fe Police Department for twelve years as a detective, following four years service with the Albuquerque Police Department as a patrolman and supervisor."

"During your time with the Santa Fe Police Department have you handled many homicide cases?"

"Most of them, I believe."

Eagle leaned over to Wolf and whispered, "Murder is pretty rare in Santa Fe. This case is the first this year."

"So you are a highly experienced homicide detective?" Martinez continued.

"Yes, sir, I believe so."

"Did you arrest the defendant, Willett, last evening?"

"Yes."

"Did you have an arrest warrant?"

"Yes."

Wolf leaned over and whispered to Eagle. "He never served me with a warrant."

Eagle nodded.

"On what evidence did you base your request for a warrant?" Martinez asked.

"The three victims were murdered in Mr. Willett's house at a time when he was present; they were murdered with a shotgun belonging to Mr. Willett; one of the victims was Mr. Willett's wife, and she was in bed, naked, at the time, with his business partner and another friend of his; I am not satisfied with Mr. Willett's account of his actions; Mr. Willett has lied to me with regard to his presence in the house at the time of the murders and with regard to his knowledge of the third victim, James Grafton. I have a witness who can place

Mr. Willett in the room where the murders occurred on the night of the murder; I have a witness who can confirm Mr. Willett's intimate knowledge of Mr. Grafton. Mr. Willett has withheld knowledge from the state that he was the principal beneficiary of his partner's will. As a result of my investigation, and based on my experience as a homicide detective, I believe that Mr. Willett's motive was jealousy over his wife's extramarital affairs and greed for his partner's estate, and I believe that he had opportunity to commit these crimes, since the murders occurred in his home at a time when he was present."

"No further questions, Your Honor," Martinez said, then sat down.

Ed Eagle was on his feet. He walked to within a couple of paces of Carreras and faced him. "Captain Carreras," he said.

"Yes, sir?"

"You say you have a witness who can place Mr. Willett in the room where the murders occurred on the night of the murder?"

"Yes, I do." Carreras permitted himself a small smile.

"Tell me, is your witness presently an inmate of the Santa Fe County Jail?"

The smile disappeared.

Martinez stood. "Objection; irrelevant."

"This is *most* relevant, Your Honor, and I will demonstrate why."

"I'll permit it," the judge said. "Answer the question, Captain Carreras."

"Yes."

"Is your witness awaiting trial on a criminal charge?" Eagle continued.

"Yes."

"Has your witness been offered a reduction of sentence or any other inducement to testify?"

Carreras looked uncomfortable. "Yes."

"Captain Carreras, on what occasion did Mr. Willett tell you—or anyone else, for that matter—that he was not present in the house at the time of the murders?"

Carreras seemed to search for an answer.

"In fact, Mr. Willett told you that he had no memory of that evening, didn't he?"

"Yes."

"So if he told you he had no memory of that evening, that is not a claim of his whereabouts, is it?"

"I suppose not."

"So your case so far is based on the testimony of an accused felon who is bargaining for his freedom, and on Mr. Willett's statements, which you have just—shall we be kind and say, *misinterpreted* for the court."

"There's also the matter of his denial of knowledge of one of the victims and the matter of Jack Tinney's will," Carreras said.

"I'll address those points, Captain Carreras. Tell me, how did you learn of Mr. Willett's alleged knowledge of Mr. Grafton?"

Carreras seemed eager to explain. "I visited Los Angeles in the course of my investigation, and I received statements from a head waitress and a waiter at a restaurant that Willett had had lunch in the restaurant in the company of Mr. Grafton."

"And, since Grafton was dead at the time, how did these witnesses identify him?"

"By a photograph."

"Can the state produce this photograph?" Eagle asked.

Martinez stood and shuffled through his files. "Here is the photograph, Your Honor."

Eagle took the photograph, looked at it, and placed it on the defense table.

Wolf picked it up and looked at it. A slim, graying man holding a placard with a number on it stared back at him. Wolf stopped breathing.

Eagle continued with Carreras. "A prison photograph, was it?"

"Yes."

"A good likeness?"

"Good enough for the witnesses."

Wolf stood up. "Excuse me, Your Honor, but I request permission to speak to my attorney for a moment."

Eagle looked surprised. "May I have a moment, Your Honor?"

"Yes, but be brief, Mr. Eagle. I have a full morning."

Eagle walked to the defense table. "What is it, Wolf?"

Wolf tapped the photograph on the table. "I know him," he said.

Eagle froze for a moment. "I'm going to put

you on the stand in a moment. Tell the truth." He turned back to Carreras. "Thank you, Judge. I have but two more questions for this officer."

"Proceed, Mr. Eagle."

"Captain Carreras, did you at any time show this photograph or any other photograph of Grafton to Mr. Willett?"

Carreras looked suspicious. "No," he said.

"One final question, Captain Carreras. You say you had an arrest warrant for Mr. Willett?"

"That's right."

"Then why didn't you serve it on Mr. Willett when you arrested him?"

Carreras winced. "I, uh—"

"No further questions, Your Honor. The defense calls Wolf Willett to testify."

The district attorney, who was halfway to his feet, sat down heavily.

The judge peered at Eagle. "You realize, of course, that Mr. Willett's testimony in this hearing can be used against him in a trial?"

"Of course, Your Honor. The defense has nothing to hide."

Wolf took the stand and was sworn in.

"Mr. Willett, let's first address the issue of Mr. Tinney's will. Were you Mr. Tinney's personal attorney?"

"I was, for many years."

"And did you ever draw a will at his request?"

"I did, about two years ago."

"And who, in that will, would have received the bulk of Mr. Tinney's estate?"

"His four ex-wives. Apart from some small bequests, the bulk of the estate was to go to them."

"At the time of Mr. Tinney's death, did you believe that will to still be in force?"

"I did."

"When did you learn that Mr. Tinney had drawn a new will?"

"A couple of weeks after his death, when our business manager sent me a copy."

"And was that will drawn by an attorney different from yourself?"

"Yes, it was."

"And you had no knowledge whatever of this will until two weeks after Mr. Tinney's death?"

"That is correct."

"Mr. Willett, in his will did Jack Tinney give any reason for leaving you the bulk of his estate?"

"Yes."

"What was his reason?"

"He stated in the will that he was making the bequest in gratitude for my friendship and my wise management of his business affairs."

"Now, Mr. Willett, I will show you a photograph and ask you if you are, or were, acquainted with this man." He handed Wolf the photograph of Grafton.

"Yes, I knew him as Dan O'Hara."

"How did you meet?"

"My wife asked me to meet with him. She said he was a friend of a friend of hers from New York."

"Why did she want you to meet him?"

"Mr. O'Hara, as I then knew him, had written

a screenplay and was anxious to have it produced. I read the screenplay."

"Did you then meet with this O'Hara?"

"I did. I took him to lunch at a restaurant called Mortons, in Los Angeles."

"What was the substance of your discussion?"

"He asked my opinion of the screenplay; I told him I thought it was very good. However, I had no wish to produce it myself—it was about a prison break, and it was not the sort of thing that Mr. Tinney and I undertook. I offered to call someone I knew at Warner Brothers who might be interested, and I later did so. I believe Mr. O'Hara entered into a contract with that studio to produce the film."

"Did you ever see this O'Hara again?"

"No. He did telephone to tell me the outcome of his talks with Warner Brothers and to thank me for sending him there. I recommended a lawyer to negotiate the contract for him."

"And that was your only contact with him ever again?"

"It was."

"One final question: Why did you tell the district attorney and the police that you did not know James Grafton?"

"I had never heard that name before. When I saw his body at the county morgue, it had no face. I had no idea that Grafton and O'Hara were the same man until I saw that photograph here this morning."

"I have nothing further, Your Honor. The prosecution may question my client."

Martinez hesitated, then said, "I have no questions for Mr. Willett at this time, Your Honor," he said.

The judge spoke up. "The witness is excused. Mr. Eagle, do you have a motion?"

"Yes, Judge. I move that the charges against Mr. Willett be dismissed, for lack of evidence."

"Mr. Martinez?"

Martinez rose. "The prosecution opposes the motion and asks that Mr. Willett be bound over to a grand jury."

The judge thought for a moment. "Motion denied," he said. "Do you have a request for bail, Mr. Eagle?"

"I do, Your Honor. I request that Mr. Willett be released on bail in the amount of one thousand dollars."

Martinez was on his feet again. "Your Honor, may I point out that this is a heinous crime? That three people have been brutally murdered? The prosecution vehemently opposes bail."

"Mr. Eagle?" the judge asked expectantly.

"Your Honor, I would like to point out that the case for the prosecution is flimsy at best. Mr. Willett is a reputable citizen with high standing in the community and in his profession. He has been devastated by this horrible crime, losing both his wife and his business partner of many years. He has cooperated fully with the investigation and has voluntarily remained in the jurisdiction in order to be of further help. He has no intention of fleeing—on the contrary, he is most anxious for the murderer or murderers of his wife and friend to be quickly brought to justice and will do anything in his power to further aid the investigation."

Martinez stood again. "Your Honor, I would like to point out that Mr. Willett has already fled the jurisdiction once and might well do so again."

Eagle spoke up. "Judge, when Mr. Willett left the jurisdiction, it was without knowledge that the murders had even occurred. When he learned of the murders, he went to Los Angeles briefly to conduct vital business to protect the health of his business and the livelihoods of the dozen people he employs. At the earliest possible moment, he returned to Santa Fe and offered his help to the district attorney. If he was going to flee, he could easily have done so immediately following the murders, since the district attorney, in his wisdom, had not bothered to check the fingerprints of the victims and did not even know that Mr. Willett was still alive. He could have remained dead, if he had wished, to avoid prosecution. I submit that, since that time, his every action has been that of an innocent man. And, Your Honor, the defense will overlook the improper arrest of Mr. Willett in the interest of speedy justice. I reaffirm my request for bail."

The judge thought for a moment. "The defendant will be released on bail of one hundred thousand dollars," he said. "Next case?"

Eagle took Wolf by the arm. "Let's get out of here," he said.

30

Wolf and Ed Eagle left the Santa Fe County Jail, where Wolf had collected his belongings taken from him the night before. They got back into Eagle's large BMW, and Eagle produced an electric razor from the glove compartment. "I expect you'd like some breakfast," Eagle said, pulling out into traffic.

"How'd you know?" Wolf asked, checking his shave in the sun visor mirror.

"Most folks have to spend longer than a night in our local slammer before they're willing to eat the food."

"You're right about that," Wolf said with feeling. "Do you know what they gave us this morning?"

"Polenta, beans, fat bacon, and green Jell-O."

"How'd you know that?"

"They've been serving the same breakfast for as long as anybody can remember. They change the color of the Jell-O at lunch and dinner, though." Eagle turned in to Guadalupe Street, drove a few blocks, and found a parking spot. He led Wolf across the street and into the Zia Café, then ordered him a big breakfast.

Wolf tore into the food. "God, this is good," he said.

"Your first meal out always is. I'm sorry you had to go through that, but even if I had been here I couldn't have prevented it. They wanted a shot at you, and they got it, for what it was worth to them. We're lucky that this guy Carreras put himself on the case. He's sloppy about his work, and that makes my job easier."

"Can you believe he forgot to serve the warrant?"

"Yes. It's one of my favorite stalling tactics, to make them rearrest my client, but in this case I didn't want to lean on a technicality. If we go to trial we're likely to have the same judge, and I didn't want to annoy him."

"I was amazed he didn't dismiss the charges when you finished in there," Wolf said, stuffing a sausage into his mouth.

"He didn't want the D.A. to look too bad, but I can tell you, if that had been their whole case at a trial, you'd have walked without its ever having gone to a jury."

"Will he go for the indictment now?"

"Maybe, but he'll probably wait until he feels he's got a stronger case. I expect Carreras instigated the arrest just so he could get you in his jailhouse."

"I think I have a better understanding now of why so many people confess to crimes they haven't committed. Just the experience of being locked up is so demoralizing that the police have you at a tremendous disadvantage."

"Did they do the 'good cop, bad cop' routine?"

"Yes, and it was surprisingly effective. It took me a few minutes to grasp what was going on."

"I see you've got Ms. Deering back on the scene."

"Now, look, Ed, I'm not flaunting her presence. She and her daughter are here for Christmas, that's all."

"Okay, but no public places, no dinners at the Santacafé, you hear me?"

"All right, agreed."

Wolf finished his huge breakfast, and they left.

"Now," Eagle said as he turned toward Wilderness Gate, "remember that I've now promised a *judge* that you won't leave the jurisdiction. That means you can't leave the county, not even to take Ms. Deering to the Albuquerque airport when she returns to L.A. Get the lady a taxi."

"All right," Wolf said, beginning to feel trapped. "I'll stick close to Santa Fe."

"Don't cross the county line, you hear me? I wouldn't put it past Carreras to put a tail on you, in the hope that you might jump bail and give him a chance to arrest you again."

"I hear you, Ed."

"There's something I want you to do, now that the police have made a move."

"Sure."

"I want you to call or write to everybody you

know who is somebody—all those movie people who have public names—and get character references. Absolutely anybody you think might be of any help. Also, any politicians you may know, and any clergymen."

"That's kind of embarrassing, asking people to do that. Is it really necessary?"

"It is. If it embarrasses you, ask somebody you know to write to them for you. And there's something else that isn't going to be easy for you."

"What's that?"

"If we go to trial, I'm going to put Julia's sister on the stand."

"What for?"

"I'll want a jury to know the kind of person Julia had been, her record of arrests, all the sleaziness. If worse comes to worse and the jury starts thinking you might be guilty, I want them to have somebody else to blame, and Julia's ideal."

"Yeah," Wolf said. "Julia won't be there to defend herself. That'll make me look just swell."

"Don't hand me that. I know enough about her now to know that the woman was a slut and a con artist, and that she never gave a fuck about anybody but herself. What you have to get used to is that she never gave a fuck about you, either."

"I don't believe that," Wolf said stubbornly.

"Well, just look at the newest wrinkle in all this," Eagle said. "She sent Grafton to you—an escaped convict, an armed robber, a con man, a *murderer*, for Christ's sake, and she snookered you into having lunch with the guy and helping him sell his screenplay."

"It was a good screenplay," Wolf said. "Crude, but that never put off a major studio. Anyway, Grafton must have been blackmailing Julia."

"How do you know that? For all you know, she could have welcomed him with open arms. I have it on good authority that he was an absolute ace in bed."

"Oh, thanks for that, Ed, that really helped."

"I hope it helped you to understand what Julia was. I deal with people like her every week of my life; I see what they're capable of and how they always blame somebody else when they get caught. Now, I'm telling you it is *critical* to your defense to make you look as good as possible and to make Julia look as bad as possible, and we're lucky that it won't be hard to do. Julia gave us that, anyway."

"All *right*, Ed, do what you have to do to get me free of this, but I don't want to hear about it until I'm in a courtroom, unless it's absolutely necessary."

"You're giving me a free hand, then?"

"Yes, a free hand."

Eagle pulled into Wolf's driveway. "I'm sorry this is so hard for you, Wolf, but I said I'd get you off; I didn't say it was going to be fun."

"All right, Ed." Wolf sighed. "I understand my position."

Eagle pulled to a stop at Wolf's door. "No, you don't. There's something else you haven't grasped yet."

"Not something else." Wolf groaned.

"Yes, and something important. Even if you're acquitted, even if you walk out of that courtroom a free man, a substantial percentage—maybe even a majority—of the people you now know and later meet are always going to wonder if you committed those murders. An acquittal isn't exoneration."

"So how do I become exonerated?"

"The only way I can do that is by proving that somebody else did it." Eagle looked away. "And considering the facts of this case—or rather, the lack of them—that may not ever be possible."

Wolf slumped. "I see," he said.

"Take care of yourself. Call me day or night, if you need me."

"Thanks." Wolf got out of the car and trudged toward the door. As he turned the knob, the door opened before him. Jane rushed to him and put her arms around his waist. "Boy, am I glad you're here," she breathed into his ear. "I was wondering if I would ever see you again."

He hugged her back. "So was I, love; so was I."

31

When Wolf awoke, someone was in bed with him. He opened his eyes, and Jane was there, asleep, wearing a sweater and jeans.

He turned to face her, and she opened her eyes. "How long have you been there?" he asked.

She looked at her wristwatch. "About half an hour."

"Oh," he said, disappointed. "I wish you had been there longer."

She laughed. "I got up and made breakfast for Sara and Flaps. They went out to build a snowman, so I thought I'd look in on you. You were sleeping like a child; I couldn't bring myself to wake you."

He leaned over and kissed her.

"Unshaven!" she said, rising to her knees. "Okay, out of bed and scrape that face. I'm not kissing whiskers this early in the morning."

He got out of bed and staggered into the bathroom for a shower and a shave. She had breakfast on the kitchen table when he surfaced.

"Yesterday was nice," she said. "Thank you for the tour; Sara liked it, too."

"Tonight we'll take a different kind of tour and look at the Christmas decorations. Is it all right for Sara to stay up?"

"We wouldn't be able to get her to bed before that time, anyway. She's a coiled spring on Christmas Eve. What's on for today?"

"If you don't mind, I'd like to spend some time working on some stuff Ed Eagle asked me to do. I've got to write some letters and make some calls."

"Okay. We'll amuse ourselves."

"Why don't the two of you take the car and do some shopping?"

"Sounds good. I've got one or two last-minute things to pick up. I'd just like to lie around and read for a while, too."

"My library is yours. Maria is coming tomorrow to cook Christmas dinner for us. I thought I'd ask Mark Shea over, if he hasn't got plans."

"He's the shrink I met at the D & D's party?"

"Right. He's probably my closest friend in Santa Fe, and I think you'll like him when you've had a chance to sit down with him for a while."

"If he's your friend, he can't be all bad."

Wolf finished his breakfast and glanced at his watch. "I'll call him now, before he starts with patients." He went into the study and dialed Mark's number.

"Mark Shea."

"Hi, it's Wolf."

"Oh, Wolf," Mark replied, sounding tired. "I've

been wondering how you were. I'm sorry I haven't called, but I've been swamped."

"Jane Deering and her daughter are in town, and Maria's cooking us a big Christmas dinner tomorrow. Why don't you join us?"

"Thanks, Wolf, but I'm committed to something. I . . . I would like to talk with you, though. Listen, do you think you could come around here late tomorrow afternoon?"

"Sure. Can I bring Jane and Sara?"

"I'd really like to talk to you alone. Do you mind?"

"No, not at all. What time?"

"Around six?"

"Fine. Mark, are you all right? You sound a bit . . . weary."

"Well, a lot has been going on; that's what I want to talk with you about. I've got some explaining to do, Wolf, and I'm looking forward to getting it off my chest."

"What on earth are you talking about?"

"I'll tell you everything tomorrow. See you at six. Oh, and Merry Christmas."

"You too, Mark."

Wolf hung up, got his address book, and started to make a list of people who would be good for character references. He had a hard time concentrating; Mark had sounded depressed, and he was *never* depressed. Well, he reckoned, he wasn't the only one with problems. He'd hear about Mark's tomorrow.

After dinner, he drove Jane and Sara around

downtown Santa Fe and the East Side Historic District.

"What are all those little lights along the tops of the houses?" Sara asked.

"They're called *farolitos*," Wolf replied. "You take a paper bag, put some sand in the bottom to weight it, then stick a candle in the sand and light it. Presto! A *farolito!* Then you line them up along the roof."

"They're beautiful," Sara said, pressing her nose to the window.

"Of course, these days a lot of them are plastic and electric, but it's the thought that counts."

They drove slowly through the narrow streets of the east side. Traffic was heavy—everybody went out on Christmas Eve in Santa Fe to see the lights.

"What's that nice smell?" Sara asked. "It's like incense, or something."

"That's piñon smoke," Wolf replied. "All the adobe houses have fireplaces, and everybody burns piñon wood. Piñons are the short, gnarled pine trees that you've seen all over the place."

"It's lovely," Jane said. "It seems to fit right into the Santa Fe atmosphere."

"We'll burn some ourselves when we get home."

By the time they got home, Sara had fallen asleep in her mother's lap. Wolf carried her into the house, and Jane got her tucked in. Flaps climbed onto the bed, tail thumping, and laid her head across Sara's small body, then gave them all a goodnight grin. Wolf and Jane tiptoed from the room.

Wolf lit a fire in the study and poured them a brandy.

"I've never seen her fold so completely on Christmas Eve," Jane said.

"It's Flaps," Wolf replied. "She's never had her own little girl before; the two of them wore each other out today."

"You're good with her," Jane said.

"I like her. I haven't spent a lot of time around children, but I feel very comfortable with Sara."

"She feels comfortable with you, too," Jane said. "That hasn't always been the case with the men in my life."

Wolf reclined on the sofa and pulled her head onto his shoulder. They kissed, then began to move against each other.

"You don't know what you're getting yourself into," Wolf said.

"Maybe not," she replied, "but I'm willing to find out."

They made love on the floor in front of the fire until only glowing coals were left.

"Best Christmas I ever had," Wolf sighed.

32

When Wolf woke on Christmas morning, Jane was under the covers with him again, this time without clothes. But they were not alone; Sara was jumping up and down on the bed, screaming "It's Christmas! It's Christmas!" and Flaps was on the bed too, dancing and barking.

"All right! All right!" Jane cried. "Just give us a minute! We'll meet you at the tree!"

The little girl and the dog bounded from the room.

"What was that?" Wolf said sleepily. "A terrorist attack?"

"That was a little girl and a dog on Christmas morning," Jane groaned. "And if we don't get up and get in there *right now*, they'll be back, I promise you."

Wolf struggled out of bed, crawled into some clothes, and moaned. "Do I have time to brush my teeth?"

"Not a chance," Jane said, zipping up her jeans. "We'll be attacked again. Come on."

When they arrived at the tree, Sara was separating the presents into three piles, while Flaps helped by sniffing everything carefully. Sara's was the biggest pile. She tore into the packages, shrieking with delight at each gift, no matter what it was. She danced around the room wearing Wolf's gift, a small sheepskin coat and matching snow boots.

"Those are for when you're in Santa Fe," he said. He opened one of his own presents—a photograph of the three of them with Flaps and the snowman that had been taken only the day before.

"That's for when we're not here," Jane said.

Maria cooked a grand Christmas dinner, and they ate formally in the dining room, stuffing themselves with the traditional dinner. After lunch, Wolf and Jane left Sara playing with her new Nintendo game and Flaps methodically removing the skin from one of her new tennis balls. They napped for most of the afternoon, and when Wolf woke, it was time to visit Mark Shea. He got out of bed, taking care not to wake Jane; he was on his way out of the house when the phone rang. He grabbed it before it could wake Jane.

"Hello?" he said.

"Wolf, it's Mark. I want to ask a favor."

"Sure, Mark."

"I remember your telling me you owned a pistol."

"That's right."

"May I borrow it? Would you bring it with you?"

Wolf was very surprised. Mark was a vigorous opponent of the right to handgun ownership; he and Wolf had argued many times about the gun control laws. Wolf resisted the urge to tease him now about his stand. "All right, Mark. I'll bring it with me."

He went to the study, opened the safe, checked to be sure the pistol was loaded, put it into his coat pocket, and left the house.

New snow had fallen during the night, and Wolf drove carefully through the nearly deserted streets. Everybody was doing what he had been doing, he reckoned—sleeping off Christmas dinner. He drove north through town and out onto the Taos Highway. When he turned left onto Tano Road, he noted how few tire tracks had marred the new snow; by the time he reached the turnoff to Mark's house, there were only the tracks of a single car. It was dark as he swung through the open gates to Mark's compound, and his lights illuminated the single set of tire tracks that had turned into Mark's place.

The only light in the compound was from the outbuilding that was Mark's professional suite, and Wolf turned toward it at the fork in the drive. The big house, off to the right, looked empty, haunted. The tracks preceding him stopped next to Mark's Range Rover, which was covered in a fluffy layer of new snow, but there was no other car. Wolf left the Porsche and trudged to the front door, following another set of footprints that seemed to be going the other way.

Wolf rapped sharply on the door and opened it. "Hello? Mark?"

Music was playing quite loudly. Vivaldi, *The Four Seasons*. There was something in the air, too, a familiar scent.

Wolf was swept back in time; he was twelve or thirteen. He'd gotten his first gun, a .22 rifle, for Christmas, and he was out in the woods at the edge of his hometown of Delano, looking for rabbits. First, though, he'd wanted some target practice. He'd found some bottles and lined them up against a mudbank, then fired his new rifle for the first time. The smell of gunpowder had filled the woods, a smell he came to associate with afternoons in the fields and mountains around his home, hunting with a friend and a dog. The smell was here now and was entirely pleasant, until he realized it was out of place.

Wolf looked around and saw no one. The music became an irritant, and he went to the stereo in the bookcase and switched it off. It was then that he heard the noise, and it made his hair stand on end—a rasping groan. He walked around the sofa and found Mark Shea, lying on his side, trying to get up.

"Mark!" Wolf managed to say. He went to his friend and turned him over onto his back. The front of his white shirt was a mass of blood, and turning him over revealed an expanding pool of red on the carpet.

Mark's mouth moved, but no sound came out, except the rasp.

"Hang on, Mark," Wolf said, grabbing for the phone. With one hand he dialed zero, while with the other he loosened Mark's shirt collar.

"Operator."

"Get me the police; this is an emergency."

The operator was matter-of-fact. "May I have the number you're calling from?"

Wolf struggled to remember the number and couldn't. "I can't remember it. Please connect me with the police—no, with the sheriff's department." Mark's house was outside the city limits, in the county's jurisdiction.

"I'm sorry, sir, but I must have the number."

Frantic, Wolf looked at the telephone in his hand, but there was no number on it.

"Listen to me, you stupid bitch," he said, "a man is badly hurt, and I want the sheriff's department right now, do you hear me?"

"All right, keep your shirt on," she said sourly.

At the moment he was connected, Wolf remembered Mark's number.

"Sheriff's department."

"Hello, I need an ambulance and the police here right away. A man has been shot." He recited directions to Mark's house.

"Your name and number?" the deputy said.

"My name is Willett." He rattled off the phone number. "Please hurry and get here."

"Is the man badly hurt?"

Wolf wanted to say that he was probably dying, but he didn't want Mark to hear that. "Yes, very."

"We're on the way."

Wolf hung up and turned his attention back to Mark. His eyes were glazed. "Mark, can you hear me?" he asked.

Mark's eyes came back into focus, and he seemed to recognize Wolf. He nodded.

"Can you tell me who did this?"

Mark's mouth moved, but no sound came out. Wolf couldn't read his lips.

"Try, Mark, try hard. I can't do anything to help you, and I have to know who did this."

Mark did try harder, and this time Wolf could understand the words. "She . . . did . . ." he managed to say.

"Who, Mark? Who did it?"

Mark tried again and failed. His eyes began to lose their focus. He jerked in a sharp breath and it came out in a rattle. Wolf saw his pupils dilate. Mark Shea was dead.

Wolf could hear a distant siren—no, two sirens. He sat back on the floor and took his friend's hand. He was still sitting there when the sheriff and the ambulance arrived.

33

Ed Eagle was dozing when the phone rang. He groaned with the effort of answering it. "Hello?"

"Ed, it's Wolf Willett."

"Merry Christmas, Wolf."

"Not anymore. I'm at Mark Shea's place, and he's been shot."

"How bad?"

"Dead. He was alive when I got here; he died a couple of minutes later."

"Were you first on the scene?"

"Yes. We had an appointment at six o'clock."

Eagle glanced at his watch: ten past six. "Have you called the police?"

"The sheriff. I can hear the sirens now."

"I'll be there in ten minutes," Eagle said. "Wait until I arrive before you talk to them."

"All right, but hurry."

Eagle grabbed a coat, headed for the BMW, then changed his mind and got into the Bronco; with new snow on the ground he might need the four-wheel drive. He drove faster than he ever had in snow, and he nearly lost it a couple of times. It was dark now, and his headlights brightly illuminated the white road ahead of him.

Tano Road was treacherous, and he could see that other cars ahead of him had skidded. The sheriff's cars, he thought; they had been in a hurry too. He skidded through Mark Shea's gates and drove toward the flashing lights. Three sheriff's cars and an ambulance were there when he pulled up in front of the psychiatrist's office.

"Just hold it right there, Mr. Eagle," a deputy said, moving in front of the door and holding up a hand.

"Fuck you," Eagle said, shouldering the man aside. "My client's in there." He strode into the office. Half a dozen men were gathered around the sofa at the end of the room, all looking down. Wolf Willett was one of them. So was the sheriff, Matt Powers. Eagle nodded at the man. "Matt," he said.

"What're you doing here, Ed?" the sheriff asked. "This is a crime scene, and you're not welcome."

"Let's start all over, Matt. I represent Wolf Willett, and he's not talking to you until I say so. Am I still unwelcome?"

The sheriff looked at the floor again.

"Yes, I am," Wolf replied.

"All right, Matt, Mr. Willett is going to answer all your questions, and I'm going to be here while he does it."

The sheriff glowered at Eagle. "Okay. Let's all

go sit down over here." He directed Wolf to a sofa at the other end of the room.

Eagle ignored them for the moment and went to look at Mark Shea's body; he was appalled at the amount of blood on the floor. He turned and joined the sheriff and his client.

Wolf began telling his story, and Eagle listened closely, ready to keep him out of trouble, if necessary. It was not necessary; Wolf was lucid and articulate. He stopped at the point when he called the sheriff's office.

"So," the sheriff said, "Dr. Shea said that 'she did it'?"

"Not exactly," Wolf replied. "I said, 'Mark, who did this?' and he replied, with some difficulty, 'She did.' There was a pause between the two words; he was struggling to say it."

Eagle broke in. "So he didn't actually say that a woman shot him?"

"Sounded like that to me," the sheriff said. "Mr. Willett asked him who did it, and he said, 'She did.'"

"Maybe," Wolf said. "How can we be sure exactly what he meant?"

"Why were you coming to see Dr. Shea?" the sheriff asked.

"We talked yesterday, and Mark asked me to come over at six; said he wanted to talk to me alone."

"Did he give you any indication what he wanted to talk about?"

"He said he wanted to tell me some things, wanted to get something off his chest, words to that effect. He sounded worried and depressed. That was very unusual for Mark."

"Sheriff?"

The group on the sofa turned and looked at the deputy standing in the doorway; he was gingerly holding a rifle.

"We found this in the snow, a few yards off the front walk; looks like somebody slung it over there."

"Bring it over here," the sheriff said, and watched the deputy as he approached. "Looks like an old Winchester," he said, looking at the rifle without touching it.

"It's a Model 73," Wolf said. "Mark bought it late last year—a Christmas present to himself, he said."

The deputy sniffed the barrel. "Been fired," he said.

The sheriff turned back to Wolf. "Mr. Willett, do you have any objection to a test to see if you've recently fired a weapon?"

"None at all," Wolf said. "Under the circumstances, I'd be grateful for such a test."

"We'll do that in a few minutes," the sheriff said. "Do you know if Dr. Shea owned any other firearms?"

"No, he didn't—not to my knowledge, anyway. He had an absolute hatred of handguns; he signed ads in the *New York Times*, he wrote letters to Senate committees—he was very strong on handgun control."

"And yet he bought a rifle."

"It was only a decoration to him, I think. I

doubt if he ever fired it; I'm astonished that he would even have ammunition for the thing."

"He owned a rifle, but he didn't shoot," the sheriff said, as if such a thing were unheard of.

"Lots of people in Santa Fe have western relics—like that," Wolf said, pointing.

The others turned and looked at an old silver-trimmed saddle, resting on a sawhorse across the room.

"He didn't ride, either," Wolf said.

"I see," the sheriff replied.

Wolf spoke again. "There's something else."

"What's that?"

"Just as I left the house to come here, Mark called and asked if I still owned a pistol—asked me to bring it with me."

"Did you ask him why?"

"No. I planned to when I got here."

"Did you bring the pistol?"

Wolf dug the automatic out of his pocket and handed it over.

The sheriff sniffed at the barrel. "Doesn't seem to have been fired recently."

"It's never been fired at all," Wolf said. "I bought it at a gun shop out on Airport Road right after I built my house here. I've never had occasion to shoot it."

The sheriff expertly fieldstripped the weapon and checked it carefully; he reassembled it and handed it back to Wolf. "It's as you say. There's still some packing grease in the barrel. How did Dr. Shea know you owned a pistol?"

"We were arguing about gun control once, and

I told him I owned one," Wolf said. "But there's something else: When I drove out here, there was only one set of tracks ahead of me from the time I turned onto County Road 84. The tracks turned into here, and there was a set of footprints between the parking place and the front door."

"Let's have a look," the sheriff said. He led the group outside and played a flashlight around. "Shit," he said. There were now many tire tracks and footprints around the house, where his department's cars and men had left them.

Wolf took the flashlight from the sheriff and pointed it at Mark's Range Rover. "Look over here," he said, leading the group to the parking area. He pointed. "The tracks weren't *to* the house, they were *from* the house. Somebody walked out of the house—only one set of footprints—got into a car parked here, and drove away."

The sheriff took the flashlight back. "We've got a good print right here, from when he got into the car." He called out to a deputy. "Jack, get over here and take a cast of this footprint, and measure it. I want one of the tire track, too." He turned to the others. "I got me a good footprint man."

Eagle spoke for the first time. "Matt, it looks like whoever did this spent the night here—or most of it, anyway. It started snowing at my house just after midnight, and it stopped around seven this morning, while I was having breakfast. That means your man—or woman—got here before it started and left after it stopped;

otherwise, there'd be tire tracks coming and going. Wolf, is there a bedroom in the office building?"

"No," Wolf replied. "Wait a minute, there's a back door and a walk leading to the main house. Maybe there are some footprints there."

The group walked back into the office and Wolf led them to the back door. He switched on the outside lights and opened the door. The walkway leading up to the main house had been shoveled nearly clean.

"I'll see if we can get some kind of footprint from what's left of the snow on the walk, and we'll go over the main house for fingerprints, too," the sheriff said.

They went back inside, and a deputy met them. "Sheriff," he said, "we're making casts of those prints, but I can give you an idea right now."

"Shoot," the sheriff said.

"The tires are Goodyear snow and mud tires; they're standard on half a dozen different new four-wheel-drive vehicles—Cherokees, Broncos, et cetera—and every tire shop in town carries them. The footprints are from some kind of snow boot; I've seen 'em before, and they're common, too."

"Man or woman?" the sheriff asked.

"They're about nine and a half inches long, so the size would work for either a large woman or a man. I stood next to them and compared 'em with the depth of my tracks; they're shallower—I weigh a hundred and eighty; whoever wore the boots, I'd put at one-thirty to one-sixty."

"Good work, boy."

"Oh, and something else; the Winchester had been wiped real good. No prints."

The sheriff nodded. "Mr. Willett, how much do you weigh?"

"A hundred and sixty pounds."

"Uh-huh. Let me have a look at your shoe soles."

Wolf displayed a leather boot with a Vibram sole.

"Uh-huh, a different boot from the print."

Another deputy called the sheriff aside and spoke with him briefly.

The sheriff returned. "Your story checks out with a lady at your house," he said to Wolf. "About the time you left, I mean. Considering what time you called us and the time we got here and the car tracks and footprints, I think we can rule you out as a suspect, Mr. Willett."

"I'm glad to hear it," Wolf said.

"So am I," Ed Eagle echoed.

"I'll admit, I'm kinda disappointed," the sheriff said. "You looked real good there for a while, considering you've already been charged with three other murders."

"Matt," Eagle said, "I'd like to point out that the murders at Mr. Willett's place have a similarity to this one, in that both were committed with weapons already on the premises—assuming that the Winchester was the weapon used here."

"That's a good point, Ed."

"Can I speak to you in private for a moment, Matt?" Eagle took the sheriff aside. "Are you entirely satisfied that Willett is not a suspect in this murder?"

"I believe I am," the sheriff replied. "Of course, there could have been an accomplice who left Willett here after the shooting, but that doesn't really make much sense."

"I'd like to point out that Shea was one of Willett's closest friends; Willett had been his patient at one time, and Shea had already told me that he'd be happy to testify on Willett's behalf, if he's tried on the other murders."

"No apparent motive, then," the sheriff said.

"What I wanted to talk to you about is, when you start talking to the press about this, I'd appreciate it if you'd go out of your way not to imply that Willett is suspected. I don't want the papers to crucify an innocent man."

"All right, Ed, I'll be careful talking to the press."

"Thanks." Eagle rejoined Wolf. "Sheriff, is Mr. Willett free to go now?"

"I guess he is," the sheriff replied. "I may want to talk to him again, though."

"He'll be available at all times," Eagle said. He shook hands with the sheriff and led Wolf to his car. "Go on home and relax; you're out of this one."

Wolf got into his car, then rolled down the window. He looked thoughtful. "Ed, three of the people closest to me have been murdered now. What do you think is going on?"

Eagle shook his head. "I wish the hell I knew, my friend. But I'll tell you this: I think you ought to have somebody up at the house with you. I can get somebody to do that."

Wolf thought about it, then shook his head. "No, I don't think so."

"All right, whatever you say, but I think it might be a good idea to keep that gun of yours handy."

Wolf nodded, then seemed to think again for a moment. "Ed, have you seen Julia's sister recently?"

A little chill went through Eagle. "Yes. Last night, in fact. She was at my house."

"What time did she leave?"

"Around midnight, I think."

"Had it started to snow yet?"

"No."

"I just wondered," Wolf said. He started the car and drove away, leaving Eagle staring after him.

Barbara Kennerly was a big girl, Eagle remembered—five ten and a hundred and thirty-five, maybe; she drove a Cherokee; and when he had kissed her goodnight, she had been wearing snow boots.

34

Wolf drove back to Wilderness Gate on automatic pilot, numb with shock and grief. He pulled up at the house, and Jane greeted him at the door.

"What's going on?" she whispered, indicating that Sara, who was setting the kitchen table, should not hear.

"I'll tell you later, when we're alone," he whispered back.

Jane had dinner in the oven, and Wolf was surprised that it was after nine o'clock. He picked at the food while trying to make cheerful conversation with Sara.

When they had finally tucked the little girl into bed and left Flaps to guard her, Wolf poured them a drink and took Jane into the study. He took a deep breath. "There's been another murder: Mark Shea."

Jane nearly choked on her drink. "Is that what the sheriff's office was on the phone about?"

"Yes. I arrived at Mark's house and found him dying."

"Who did it?"

"I don't know. Nobody knows."

"Wolf, what is going on here? I mean, how many more of your friends are going to die before this is over?"

"I don't know, but I think it would be best if you and Sara were on the noon plane from Albuquerque tomorrow."

"I don't want to go and leave you in this state."

"Thank you, love, but we don't want Sara to know about this, and to tell you the truth, I don't think I'm going to be fit company for anybody until this is over."

Jane looked sad. "I'm sorry I can't help."

"I wish you could help, but nobody can until we find out who's doing this and why. Believe me, I hate to see you go; these few days have been the happiest I've had since I left you in L.A."

"I'm glad to hear it," she said, kissing him.

"I don't know what I'd have done without you, being in this house alone at Christmas. I'm going to hate being alone again, too."

"Well, just as long as you miss the hell out of me."

"I will, I will." He pulled her into his arms.

In the middle of the night, Wolf woke and couldn't go back to sleep. He extricated himself from Jane's arms and, careful not to wake her, got into a robe and slippers and went into the study.

The moon was high, and there was no need for a light. He poured himself a brandy and stretched out in the Eames lounge chair, looking down over a snow-covered Santa Fe gleaming in the moonlight.

He hadn't said anything to Ed Eagle, but he felt strongly now that Mark Shea had known more about the murders of Julia, Jack, and Grafton than he had previously been willing to say. There was nothing else the psychiatrist could have meant when he said he had some things to tell Wolf, things to get off his chest.

Who would have wished the deaths of, first, his wife and his partner, then his friend and doctor? He wrestled with this for a long time, then gave up. He knew no one who was the enemy of any of them, no one who would profit from the death of any of them, let alone all of them.

He had to consider, too, whether he himself was in any danger. After all, Grafton may have died because somebody thought he was Wolf Willett. Suddenly he was frightened again. He went to the hall closet and retrieved the pistol from his coat pocket, then slipped it into the pocket of his robe. It weighed heavily there, felt odd, unnecessary. He had bought the thing while in some paranoid delusion of having to defend the house, and now it looked as though he might need it to defend his life.

He poured himself another brandy and sat down. The moon had set now, and only the quiescent lights of the town could be seen. He was tired and thought of going back to bed; instead, he dozed.

Some time later, he jerked awake. A noise had woken him—or had he dreamed it? He reconstructed the sound from his memory; it had come from the kitchen door. He got up and padded into the kitchen. The noise came again, but fainter this time. His hand closed on the pistol.

He tiptoed to the door and peeped out through the glass pane next to it. He could see nothing; he heard only the sound of a light wind through the piñon trees above the house. He grasped the knob and turned it as silently as he could. Slowly, he opened the door and stepped outside, the pistol before him.

A shock sent him back through the door; he had stepped into loose snow on the doorstep. He walked out again, avoiding the pile; it hadn't been there when he'd returned to the house earlier.

The wind blew again, and a handful of snow went down his neck. He danced around, pulling at the cord of his dressing gown, shaking the snow away. Then he looked up. A limb of a ponderosa pine extended over the kitchen door. The wind had blown off its load of snow and deposited it on the doorstep; that was the sound he had heard.

He walked quietly back through the house, still squirming from the cold dampness on his back and in his slippers. In the bathroom he dried himself with a towel, then crept back into bed with Jane. She accepted him as if he'd never left, came into his arms and rested her head in the hollow of his neck. The only sound he heard

before falling asleep was a tiny groan of content-
ment from her.

The following morning, he put Jane, Sara, and a
great many shopping bags into a taxi and sent
them to Albuquerque Airport. He watched the
cab disappear down the road to Santa Fe. He had
never felt more alone.

35

Ed Eagle was up early the day after Christmas. He had breakfast, then got into the Bronco and drove into Santa Fe. The snow of Christmas Eve had frozen solid, and the streets were icy. Those drivers who had ventured out drove with exaggerated care, and so did Eagle.

He made his way to the east side, through the warren of streets with their adobe houses, some of them antiques, the others designed to seem antique. He found the little apartment house where Barbara Kennerly lived, parked the car, and walked through the archway toward the staircase that led up to her apartment.

As he approached the stairs, Barbara came down, wearing a heavy coat over a nightgown and snow boots.

"Well, good morning," she said, surprised. She picked up a newspaper and brushed the snow off it.

"Good morning," he replied. "I was in the neighborhood. Will you buy me a cup of coffee?"

"Sure." She smiled. "But the place is a mess. Come on upstairs."

He let her precede him up the steps, which had not been cleared of snow, and he looked closely at the tracks she made. The imprint of the soles was familiar.

She opened the door and waved him in. "You haven't seen my place, have you?"

"No," he said, stepping inside. He found himself in a small living room; he could see into the bedroom, only a few steps away, and a tiny kitchen was on the other side of the apartment. "I like it." He sat down on the sofa.

"It suits me, for the time being," she said, shrugging. "There's enough room for one, and the furniture's not too bad. I'm going to need some pictures, though; I've already started looking." She busied herself in the kitchen and returned with two cups of coffee. "Listen, Ed, I'm sorry about leaving you on Christmas Eve, but I just felt like sleeping alone. Can you understand that?"

"It's all right, Barbara. I'm accustomed to spending a lot of my time alone. I've made a point for a long time to spend Christmas Day by myself."

"I hope I didn't hurt your feelings."

"You didn't." He changed the subject. "I like the boots. Where'd you find them?"

She held one up for inspection. "A Christmas present to myself. I got them at the Overland Sheepskin Company."

He knew the place; he'd bought boots there

himself. "I like fur boots," he said. "Do they have them in men's sizes?"

She laughed. "These are a man's size nine," she said. "I've got a big foot."

He was stuck for something to say. "They look warm," he managed.

"They are," she said, kicking off the boots. "Just the thing for going out in the snow for the papers."

"Yes." A long silence.

"Ed, what brings you over here to see me so early in the morning?"

He shrugged. "The office is closed today. I just thought I'd drop by."

"Come on, Ed," she coaxed. "Something's on your mind; why don't you tell me about it?"

He couldn't bring himself to question her as he had intended to, and he looked for another subject. "Barbara, I've wanted to talk with you about Wolf Willett's trial."

"Is he going to be tried?"

"I expect so, and his case has become more complicated with the death of Mark Shea. Did you know Mark?"

She shook her head. "I saw him at Santacafé a couple of times; he came in for lunch. I never actually met him, though. I heard about his murder on television last night. Have they caught anybody?"

She seemed innocent of any knowledge of Shea, Eagle thought. "Not that I've heard. You know that Wolf found him dying?"

"That was on the news." She looked alarmed. "He's not a suspect, I hope."

Eagle shook his head. "No. I was out there, and I talked with the sheriff about it. At least we don't have to worry about that one."

"You're worried about the trial, though?"

"Yes. Mark Shea would have been a principal witness for us. He had been Wolf's psychiatrist, and he would have been good on the stand."

"I'm sorry," she said. "I wish there was something I could do to help."

"There is."

"What's that?"

"I'd like you to testify about Julia. About her background, I mean, and . . . her character."

Barbara was quiet as she thought about this. "Oh, I think I get the picture," she said. "You want me to go into a courtroom and trash my sister in front of a jury in order to get your client off?"

"I want you to tell the truth about Julia; if that constitutes trashing her, then so be it."

Barbara stood up and began pacing the room, sipping from her coffee cup. "You want me to stand up in public, reveal my own past, and help you make Julia the villain," she said.

"I can protect your identity; you can testify as Hannah Schlemmer, and I can ask the judge to exclude the public and the press during your testimony. Nobody need find out your new name."

"I don't believe that for a minute," she said. "It's bound to come out—I could lose my job, and worst of all, lose the anonymity I've found in Santa Fe."

"I'll do everything I can to prevent that happening."

"What really gets me is that I thought you and I were forming some sort of relationship. Did I dream that, or am I just your Saturday night fuck?"

Eagle stood up and took her by the shoulders. "No, you didn't dream it; you and I have come to mean something to each other. That doesn't have anything to do with the trial."

"You're willing to expose me in Santa Fe to protect your client," she said bitterly. "A man who may have murdered my sister."

"The only thing Wolf ever did to your sister was take her out of the criminal life she had always led and give her respectability and everything she could ever have dreamed of having. He didn't know he was being lied to, of course. I believe Wolf Willett is innocent of any involvement in Julia's death; I think she may be a great deal less innocent. Who's the real victim here?"

"But Julia can't defend herself."

"Could she defend herself if she were here?" Eagle demanded. "Could she justify deceiving the man she married? Did she have innocent reasons for forcing a sleaze like Grafton on him?"

Barbara looked surprised. "What do you mean?"

"Julia talked Wolf into meeting Grafton and helping him with some screenplay he had written—about a prison break—that's amusing, isn't it?"

"Jimmy was in L.A.?"

"Yes, and I think he went out there to blackmail Julia, who was eminently blackmailable."

"Jesus, that creep. How could I ever have gotten involved with him?"

"That's a good question. I've always believed you were an essentially innocent person who was duped by a con man, and I'd like to go on thinking that. But you have to face the fact that your relationship with Grafton is probably what launched the whole series of events that ended in Julia's murder. I don't know how, exactly, and I may never know, but you are the connection between Grafton and Julia and Wolf, and whatever brought them together in Wolf's house that night led directly from that."

"So now you're blaming me for all this, is that it?"

"I've already told you that I regard you as innocent, but surely you can see how the consequences of your . . . your *stupidity* in falling for Grafton have been disastrous for everybody involved."

Barbara sat down and began to cry.

Eagle, who did not know how to deal with a weeping woman, sat down opposite her and waited uncomfortably for it to pass. His instinct was to sweep her into his arms, but he resisted that.

Finally Barbara composed herself. "You're right," she said. "I thought when I got out of prison it was over, but it isn't. I've got to go on paying, haven't I?"

Eagle put a hand on her cheek. "It will be over soon, I promise you."

"You can make that happen? You can make it end?"

"I think I can bring all this to a conclusion eventually, and I want to do it without either you or Wolf getting hurt. You have to understand that New Mexico has the death penalty, and as a decent human being, you have to do what you can to see that an innocent man doesn't face that."

"But you don't know if he's innocent," she said. "You told me yourself that he doesn't remember anything. Not remembering isn't the same as being innocent."

"Barbara, I've represented a lot of people charged with murder over the past twenty-five years—some of them guilty, some of them innocent—and I think I've come to know the difference."

"All right." She snuffled, dabbing her nose with a Kleenex. "I'll do it."

"Thank you. And I'll do everything I can to see that no one connects Hannah Schlemmer with Barbara Kennerly." He leaned over and kissed her.

She looked at her watch. "Oh, God, I'll be late for work."

Eagle stood up, and she followed him to the door.

"Will you be all right?" he asked.

"Of course I will," she said. "I just have to face the reality that my past isn't going away."

"When this is over," Eagle said, "you can lead your life without any fear of that. The last link with the past will be broken."

She kissed him lightly. "I wish I could believe you," she said.

Eagle walked carefully down the icy steps. He stopped and looked back at her.

"Ed," she called.

"Yes?"

"If I had refused to testify, you'd have subpoenaed me, wouldn't you?"

"Yes," he said, "I would have. I'm glad you didn't make it necessary."

She nodded. "I'm glad, too."

"Dinner tonight?"

"Sure."

"I'll call you later, and we'll figure out when and where."

She waved and stepped back into the apartment.

Eagle crunched through the snow to his car. As he was about to get into it, he looked up and saw Barbara's Cherokee parked a couple of spaces away. He walked over to the rear of the car and looked at the snow behind it. One set of tracks led to the rear tires. Goodyears.

Barbara Kennerly had come home after the snow had stopped.

36

For a week, Wolf hardly left the house. He tried to stay busy, making and taking frequent calls from Hal Berger about progress on the new film—if he should ever be free to shoot it. He began laying out the film scene by scene, drawing storyboards and making lists of actors for roles.

He refused all comment on Mark Shea's death, referring callers to Ed Eagle. He heard through Eagle that some friends of Mark's were arranging a memorial service, but no one called him about it.

He and Jane talked every day—sometimes about the new film, sometimes about the editing jobs she was doing on commercials and industrial films. She had given her agent notice, and he had arranged for her to sign with the agent at the Creative Artists Agency, who would henceforth handle her career. He assured her that she wouldn't be doing commercials much longer.

He asked Hal Berger to find some charity to give Julia's clothes and personal belongings to, and to have her jewelry appraised for a possible sale. He had reached a point where he wanted any vestige of Julia gone.

On New Year's Eve, he had a call late in the afternoon from Hal.

"Wolf, I'm at your house in Bel Air, and I'm afraid things aren't right here. There are some big problems."

"What sort of problems, Hal?"

"Let me start at the beginning. You remember that when you and Julia were married, she insisted on taking over the household accounts. I had been paying the household bills from the office, but she wanted to do it."

"Yes, Julia seemed to want to run as much of my life as possible, outside the office, anyway."

"Well, since her death, your housekeeper, Bridget, has been forwarding the mail from the house about once a week, and I've been paying the bills from the office."

"That's what I asked you to do, Hal."

"I hadn't received any mail from Bridget for a couple of weeks, and also, I wanted to get an idea of what things of Julia's you might want to give away, so I came over here. No one was answering the phone."

"What's happened there?"

"The house is a mess, for starters. It obviously hasn't been cleaned in weeks—probably not since you were here. The place reeks of booze, and there are a lot of dirty glasses scattered around. Bridget was nowhere to be found, so I went upstairs to check on Julia's things, and I found the maid passed out, drunk, on the bed in the master bedroom, wearing a dress of Julia's. She's up there now. What do you want me to do about it?"

A wave of anger ran through Wolf; he should have gotten rid of that woman a long time ago, he thought. "Fire her, Hal. Give her a month's pay so she won't have anything to bitch about, and get her out of the house today."

"Consider it done, Wolf; I never liked her, anyway, I have to admit."

"Neither did I. Julia hired her; I had nothing to do with it."

"That's not the only problem, though. There's worse to come."

"What else?"

"Bridget had apparently gone through Julia's dressing room looking for something—my guess is the jewelry—and she had ransacked Julia's desk, too. There were a lot of bank statements and other documents, and I gathered them up."

"Her jewelry is in the safe in the study; you've got the combination. You may as well take everything to the office," Wolf said. "I suppose we had better go ahead and wind up Julia's estate and close her bank account."

"Sure, I'll do that, but I found something else among the papers."

"What, Hal?"

"Are you sitting down?"

"Yes."

"Wolf, I found some correspondence with your

stockbroker. Did Julia have anything to do with your investments?"

"Yes, she had an interest in the market. She read the *Wall Street Journal* every day, and occasionally she would buy or sell something. I gave the broker a power of attorney so she could do that, but she always checked with me first. I believe she even made me some money."

"Maybe so, Wolf, but it's gone now."

"What do you mean?"

"I mean Julia sold everything less than a week before she died."

Wolf sat down. "Everything?" he asked weakly.

"Everything—the stocks, T-bills, those bonds you bought a couple of years ago, and your Keogh and 401K retirement plans. The total value was a little over three million six hundred thousand dollars."

"What did she do with the money?" Wolf asked, trying to grasp what Hal was saying.

"It went into her bank account first, then she wire-transferred the whole amount, plus about thirty thousand dollars, to a bank in the Cayman Islands."

"*Three million six?*" Wolf asked, beginning to get a grip on what had happened to him.

"That's right," Hal said. "And that's not all. Just over a million of that was from the two retirement accounts; that means you're going to have to pay tax on that amount come April 15th—that'll be, say, three hundred and fifty thousand, plus a ten percent penalty for cashing in a retirement account before you're sixty-five. Your total loss is looking like about four million dollars, plus tax on whatever profit might have been made on the other stocks."

Wolf was breathing deeply, trying to keep a grip on himself.

"Wolf, I'm sorry. I know what a blow it must be, but I had no oversight of any of this, so I had no idea it was happening."

"Of course not, Hal; it's not your fault."

"What do you want me to do?"

"Jesus, what *can* I do, Hal? The money's out of the country, and Julia's dead. Is there any way I can get it back?"

"I don't know. There's an account number for the Cayman bank on the wire-transfer receipt; I guess we can start there, but the Caymans have a very secretive banking system."

"Christ, there must be *something* we can do."

"Wolf, I know this idea won't appeal to you, but I think we ought to call the police."

"You're right; that doesn't appeal to me."

"I think you have to do it to protect yourself. It could be that some of the insurance you have might cover at least some of this; I don't know that, but I can check. The first thing the insurance company would want is the police in on this."

"Hal, I don't know how that would affect my current position in Santa Fe. I want to talk to my lawyer before we do anything."

"All right, what do you want me to do here?"

"Just take all those statements back to the

office and see if you can find out anything else
from them. Talk to my broker, too, and see if he
has anything to add. And, Hal, *fire Bridget now*.
Don't leave the house until she's gone, and be
sure and get her keys."

"Right. Call me at the office after you've talked
to your lawyer."

Wolf hung up and called Ed Eagle.

"Yes, Wolf?" Eagle said when he came on the
line.

"More complications," Wolf said, then told him
what had happened."

Eagle whistled. "That lady was some piece of
work, wasn't she?"

"She was that," Wolf agreed. "What is this going to do to my case, if it comes to trial?"

"If we try to pretend this isn't relevant, and it
comes out later, it could reinforce the D.A.'s case
with regard to your motive—that is, he could
claim you killed your wife not only because she
was sleeping with other men, but because she
was stealing from you."

"Swell."

"I do think you have to get the L.A. police in
on this without delay; call your man back and
tell him to scream bloody murder to the cops."

"All right. Ed, do you think I could get permission to go to L.A. and look into this?"

"No, I don't think that would work; I don't
think we should even ask the judge."

"All right, whatever you say."

"One good thing about this, Wolf, though it
may not be equal to four million dollars."

"What's that?"

"It'll be the final nail in Julia's coffin, where her character is concerned. It'll make a jury more sympathetic."

"You're right," Wolf said. "It isn't equal to four million dollars."

37

Ed Eagle rang Barbara Kennerly's bell at eight-thirty on New Year's Eve. She greeted him wearing a dress that he could only think of as sensational; it was tight, black, and showed an entertaining amount of cleavage and her tattoo. A diamond choker encircled her neck.

"You are beautiful," he said.

"So are you," she replied, kissing him. "I love a man in a tuxedo. Would you like a drink here before we go?"

"We should probably move on," Eagle said. "I think our hosts plan to sit down for dinner at nine."

Barbara produced a full-length mink coat, and Eagle helped her into it. "Something else left over from the marriage?" he asked.

"I told you," she said, "my husband was a generous man—and he had a brother in the fur business."

He opened the door for her.

"Just pull it shut and it'll lock itself," Barbara said.

She stepped out the door, and as she started down the stairs, Eagle found the night-latch button and switched it off. He closed the door firmly and followed Barbara down the stairs.

"Tell me about these people," Barbara said as he started the car.

"Tom and Susan Taylor," Eagle said. "He's a trial lawyer, too, but on the civil side; he sends me a lot of work. Susan's a sculptor; she does quite well at it, I think. I'm not sure who they've invited, but there'll be quite a mob. They do this every New Year's."

"Will I like them?"

"I like them; we'll see if you do."

He drove out Camino del Monte Sol and turned into the courtyard of a large adobe house. They were greeted at the door by the Taylors, and Eagle made the introductions.

"You were right," Barbara said, "there's a mob. Oh, my God, it's that movie star—what's his name?"

"That's him," Eagle said. "Would you like to meet him?"

"Absolutely."

Eagle introduced her to the man and relieved a passing waiter of two glasses of champagne.

After a sumptuous buffet dinner, there was dancing to a small band, and Eagle was relieved when the movie star asked to dance with Barbara.

"Good timing," he said to the man. "I've got to go to the john, anyway."

"Take your time," the movie star said, and Barbara laughed.

Eagle headed out of the living room, then left the house by a side door; he got into his car and drove as quickly as he dared, considering the cops were out in force on New Year's Eve. He parked at Barbara's place and let himself into her apartment. She had left a light on, and he pulled down the shades of the living room windows.

Eagle wasn't sure what he was looking for, but he immediately found something interesting; when going through the chest of drawers in her bedroom, he came across a gun, a snub-nosed Smith & Wesson .38-caliber revolver, meant for close work. He checked the cylinder; it was loaded. He wiped it and replaced the pistol exactly as he had found it.

There was a hell of a lot of jewelry in a box on her dresser; he'd expected jewelry, but not so much of it, and it was beautiful stuff. The woman should have a safety deposit box. He worked his way around the apartment, checking every drawer and cupboard, even going through the kitchen thoroughly. Apart from the pistol and the unusually large amount of jewelry, there was nothing he might not expect to find in a single woman's apartment. There was a diaphragm in the bathroom medicine cabinet, but he had known about that.

The books in the bookcase were mostly popular novels and art books, some of them obviously acquired locally, such as *Santa Fe Style*, the bible of southwestern design that seemed to be on every coffee table in the city, if not the country. One other book caught his eye, because it seemed so out of place. It was called *Beautiful Girlhood*, and the style of the cover placed it in another era. He opened it and checked the chapter titles: it seemed to be a guide to maintaining virginity. Written on the title page was the name Leah Schlemmer. It must have be-longed to her mother, he thought.

As he was about to replace the book, his fingers came into contact with something protruding from the pages. He opened the book again to a page where two pieces of an old photograph had been inserted. It had apparently been torn in half, but when he tried to put the two pieces together they did not fit. Each of the two pieces contained a snapshot of a girl, and, judging from a disembodied hand resting on the shoulder of one of them, there had once been another girl between the two. The hairdos and clothes seemed to place the photograph around the late sixties. The two girls might have been twins; he could not tell which one was Barbara. Eagle replaced the photograph in the book and returned it to the bookcase.

He stood in the middle of the living room and looked for some other item in the little apartment that might give him further information about Barbara, but there was nothing. There was a lack of pictures on the walls, as Barbara had mentioned, and the furniture seemed out of the landlord's attic.

He raised the shades in the living room, opened the door, flipped on the night latch, and closed the door behind him. He drove quickly back to the Taylors' house, let himself in through the side door, locked it, and returned to the party.

"There you are," Barbara said as he took a seat beside her on a cushion before the fireplace.

"Here I am," Eagle said. "I got into a discussion in the kitchen."

The movie star's wife had materialized and seemed to be relieved to see Eagle.

"I hear you're representing Wolf Willett," the actor said. "I know him slightly; I did a walk-on in one of Jack's early films. Are you going to get him off?"

"I don't expect to have to," Eagle said confidently. "He shouldn't have to go to trial; Wolf is an innocent man, and if the police were willing to do their work, they would have probably already found the real murderer."

"I'm glad to hear that," the man said. "I always liked Wolf." He turned to Barbara. "You look a lot like Julia," he said.

Her eyebrows went up. "Do I?"

"You could be sisters."

Eagle stepped in. "That's high praise," he said to Barbara. "Julia was a knockout, by all accounts."

"Thank you, kind sir," Barbara said to the movie star.

The music stopped and there was a drum roll.

"Ladies and gentlemen, dear friends," the host said, "Happy New Year!"

Everybody sang "Auld Lang Syne" and kissed. Eagle was a little jealous of Barbara's bussing of the other man, but what the hell, he *was* a movie star.

Barbara kissed Eagle even more avidly, then raised her glass and looked him in the eye. "To the New Year," she said, "and to new beginnings."

Eagle raised his glass. "New beginnings," he said. He had the feeling that her new beginning might be cut short, and he hoped he was wrong. She'd had a lot to drink; he'd ask her some questions later.

38

About halfway through New Year's Eve, Wolf started to hate Julia. He hadn't hated her until now, not even when he'd learned about her past life; he'd had a certain amount of sympathy for her wanting a fresh start, even if she had lied to him.

Now it was different; he had trusted her completely, and she had stolen as much from him as she possibly could. It had taken him twenty-five years to amass his small fortune, and she had stolen it from him in the blink of an eye.

He ate half the steak he'd cooked for himself and opened a second bottle of wine.

What she'd stolen was enough for a girl to start over somewhere else with a new name. Only Julia had run into a shotgun before she could bolt. Maybe there was some justice, after all.

He drank the wine and tried to figure out what this was going to mean. He couldn't direct the new picture, that was for sure. If he tried to, Centurion would beat him down on his price, make him practically pay them to let him direct. He couldn't afford that now, not unless he sold the Bel Air house; and if he did that, if word got around that he needed money, there would be blood in the water, and the sharks would tear him apart.

He laughed aloud. He was thinking too far ahead. How could he make the picture when he might be spending the next few years in a New Mexico prison? He might even be spending them on death row while the appeals sucked up every dime he had left. The best he could hope for would be parole in seven years. Then he'd be free again and penniless; nobody in the film business would ever take his phone calls again.

It might almost be worth it, if he could only know what had happened the night Julia, Jack, and Grafton were murdered; the knowledge might kill him, but at least he'd know. Mark Shea had been the only man who might have helped him find out, and now he was gone.

Wolf took the second bottle of wine into the study and switched on the television, flipping through the satellite channels. Suddenly a movie of his and Jack's was on the screen, and Julia was there, playing her hooker—a role she knew so well. He and Jack were seated at a table at a side-walk café—it had been a joke, a Hitchcockian walk-on—and they gaped at her as she walked by. Tears welled up. They had all been so happy on that shoot. He switched off the TV and swiveled his chair to face the lights of Santa Fe.

People were down there toasting the new year,

whooping it up, having a good time. Tomorrow they'd have hangovers, but they wouldn't be facing financial ruin and prison; they weren't murderers who couldn't remember their crimes; they weren't suckers with whores for wives, who'd had everything they'd earned stolen.

He remembered the pistol. It lay on the coffee table before the fireplace, ready for self-defense. Or self-destruction. He resisted the urge to pick it up. On the other hand, why shouldn't he? Why shouldn't he save everybody the trouble of dealing with him? It would be easier for Hal Berger to simply wind up his estate instead of trying to help him hold the company together while the criminal justice system dangled him from a slender thread. Dead, maybe he could face Julia and hear from her what had happened, what her plans had been, how she had lost her life.

Was there some part of his life worth saving? Something worth staying alive for? He thought about that, and he came up with Jane Deering. Jane was worth it, and so was Sara, but what would he do to them by going on living? Sara was ignorant of his troubles now, but soon she'd see his picture in the papers, being led to trial. Suppose he was acquitted? Ed Eagle had said that a lot of people Wolf knew—his friends—would still think he had done it, and God knew, he might very well have done so. How would Jane and, most of all, Sara handle that? The wounds he could hand out by staying alive might be worse than those inflicted by his death.

The idea of death had always horrified him;

he'd feared it, driven by the Baptist upbringing his mother had given him. Hell was out there waiting, just as heaven was. They had both always been real places to him. Who knew which he would find himself in? Julia was in hell, certainly; he might join her there. She might have the last laugh, after all. He hated the idea of Julia laughing.

The phone rang. He didn't pick it up. No last-minute reprieves for him; that was for the movies. It rang three times more, then the answering machine picked up.

"This is Wolf Willett. Please leave your name and number, and I'll get back to you." Beep.

"Wolf? I know you're there; pick up the phone."

It was Jane; he picked up the phone. "You're right, I'm here."

She was at a party. He knew that; she had told him she was going. He could hear people singing in the background.

"I knew you'd be there alone, and I wanted you to know something," she said. "I love you, Wolf, and you and I are going to face whatever happens together, do you hear me?"

He couldn't speak, so he nodded.

"Wolf, goddammit, say something!"

"Yes," he managed to say. "I love you, too. I'm awfully glad you called."

"Happy New Year!" she said. "It's going to be; trust me."

"I trust you. Happy New Year to you. I love you, Jane, I really do."

"Sara loves you, too. She told me so. She's never said that about anybody else but me."

"I love Sara, too; tell her for me."

"I'll tell her. Now, I want you to put down your drink and go straight to bed. I'll call you again in the morning and make your hangover worse."

"I'd love that," he said, putting down his wineglass. "I'll do it, if you promise to make my hangover worse."

"I promise."

"I love you, Jane."

"I love you, Wolf. Goodnight."

"Goodnight."

Wolf hung up the phone and went straight to bed.

39

On the morning of January second, Wolf left the house and went shopping. He drove downtown and parked near the plaza, then combed through the shops, looking for bargains on sale. He couldn't afford it anymore, but he bought a new leather coat and a good piece of pottery, and he was looking at a picture in a gallery when a young woman ran into the gallery and grabbed him by the elbow.

"Oh, Mr. Willett, I'm so glad I found you," she said. "I'm from Ed Eagle's office."

"What's wrong?" Wolf asked.

"You have to call Mr. Eagle right away, that's all," she panted.

"Why did he send you looking for me? Why didn't he just leave a message on my answering machine?"

"He got your maid on the phone, and she said you'd gone shopping, so he sent me out looking for you. Please call him right away."

Wolf asked the gallery manager if he could use the phone, then called Eagle.

"I'm glad we got hold of you, Wolf," Eagle said.

"What's up, Ed?"

"You've been indicted. The police have already been to your house with a new warrant looking for you, and it's important for appearances that you surrender before they can arrest you."

"I'm on the east side of the plaza now, at a gallery. What do you want me to do?"

"Stay where you are. I'll pick you up in five minutes. And don't go out onto the streets; I don't want you picked up."

"All right. Ed, does this mean I'll have to go back . . ." he glanced at the woman behind the desk, who was taking an interest in his conversation, "back where I was before?"

"I hope not. We'll talk about it when I see you."

"Fine, I'll wait here." He hung up the phone and tried to appear calm. He went back and looked at the picture again. "Tell me something about the artist," he said to the gallery manager.

Eagle drove quickly through the downtown sale traffic. "What we do now is, we turn you in. I've already phoned the judge and asked for an immediate hearing on continuance of bail."

"Are we likely to get it?"

"It depends on what the D.A. might have in the way of new evidence. He'll have to tell the court, in general terms, what he's got. He'll certainly ask that bail be revoked, and he might get it. At the very least, we'll have to come up with a higher bond. I know your financial circumstances have changed drastically, so I think we'll have to pledge your house. How much is it worth?"

"It cost a million and a half to build." Wolf tried to calm his racing heart.

"That should do it." Eagle found a parking place at the detention center, and as they got out of the car, Wolf looked up and saw Carreras across the parking lot running toward them.

"Have a look at that, Ed," he said.

"Uh-oh, let's hurry," Eagle said. They hurried into the building. Eagle led Wolf to the high desk and said to the sergeant in charge, "Mr. Wolf Willett is here to surrender himself on a charge."

Carreras burst through the front door, panting.

"Good morning, Captain Carreras," Eagle said, beaming at him.

"You're under arrest, Willett," Carreras said, producing a warrant.

"Too late," Eagle said. "He's already turned himself in, and the judge is waiting for us now for a bail hearing."

Carreras glowered at Eagle, then turned on his heel and stalked off toward his office.

They sat in the courtroom until the morning's arraignments had been completed, then the judge looked at Eagle and said, "Any further business?"

Eagle rose. "Matter of continuance of bail for

Mr. Wolf Willett, following an indictment," he said.

"Bring your client forward, Mr. Eagle," the judge said. "Mr. Martinez," he said to the district attorney, "may I hear from you on this subject?"

"Your Honor, the state requests that bail be revoked and that the defendant now be incarcerated until his trial. We have evidence placing him at the scene of the crime on the day of the murders; we have evidence of a further motive. The state believes that Willett is a dangerous man and should be jailed immediately."

The judge turned to where Eagle and his client now sat at the defense table. "Mr. Eagle?"

Eagle rose and took a sheaf of papers from his briefcase. "Your Honor, I would like to present to the court nine letters from prominent figures in the film industry, attesting to the good character of Mr. Willett." He handed the letters to the judge, who began leafing through them.

Wolf had written to fifteen people; he wondered who were the six who had not come through.

Eagle continued. "I would like to point out that Mr. Willett has kept the terms set for his current bail, that he has not left the jurisdiction, and that immediately on being informed of his indictment, he voluntarily surrendered himself to the authorities. Mr. Willett has no intention of fleeing; he looks forward to a trial so that he can clear his name. I would also like to point out that the state's case is no stronger than it was at Mr. Willett's last hearing. Mr. Willett has never denied being in his own home, and I believe that

Mr. Martinez's reference to a new motive is based on information that will, in fact, strengthen Mr. Willett's defense. We are ready for trial, and request an early court date." He sat down.

The judge continued reading the letters, then spoke again. "I am impressed with Mr. Willett's references, and I am pleased that he has kept the terms of his bail and that he surrendered voluntarily. I will continue bail; however, in light of the seriousness of the charges, I will increase the amount to one million dollars. Can your client raise that sum, Mr. Eagle?"

"He can, Your Honor; he has already posted one hundred thousand dollars cash, and he will offer his house in Santa Fe, which is unencumbered and is worth well in excess of one million dollars."

"That will be acceptable to the court. I will release Mr. Willett in your custody, pending receipt of the deed to the house by close of business today." He flipped through a large desk diary. "I have had a postponement of a case, leaving a gap in the calendar, so I will set trial for January tenth. Is that acceptable to the state?" He looked at the district attorney.

Martinez rose. "It is, Your Honor."

"There being no further business before me, this court is adjourned."

"Thank you, Ed," Wolf said when they had left the courtroom.

"Not at all. Where is the deed to your house?"

"In the safe in my study."

"I'll drive you back to your car, and you can have it delivered to the court later today."

"Fine."

When they were back in his car, Eagle raised another point. "Wolf, I want your authorization to hire two investigators. I know a good man who can look into Grafton's activities in Los Angeles—Julia's sister gave me the name of a man Grafton knew there who he might have contacted."

"Fine, go ahead. What's the other investigator for?"

"I want to send a man to the Cayman Islands and see what he can find out from the bank there."

"Aren't those banks very secretive?"

"Yes, but if we can present evidence of a crime in connection with funds they are harboring, they can choose to give us information. I know a guy in Washington who until recently was an investigator for the I.R.S., and who has a lot of experience looking into Cayman accounts. He's a C.P.A. in Virginia now. He'll be expensive, but he's damn good."

"All right, go ahead."

"What are your resources following Julia's theft of your investments?"

"I'm pledging the Santa Fe house, of course, but there's the Bel Air house, and my company has got some cash; I can draw on that, if I have to."

"Good. That should see us through."

"When did Julia's sister become so cooperative?"

"I had a chat with her last week, and she agreed to testify for us; then, when she had had a lot to drink on New Year's Eve, I went over the Grafton business with her again. I don't think she had really been holding back, but she came through with the name of a man in L.A. that Grafton had mentioned several times in the past. We may have to spread some money around to get information."

"How much money?"

"Will you authorize twenty-five thousand dollars?"

"Yes, go ahead. I'll have my office in L.A. wire-transfer, say, fifty thousand to you today."

"That should cover everything." Eagle stopped the car next to the Porsche, and Wolf got out.

"Ed, keep me posted on these investigations, will you?"

"Sure, I will; I know how anxious you are."

No, Wolf thought as he watched Eagle drive away, *you don't have* any idea *how anxious*.

40

Cupie Dalton sat in the tiny second bedroom of his small apartment in Santa Monica, which served as his office, and worried. He had earned his nickname when he had been on the force, because he was plump, pink, and resembled the prize dolls at carnival shooting galleries, and he was worried because he had four dollars in the bank and his pension check didn't come for another week. "Please, God," he said aloud. "I need some work." The phone rang.

"Dalton Investigations."

"Cupie, it's Ed Eagle. How are you?"

He tried not to sound excited. "Okay, Ed. You?"

"Not bad. I need a guy looked into."

"Okay. Who is he?"

"His name is—or rather, was—James Grafton, known as Jimmy, recently known in L.A. as Dan O'Hara. He caught the wrong end of a shotgun around Thanksgiving in Santa Fe."

Cupie wrote down the names. "Never heard of him."

"Armed robber, con man, escapee, murderer. He bounced out of a New York prison earlier this year and ended up in L.A.; apparently sold a screenplay to Warner."

"That's cute. You got anything else?"

"A name: Benny Calabrese, somebody he knew."

"I know him; a sleaze."

"What did you expect?"

"So what do you need on this guy?"

"I want to know every move he made in L.A., and anything else you think might interest me."

"You know my rates."

"Forget rates," Eagle said. "I don't have time for you to chalk up hours and an expense account. This is five grand straight, and anything you have to fork over comes out of that. I'll have a messenger there in an hour with cash."

"That would be nice."

"It's not a gift, Cupie; it's for results. I want to hear from you tomorrow, and I want to hear a lot."

"You got it, Ed."

"I better have it, or this is the last you'll see any of my money. Call me."

Cupie hung up and raised his eyes to the ceiling. "Thank you, God," he said.

When the messenger had gone, Cupie put four thousand dollars into the cheap safe that was bolted to the floor in the bedroom closet, then folded ten hundreds into his pocket. Feeling lighter than air, he strolled down to the parking lot and got into the elderly Continental that he loved so much. He took the freeway to Sunset and drove slowly through Beverly Hills to the Strip. Here he slowed even further and began looking. It took less than fifteen minutes to find Benny Calabrese's red Camaro with all the stripes, parked in front of a fast-food joint near the corner of La Cienega. Cupie invented a parking place and walked into the restaurant.

Benny was heavily into a double cheeseburger, alone in a back booth; he had just taken a huge bite when he saw Cupie. He stopped chewing.

Cupie sat down and put a hundred-dollar bill on the table between them. "Now, listen to me, Benny," he said. "You and I ain't ever liked each other too much, so this is going to be a brief meeting. I'm going to ask you some questions, and you have two choices: first, you can take the hundred and talk to me good, or second, I can beat the shit out of you."

Benny started chewing again. Cupie had his attention.

"Now, by the time you finish chewing, you better be talking to me about a guy named Jimmy Grafton." He held up a hand. "Don't worry, this won't bounce back on you; Grafton ate somebody's shotgun a while back. Now, what's it going to be?"

Benny swallowed hard. "Jimmy's dead? You ain't shitting me?"

"Grafton is in somebody's landfill by now. Trust me, Benny."

Benny's hand snaked out and snagged the

hundred. "Me and Grafton did some time to-gether—Riker's Island, a few years back. We kept in touch, even after I came out here."

Cupie made a beckoning motion. "Don't pause for breath, Benny; keep it coming."

"Jimmy was doing life in New York, and he busted out, turned up here calling himself—"

"Dan O'Hara," Cupie said, completing the sentence for him. "I know just enough to know if you're holding out on me."

"We did some drinking together. Jimmy said he was writing a movie about busting out of jail. He even said he sold it to a studio—that's what he said, anyway; who knows?"

"He must have had some other scam going. What was it?"

"He never told me about nothing else. He had money; he didn't seem to be looking for anything to do. He was living in one of them suite hotels in West Hollywood, off Melrose—a hundred and twenty a day, easy—but Jimmy always had style."

"Was anybody with him? A woman, maybe?"

"He said he was all fixed up in that department, no problem, you know? But I never saw him with a woman. We'd meet at some bar in the late afternoons and have a few, then he'd go off on his own at night."

"When was the last time you saw him?"

Benny screwed up his face and thought hard. "End of October. Jimmy had some Lakers tickets, and we went—the only time we spent an evening together."

"You never saw him again?"

"Nope. That was the last time."

"Come on, Benny, there's something you're not telling me. Don't make me ask you the hard way."

Benny looked around the restaurant as if he thought somebody might be watching him. "This goes no further?"

Cupie made a zipping motion across his lips.

"Jimmy wanted some paper."

Cupie sat up. "Counterfeit money?"

"No, no: paper. Papers, like—you know, social security card, driver's license, passport."

"False documents."

"No, not false; he was very up-front about that. Jimmy wanted the real thing, stuff that would work, you know?"

"And where would he get that?"

"Well, I had to ask around, you know? It wasn't easy."

"So you worked hard, Benny. Where'd you send him?"

Benny looked around again. "There's this guy in Venice."

"What guy, Benny? I'm getting short-tempered."

"Around town he's called Doc Don."

"What kind of name is that?"

"Document Don. Last name's Dunn."

"Document Don Dunn."

"He's a photographer—you know, the wife and kiddies? Passport pictures? Right along the beach-front. I don't know the exact address, but I didn't hear from Jimmy, so he must have found it."

"So how does Doc Don produce the real thing?"

"He's got some system of getting hold of birth certificates and other I.D., so he can get real stuff instead of forging it; it's like you buy a new identity, you know? The real thing."

"Anything else, Benny? Search your heart."

Benny thought. "Nope, that's it. I didn't see Jimmy after the end of October."

"I found you this time, Benny; I can find you again."

"Honest, Cupie."

"Honest," Cupie repeated, then he burst out laughing. Honest? From Benny Calabrese?

41

Russell Norris stepped out of the airplane in George Town and into the hot Cayman sun. Sweat immediately broke out on his forehead and under his arms, and he was glad he'd worn one of his old Brooks Brothers I.R.S. suits instead of something better. He'd be soaked by the time he got out of here. He walked straight through the airport and found a cab. It was a measure of his confidence that he carried no overnight bag, only a briefcase.

Norris had labored in the Internal Revenue Service vineyard for twenty-five years, had retired with a pension that covered his mortgage payments and basic expenses, and had promptly begun offering himself as a hired gun against the auditors who had been his colleagues for so many years. Mostly he represented taxpayers who had trod too near the line and were being audited; he negotiated settlements that only a former auditor could manage, and his clients loved him for it.

For the last years of his career, Russell Norris

had headed a service task force that had put the fear of God into Cayman banks. He had begun by simply auditing the hell out of anybody who had a Cayman account and prosecuting those who had lied about such an account; this made many people reluctant to deal with the banks, and finally, as a result, in 1986 he had been able to negotiate a new treaty with the Cayman Islands government which significantly altered the terms under which the banks could surrender information to the American authorities, principally the I.R.S.

Beyond that he had made himself personally felt in the Cayman banking community in such a way as to enable him to successfully elicit information not covered by the treaty—on a strictly confidential basis, of course. He had done this by force of personality and by implied threats—in fact, not always implied.

As he shuffled through the copies of bank statements and other documents faxed to him by Ed Eagle, he recalled the past hoops through which he had put this particular organization. They would stand him in good stead today.

The taxi stopped in front of the bank, and Norris got out into the burning sun once more. Tourists were paying thousands to experience this climate in January, but Norris was warm of nature and could not wait to get back to the chilly joys of a Virginia winter. He walked into the bank, marched straight through the customer area until he came to a mahogany railing broken by an electrically operated gate. He cast an eye around the small sea of desks until he found a bank officer who knew him, then stood quietly, burning his gaze into the fellow's face until he caught the man's eye. The officer blanched, frowned, and looked around for assistance. Everybody else had busied himself with work. Forced to make a decision, the man pressed the release button, and Norris proceeded through the gate.

He kept straight on toward a paneled wall, opened a door, walked past a secretary who had not been quick enough to halt his progress, and stepped into a large, beautifully appointed office.

The president of the bank, a Cuban named Rouré, nearly bit through the Upmann cigar clenched between his teeth. Norris waited a moment for the full effect to set in. This was why he had worn the old suit, instead of one of the more recent ones from the Polo Shop; he wanted the memory in the man's mind to match what he now saw—a hard-nosed, no-nonsense civil service warrior. Norris walked over to the desk, sat down in a large chair, and pulled out the stenographer's shelf from the desk.

"Now," he said, opening his briefcase, "let's begin."

"I thought you had retired," the astonished Cuban managed to say.

"You don't believe everything you hear, do you, Mr. Rouré?" He took a sheet of paper from the man's desktop and wrote down a number, then handed it to him. "I want to see the records on this account," he said. "All the records."

The banker did not look at the number. "You must be mad," he said. "You know very well I would be breaking Cayman law if I disclosed any information about one of our accounts."

"I am mad," Norris replied calmly. "Imagine how much trouble a madman in my position could cause you."

Rouré stared at Norris for a moment, and Norris could almost see the wheels turning. He picked up the sheet of paper. "I'll be back in a few minutes," he said.

Norris held up a hand. "No," he said. "Sit down."

The banker sat down.

"I don't want you to go and get the records; I want you to pick up the telephone and order the records brought in here. We'll see them together." Norris smiled.

"I am of a mind to telephone the American ambassador right now," Rouré said.

"You may do that if you wish," Norris replied, "and if you do, the world will fall on your bank from a great height. I know a federal prosecutor in Miami who is working on the Noriega case, and he would just love to know a few things I could tell him." Norris tried not to hold his breath. This was a bluff, and if the banker called it, he wouldn't have the cards. He did have one more card, though. "There's also the business you were doing with BCCI." The huge international bank had collapsed recently, and it was likely that Rouré had done business with them.

He knew he had won when beads of perspiration

appeared on Rouré's forehead. He filed the Noriega and BCCI connections away in his memory for possible future use.

"Why do you want this information?" Rouré asked, obviously buying time while he made a decision.

"Señor Rouré," Norris said placatingly, "let us say that these records are not yet the subject of an official investigation; I emphasize, *not yet*."

Rouré puffed rapidly on his cigar. A cloud of smoke rose above him and drifted toward an air-conditioning intake. "Your sight of this file will not go beyond this office?"

"I didn't say that. You should know that the funds in this account are stolen. Not simply illegally earned, not borrowed, not laundered to prevent payment of taxes. These funds were stolen outright. I should think that would make some difference to you."

"Of course, this bank would never knowingly receive stolen funds," Rouré said, spreading his hands. "Why didn't you say so to begin with?" He picked up a telephone and tapped in a number. "Bring me the file on account number . . ." He read the number from the sheet of paper, then put the phone down and smiled at Norris.

"Of course, I am willing to cooperate with you, if you can substantiate what you have just said to me."

Norris took a thick sheaf of papers from his briefcase, walked around the desk, and placed them before the banker. "These are brokerage account records substantiating the ownership of these funds," he said, turning pages and pointing at figures. "As you follow through the paper trail, you can see how the woman of the house initiated purchases of shares for her husband's account. Finally, you see how she ordered all three accounts to be liquidated and the funds transferred to her checking account. Then you see, here, how she wire-transferred the funds to the account in this office."

"Yes, yes, I see," Rouré said. "A substantial amount of money."

"A very large theft," Norris said. He knew Rouré was relieved to find that the amount in question was only three million six instead of a hundred times that, and that the account holder was a California housewife instead of a Colombian drug lord; he would have had second thoughts about revealing confidential information about a client who might put a bomb in his car.

A young man entered the office and placed a thin file folder before Rouré, then said something in Spanish.

"Wait a minute," Norris said. "Let's stick to English, here."

"My colleague has told me that we have just received coded instructions to wire-transfer nearly the entire balance in the account to a bank in Mexico City," Rouré said.

"Just now?"

"Only a few minutes ago. He was on his way to my office for approval."

"I don't think we need detain your colleague further," Norris said. When the young man had left, he walked around Rouré's desk, rummaged in the man's humidor, chose a Romeo y Juliet, and sat down.

Rouré leaned across the desk and lit the cigar with a gold lighter.

"Señor Rouré," Russell Norris said, puffing on the cigar, "I believe I may have a solution to your problem."

"Problem?" Rouré asked, raising his eyebrows. "I have a problem?"

"Of course you do," Norris replied, smiling. "For the past three minutes or so, you have been dealing in stolen funds." He raised a hand to stave off the banker's protestations. "Ever since I told you they were stolen. But if you follow my instructions exactly, you can forget about it. The matter will never arise again."

Senor Rouré looked interested. Norris began telling the banker how he could save himself an awful lot of trouble.

42

Cupie Dalton parked as close as he could to Venice Beach, then walked the rest of the way. It was a warm day for January in L.A., and the sun had brought the Venetian insects out of their holes. The muscle freaks were lifting away in the weights area, pausing only to rub oil onto their bodies and flex for the gawking passersby; small-time pushers were selling dope by the joint; T-shirts and cheap sunglasses were the sale items of the day; and every third creep seemed to be on roller skates.

Cupie found the Don Dunn Studio of Artistic Photography with no trouble; the owner had opened his front doors wide to admit the warm air and hot prospects. Dunn himself was bent over a contact sheet with a large loupe pressed to the pictures.

"Hang on a sec," he said, squinting through the magnifier. He made a mark with a grease pencil, then stood up. "Good day to you," he said.

Cupie thought him surprisingly formal for a

skinny man with shoulder-length hair and a
scraggly beard, dressed in a tie-dyed T-shirt and
greasy dirty jeans. He was like a wraith from the
sixties.

"And good day to you," Cupie said. He'd hated
hippies in the sixties, and he hated them now,
although this one, at least, seemed to be working
for a living. It was for this reason that Cupie
didn't hit him right away. "Doc Don, I presume."

Dunn's eyes narrowed. "We have a mutual
friend, do we?"

"Yeah, but I think he'd rather I didn't use his
name. I'm not here to get my picture took, you
see; I'm here to find out about somebody whose
picture you took."

"I'm in the photography business, pal," Dunn
said, "not the information business."

"That ain't the only business you're in," Cupie
said, smiling. "You're a purveyor of funny paper,
pal, and you and me have some talking to do."

"Take a hike, mister. I got a business to run."

Cupie produced the photograph that Ed Eagle
had sent with the money. "This guy came in here
at the end of October and placed an order, maybe
even had his picture taken."

Dunn barely glanced at the photograph. "Never
saw him before," he said. "Good day to you."

Cupie glanced at the swinging doors behind
the photographer; the angle was good. "And good
day to you," he said, shooting a swift right to the
man's solar plexus.

Document Don Dunn left his feet and flew

backward through the doors, leaving them flapping.

Cupie followed him at a more leisurely pace. He produced a hundred-dollar bill and waved it before Dunn's eyes, which were tightly closed as he sucked in air. "Now, just so you won't think I'm not polite, I'm going to offer you this for your assistance."

"Go fuck yourself," Dunn said, struggling to his feet. He pushed off the wall behind him and launched a backhanded chop toward Cupie's throat.

Cupie had not been expecting this, and he barely got a forearm up in time to block it. Having done so, he got hold of Dunn's skinny wrist and twisted his arm up high behind his back. Dunn was a lithe fellow, and the hand went right up to the nape of his neck before he complained.

"Let me explain something to you," Cupie said, pushing the man hard against a wall and pinning him there. "You're in a business like this, every once in a while somebody like me is going to wander in here and want to know something about somebody. The way to handle that is to charge for it and send the guy on his way happy; that way you don't get an arm broken." He jerked up on Dunn's wrist for emphasis. "If you get my meaning."

"I get it, I get it," Dunn said.

"I think you do," Cupie said, "but before I let go of you, I want to be real sure. Y'see, I could just beat the shit out of you, then destroy this place looking for what I want, and that's what I'm going to do if you give me the least bit of trouble when I let go of you. Do we understand each other?"

"We understand each other," Dunn gasped.

Cupie let go of the man's arm and stepped back, just in case Dunn didn't really understand.

Dunn grasped his shoulder with a free hand and whimpered.

Cupie pulled his jacket back to reveal the automatic pistol on his belt. "And just in case you think you can go for a shooter or something, I want you to forget about that, too."

"Okay, okay," Dunn said. "What do you want?"

Cupie held up the photograph again. "He was in here around late October."

"Yeah, I remember."

"What's his name?"

"People don't tell me their names," Dunn said. Cupie was drawing back to swing again when Dunn started talking faster. "I mean, not their real names."

"Of course not," Cupie said. "What was the name he wanted on whatever he ordered from you?"

"Look, mister, that was three, four months ago, you know?"

"Listen to me, Doc. This guy came in here for genuine paper; that means you had to produce a real birth certificate. What was the name on the certificate?"

"I'll have to look it up."

"Look it up where?"

Dunn nodded toward a big filing cabinet. "There."

"All right," Cupie said. "You walk over there and open the file drawer, and when your hand comes out of it, there better not be anything but a file in it, you hear me?"

"Listen, pal, all I want to do is give you what you want and get you out of here."

"Fine," Cupie said. "Give me what I want."

Dunn went to the filing cabinet, produced a clump of keys from his pocket, and opened the top drawer. He rummaged through the files and came up with a manila folder. "I remember something now; this guy wanted a passport in his own name, the name he came in here with: Daniel O'Hara. I called a guy I know in Boston, where there's lots of Irish, and he got it for me."

Cupie opened the file and looked at the top sheet of paper. There was a Polaroid passport photo clipped to a photocopy of an American passport, open to the page containing O'Hara's personal information. There was a second sheet of paper in the file as well. "Who's the lady?" he asked, pointing at a photocopy of another passport.

"She was with O'Hara," Dunn replied. "A real looker, too. Dynamite."

"Frances B. Kennerly," Cupie read from the document. "Was that a special-order name, too?"

"Yeah," Dunn replied, "but I couldn't come up with the first name she wanted, so I matched the last name she asked for, and she was happy with

Frances B., because the middle initial was the same as her first name."

"What was the first name she wanted?" Cupie asked.

"Uh . . ." Dunn thought hard. "Betty—no . . . ah, Barbara. That was it, Barbara Kennerly."

Cupie looked at the addresses; they were the same. "Stone Canyon, in Bel Air," he read aloud. "Pretty fancy address."

"Yeah. 'Course, it might not be a real address," Dunn said, "but they were a pretty slick couple."

"What else did you get for these people besides passports?"

"The works: driver's licenses, social security cards, voter registration cards."

"What address did you send them to?"

"They picked up the paper here."

"You say these people were slick; tell me some more about them."

Dunn shrugged. "Not much to tell."

Cupie frowned. "You want to help me out, don't you, Doc?"

"Oh, sure, sure. Let me see, well, they were slick, like I said; the guy was wearing a blue blazer that looked custom-made. The girl was wearing a low-cut black dress with a short skirt. Like I said, she was a real looker."

"Any identifying marks?" Cupie said. It was a cop's question, and Dunn looked at him sharply.

"Just one," the photographer said. "The girl had a flower tattooed on one of her tits. I remember that; I couldn't take my eyes off it."

"Gimme something else," Cupie said. He thought the photographer was dry, but it was worth trying.

"That's all I can remember about them," Dunn said. "I swear it."

Cupie tucked the file folder under his arm and fished out the hundred-dollar bill. "Here you go, Doc," he said. "You earned it."

On the way home, Cupie considered trying to milk a little more money out of Ed Eagle, but he put the thought out of his mind. Eagle wasn't his best customer, but he'd paid well and up-front. He stopped at a Federal Express office and over-nighted the folder to Eagle.

43

Ed Eagle opened the Fed Ex package and removed the file. The face of James Grafton was becoming familiar now, and he read quickly through Cupie's report, written in a surprisingly clear hand.

Eagle came to some conclusions: Grafton hadn't planned to run—not unless he was forced to. The passport was for just in case; the driver's license and social security card were for respectability and safety. It wouldn't have done for Grafton to get stopped by the police for, say, running a stop sign, and not have a license; that way led back to a New York state prison. Something else: Grafton had ordered the documents in the name of Daniel O'Hara, the name he had been using in Los Angeles, so they were to support that identity instead of supplying a new one to run with.

Eagle looked at the second photocopy—the one of the woman's passport—and his heart stopped. He looked at the photograph more closely, got a magnifying glass from a desk drawer, and examined it minutely. It looked for all the world like Barbara with a blond wig, but Barbara had been in prison in late October, when Grafton and the woman had turned up at the photographer's. It had to be Julia, but what about the name? Julia had specified the name and had nearly gotten what she asked for, and it was Barbara's new name. His impulse was to go over to Santacafé, take Barbara by the throat, and shake some answers out of her. But did she have any answers? The phone rang.

"A Mr. Russell Norris for you, Mr. Eagle."

"Hello, Russell?"

"Hi, Ed. I just got back. I would have called you from the airport, but there was a big rush to make the plane, and it was late when I got home."

"That's all right. What did you find out?"

"The Cayman account was in the name of a Frances B. Kennerly."

"That fits with some other information I have. How much was in the account?"

"Three million six and change, but if I'd been a few minutes later, there would have been nothing."

"What do you mean?"

"I mean that while I was sitting in the bank president's office, a coded instruction came in to wire-transfer virtually the whole amount to a bank in Mexico City."

"*What*?"

"Why does that surprise you, Ed? When people steal money they like to cover their tracks."

"But Frances B. Kennerly, as she wanted to be known, is *dead*."

"Then she gave somebody her account code—a friend, maybe."

"A friend or a relative," Eagle muttered.

"What was that?"

"Nothing. How was the account opened?"

"Through a proxy corporation set up in the Caymans. I didn't dig into that, since you only hired me for the day, and anyway, it would have been extremely complicated and expensive. I don't have quite the same influence with Cayman lawyers as with bankers."

"What can we do about this account, Russell?"

"Everything we can do is already done," Norris replied. He explained in detail his conversation with the banker.

Eagle slapped his desk in glee. "That's wonderful, Russell, wonderful!"

"Well, don't count on it until it actually happens; there's still a lot that can go wrong. I wouldn't tell your client about it yet, either—not until we know for sure."

"Russell, I can't thank you enough, but if this comes off, I'll double your fee."

"That would be much appreciated, Ed."

"Were you able to find out anything more about the account holder?"

"No. If she had opened the account personally, they might have had a photograph, but as I said, it was done through a proxy corporation. All the bank had was a signature sample; I'll fax that along to you, along with the coded wire-transfer order."

"I'd appreciate that," Eagle said. "It might help at some later date." He thanked Norris again, then hung up.

Eagle waited by the fax machine until the signature sample and the wire-transfer order came in, glanced at them, then put them into his briefcase and left the office. "I'll be back in an hour," he said. He drove up to Wilderness Gate.

Wolf opened the door before he could ring the bell. "Hello, Ed. You look as though you might have some news."

"Not as much news as I'd like, Wolf, but let's sit down for a minute."

Wolf indicated a chair at the kitchen table. "Would you like some coffee?"

"No, thanks. I want to show you what I've got here."

"I'm anxious to see it."

Eagle spread out the two photocopies on the kitchen table. "Is that a photograph of Julia?" he asked.

Wolf looked closely at the picture. "The photocopy's a little fuzzy, but yes, that seems to be Julia. Who is Frances Kennerly?"

"I'll get to that in a moment," Eagle said. "First let me take you through what we know so far."

"I'm all ears."

"When Grafton broke out of jail, he headed straight for L.A., and he looked up an old prison pal there. The pal sent him to a man who can arrange for passports and other I.D. Around the end of October, Grafton and a woman turned up at this guy's place of business, had their pictures taken, and paid for some documents. Grafton picked them up a couple of weeks later. That would have been a week or so before Thanksgiving."

Wolf interrupted. "Meantime, Julia was rifling my brokerage account and wiring the money to the Cayman account."

"Exactly, and the Cayman account was in the name of Frances B. Kennerly."

"Kennerly is the name that Julia's sister is using, isn't it?"

"That's right; Barbara Kennerly. Which is the name Julia wanted on the passport, but Frances B. was as close as the guy could come."

"So she's in on this?"

"I don't see how she could be; she was in prison at the time. I met with her there, remember?"

"That lets her out, I guess."

"It would seem so, except for one thing."

"What's that?"

"Somebody, using the account code that Julia had established, sent an order to the Cayman bank to transfer the funds to an account in Mexico City. And that happened yesterday." He handed Wolf the signature sample and the wire-transfer order.

Wolf seemed too stunned to look at them. "*Yesterday?* That means that somebody else is in this, doesn't it?"

"I think it does, probably whoever killed Mark Shea. First of all, I'm surprised that Julia would give anybody else the code; from what I know about her, it just doesn't sound like her. But she obviously gave the code to somebody, so it had to be somebody she trusted implicitly. That person waited until he—or she—felt the heat was off, then made a run on the money."

"Well, Barbara Kennerly isn't in prison anymore, is she?"

"No, she's a free woman."

"Then she's got to be the one."

"Maybe, but I've got some problems with that."

"What problems?"

"Wolf, why would she come to Santa Fe and start a new life? She knew Julia was dead; she'd read about it in the papers while she was in prison. So if she had the bank account code and knew the money was there, why didn't she just immediately transfer the money to a bank of her choice, take her new money and her new name, and disappear?"

Wolf thought about this. "It must mean that there's something in Santa Fe she wants, something she has to have before she takes a hike."

"But what? If she's really in this, then all that's in Santa Fe for her is the possibility of getting arrested and sent back to prison. Why would she come out here and ask your lawyer, of all people, for a job? Why would she agree to take the witness stand in your defense? It just doesn't make any sense."

"I agree," Wolf said. "It doesn't."

"Also, her every action since arriving here has

been that of a person who was beginning a new life. She found a job and an apartment, she's buying things for the place, and she bought a new car."

"Where did she get the money for a new car? She's just out of prison."

"Perfectly reasonable explanation for that: When she was married, her husband bought her a lot of jewelry—I know that's true, because I've seen it; it's good stuff. She sold some of it to establish herself here."

Wolf shook his head. "None of this makes any sense."

"No, it doesn't; but I've got a dinner date with your sister-in-law tonight, and I'm going to put her through the wringer. If she knows something about this, I'm going to find it out."

Wolf turned his attention to the two documents before him. Then he stopped talking and stared at the wire-transfer order.

"What is it, Wolf?" Eagle asked.

"This order to transfer the money was faxed to the bank," he said.

"So?"

"Look at the logo at the top of the page."

Eagle looked at the page. "What do you mean, 'logo'?"

"You can set up a fax machine so that it has something to identify the sender at the top of the page."

"Oh, sure. There's no name, just a phone number." His mouth dropped open. "Area code 505; it was sent from New Mexico."

Wolf nodded. "From Santa Fe," he said. "That's *my* fax number. This wire-transfer order was sent from *this house*."

The two men sat and stared at each other.

"When?" Eagle said, grabbing the paper. "Here it is, stamped at the top: twelve-twenty today."

"I went out to lunch," Wolf said. "I left at just about that time."

"So somebody saw you leave and came in here and used your fax machine?"

"Let's double-check," Wolf said, rising and heading for the study. He pressed a key, and the fax machine printed out a journal. "Here it is: a fax was sent at twelve-twenty."

"Was the house locked?"

Wolf shook his head. "I never lock the place unless I'm going to be gone overnight."

"Who knows about that?"

"Just about anybody who knows me well, I guess."

"Would your cleaning lady have been here?"

"No, she leaves at noon sharp every day. She has another job in the afternoons."

"All right," Eagle said, "that means there's somebody in Santa Fe who knew about the theft of the money before we did. Somebody Julia would have trusted."

Wolf nodded. "And maybe the same person who shot Mark Shea?"

"And who spent the night before at his house. So it was somebody who knew both Julia and Mark well. Did Julia have any close friends in Santa Fe?"

"Monica Collins," Wolf said.

"Yes, yes, yes," Eagle replied, his eyes widening.

"She was the only person Julia was really close to here, and Monica knew Mark well, too. She was his patient."

"Could Mark have been screwing her?"

"I wouldn't be surprised," Wolf replied. "Mark had a reputation for sleeping with the odd patient."

"I think I'll drop a word to the D.A. about Monica. It would be interesting to know if she could substantiate her whereabouts the day Mark was shot."

"It certainly would be interesting to know that," Wolf agreed. "It would be interesting to know her whereabouts on the night of the murders here, too."

"Wolf, did Monica come to your house a lot?"

"Yes, she was here often. She and Julia would lunch when we were here, and if we had people in for drinks, Monica would always come."

"So she could have been here the night of the murders?"

"Yes. Yes, she could well have been."

"Would she have known your house would be unlocked when you were in town?"

"She was in and out of here with Julia all the time. Yes."

"Can I use your phone?" Eagle asked.

"Sure."

Eagle dialed Santacafé and was connected to the owner. "Jim, it's Ed Eagle. Can I ask you something in confidence? I wouldn't like anyone to know I asked."

"Sure, Ed."

"Did Barbara Kennerly work lunch today?"

"No, I sent her home. She obviously hadn't been feeling well all morning, and by lunchtime she looked like death. Female problems, I think."

"What time did you send her home?"

"A little before twelve, I guess." He laughed. "Ed, you and your romantic problems are something."

"Thanks, Jim. Remember, don't tell her I asked." He hung up and turned to Wolf. "She wasn't at work."

"So she could have sent the fax?"

"I'm damned well going to find out," Eagle said.

44

Eagle had most of dinner prepared before Barbara arrived. "What can I get you to drink?" he asked as he took her coat.

"I think I could stand a stiff vodka," she said. "I'm really tired; maybe it will help. Do you have any Stolichnaya?"

"Sure," Eagle replied, taking a bottle from the refrigerator. "You're not feeling well?"

"Better than yesterday."

"What was wrong yesterday?"

"You really want to know?"

"Sure." He handed her a stiff shot of the vodka.

"I thought I was bleeding to death," she said. "Once in a while I have a really rough period, and yesterday was the worst I can remember."

Eagle poured himself a single-malt Scotch; it might help with what he had to do, he thought. "I'm glad you're feeling better," he said, handing her the drink.

Barbara took a long pull of the vodka. "Wow," she said.

"It's good for what ails you," Eagle said.

"Well, I asked for it. Yes, I am feeling better, but just so you know before you start breathing in my ear, not *that* much better. I won't be very good company tonight, and I'm going home early."

"As you wish," Eagle said.

He quickly sautéed some boned chicken breasts and made a cream and tarragon sauce while the rice and vegetables cooked. By the time they sat down with a bottle of wine, Barbara was clearly a little looped, and she drank most of the cabernet. After dinner, Eagle steered her to the sofa before the fireplace in the study, then poured her a brandy.

"I'm a very drunk lady," Barbara said, lifting the snifter to him.

"I think you'd better sleep here tonight," Eagle said. "You shouldn't drive."

"As long as you don't tamper with me," she said.

"I promise."

The file folder was on the coffee table in front of them, and he picked it up. "Barbara, I've got some bad news for you."

"Great," she said, "that's all I need."

"The wire-transfer didn't work."

"Huh?"

"The money isn't in Mexico City. The really bad news is, it isn't in the Caymans, either."

Barbara put her drink on the coffee table and put her face in her hands.

At last, Eagle thought, *I've cracked that seamless surface*. He hadn't wanted it this way; he was half in love with her, and he wanted her to be what she seemed—nothing more. "Did you hear me?" he asked gently.

She shook her head. "I heard you, lover, but it was Greek to me. What on earth are you talking about?"

He took out the copy of the wire-transfer order and read aloud. " 'Dear Sirs: Please wire transfer contents of account 0010022 to account number 4114340, head office, Banco Nacionale, Mexico City. Abracadabra. Voilà.' It's signed Frances B. Kennerly."

Barbara picked up the brandy again and tossed the contents of the glass down her throat. "Ah, the pain is going away," she said. Then she frowned. "What was that you just said?" she asked. She was very drunk now.

"You want me to read it to you again?"

"No, just the last part. Acabra . . . something."

" 'Abracadabra. Voilà.' "

"Where on earth did you hear that?" she asked.

"It's in the fax you sent."

"What fax?"

"The fax I just read to you."

"Is it from Julia? Can't be. Julia's dead."

"No, it's not from Julia."

Barbara helped herself from the brandy bottle. "That's what she always used to say."

"What?"

"Acabadabba—" she broke into giggles. "I can't say it."

"Abracadabra. Voilà."

"That's it! That's what Julia used to say when she was proud of herself, like when she cheated on a test in high school and got an A."

"It was the code for the Cayman account," Eagle said.

"Who Kamen?"

"The bank account in the Cayman Islands."

"Ed, what the hell are you talking about?" She tossed back some more brandy. "No pain," she said. "No pain, no gain, no pain." She looked glassily at her glass. "No brandy, either."

"I think you've had enough of that," Eagle said, taking the glass from her. He was baffled now.

"I think you're right," Barbara said. She crawled across the sofa and laid her head on his shoulder. "When you're right, you're right, Ed."

"You sent the fax, didn't you?" he asked, worried now.

"Just the fax, ma'am," she said, then giggled sleepily.

Eagle turned her face up to him. "You don't know what the fuck I'm talking about, do you?"

"Can't fuck," she replied. "Like to fuck, but can't."

"You're going to bed," Eagle said, getting an arm under her legs and another under her shoulders and lifting her from the couch.

"Going to be sick," Barbara said.

"Oh, no," he whimpered.

45

Ed Eagle sat at his desk with his face in his hands. He had left Barbara asleep in his bed, then had rung Jim at Santacafé and told him she was still unwell, wouldn't be in. He wondered why he himself was in the office this morning, when he wasn't much better off than Barbara. The trouble with getting somebody drunk, he thought, was that you had to get snockered yourself.

His secretary came into the office and placed an envelope on his desk. "By messenger from the D.A.'s office," she said.

Eagle slit open the envelope, and the sound of tearing paper seemed much too loud. "List of witnesses in the matter of New Mexico vs. Willett," it said at the top of the page.

(a) Enrico Alvarez: testimony of whereabouts of defendant at time of crime.
(b) Marcia Evans: testimony of defendant's knowledge of victim James Grafton.

There were other witnesses: Captain Carreras, the medical examiner, a fingerprint expert. It was at the very bottom of the list that the surprise came:

> (f) Monica Collins: testimony on defendant's relationship with victim Julia Willett.

Eagle did not like the sound of that at all. He picked up the phone and called Wolf Willett.

"Wolf, it's Ed. I just got the D.A.'s list of witnesses for the trial, and Monica Collins's name is on it, for testimony about your and Julia's relationship."

"I don't understand," Wolf said.

"Neither do I. I'm about to give Martinez Monica's name for investigation in Mark Shea's death, and now she turns up on his list of witnesses. Tell me as much as you can about your and Julia's relationship with Monica."

"Julia and I met Monica at a benefit for AIDS victims last Christmas at the Eldorado Hotel; the two of them seemed to hit it off. After that, they had lunch often whenever we were in Santa Fe, and a couple of times we got together with her when she was in L.A."

"Did you ever have any arguments or fights with her?"

"No, we got along quite well. Not as well as she and Julia, though."

"Apart from the two occasions when the three of you got into bed, do you think Julia could have been having a sexual relationship with Monica?"

"That never occurred to me, but they certainly were enthusiastic about each other when I was in bed with them—especially Monica. I think she could have been a little in love with Julia."

"Do you think Julia confided in her about personal things?"

"I don't know. Maybe. In some ways, Julia's relationship with me was pretty superficial; maybe she needed somebody to talk to. She didn't seem to have anybody like Monica in L.A."

"We could haul her into a deposition, I guess, but I don't think it's worth the trouble. It sounds as though her testimony would be hearsay, and that would be inadmissible."

"Why would the D.A. call a witness whose testimony he knows would be inadmissible?"

"Never underestimate the stupidity of a prosecutor," Eagle said.

"If you say so, Ed."

"I have to send Martinez a list of our witnesses today. I want to call Hal Berger and Jane Deering."

"Why do you want to call Jane?"

"Because I think she will be a credible witness to your good character, and she can testify about your state of mind since the murders."

"I'm reluctant to do that, Ed, unless you think we really need her."

"I think we do. I don't want to call a lot of witnesses, especially character witnesses; we'll admit the letters we have as evidence for the jury to consider. Hal can testify about Jack's will and the theft of your brokerage accounts, but I want one very personal witness, and Jane is the logical choice for that."

"All right, I'll ask her."

"I also want you to see a psychiatrist I know this week," Eagle said.

"What on earth for?"

"Since Mark Shea is not available to testify, we need someone who can give a rational explanation to the jury of your blackout periods. This is very important, and when the D.A. sees our man on the witness list, he may want you examined by somebody for the state as well, so you'd better be prepared for that. Just tell them both the truth, and you'll be all right." He gave Wolf the name and address of the doctor and the appointment time, then hung up.

Eagle spent the rest of the morning with an associate, sifting through documentary evidence and making up his list of witnesses. By lunchtime he felt ready for trial, and he still had a few days to go. His hangover had not abated, though; he was going to need the hair of the dog at lunch, he reckoned, just to get through the day.

The phone rang.

"Good morning," Barbara said.

"How are you feeling?" he asked.

"Not as bad as I expected," she replied. "Throwing up must have helped. It was sweet of you to get me off work today, but I'm going to go in for lunch."

"If you're feeling up to it."

"How are *you* feeling?"

"I've been better."

"What was all that last night about a fax and the Cayman Islands?"

"It's nothing, forget it."

"I very nearly have. I did have the feeling that I was being grilled about something, though."

"Forget it. There is something I want to ask you, though."

"Shoot."

"When was the very last time you talked to Julia?"

"Last spring, on the phone."

"What did you talk about?"

"Her marriage, my plans when I got out."

"Had you changed your name by that time?"

"No, but I had been thinking about it."

"Did you tell Julia what name you had chosen?"

"We kicked around a few names; Julia liked 'Barbara' best. So did I."

"So she knew your name was going to be Barbara Kennerly?"

"Yes. I wrote her about it after it had been legally changed. Why are you interested in this?"

"I don't want to go into details right now; suffice it to say that Julia took a strong interest in your new name. It looks as though she had planned to decamp with Grafton, and she obtained a passport in the name of Frances B. Kennerly."

There was silence at the other end of the line. "Why Frances?" Barbara asked.

"She had to get hold of a real birth certificate in order to get the passport, and that name was as close as she could come to Barbara Kennerly."

"I see."

"Does this sound like something Julia would do?"

"Yes. From the time we were children, she always seemed to want the things I had. Now, it seems, she wanted Jimmy, and she wanted my name, too. It bothers me about her wanting Jimmy, though."

"I'm sorry if I troubled you."

"That's not what I mean. I can't see her being interested in him for very long, but he could be useful; I bet it was Jimmy who got her the passport."

"It was."

"Jimmy was clever; he knew a lot of dodges, knew how to live on the run. Julia would have used him, then thrown him away when she was finished with him."

"That seems to fit with what I know about her character."

"You know," she said slowly, "I think this tears it with Julia and me. The fact that she would take up with the man who got me sent to prison . . . well, that just about does it. I had always felt a lot of sympathy for Julia, in spite of what she was, but Jimmy Grafton is the last straw. I feel . . . *released*, somehow. Free of her."

"I'm glad of that, Barbara," Eagle said. "It makes it easier for me to feel something for you that I was afraid to feel before. I didn't trust you, I admit that; I thought you might have been mixed up with Julia and Grafton in something. I don't feel that anymore."

"I can't blame you for thinking that," she said. "I'm not sure I deserved better."

"You deserve a lot better."

"I'm glad somebody thinks so."

"Dinner tonight?" he asked.

"Let's make it tomorrow night. I'd like to feel a whole woman again when I see you."

"Plan on staying the night; we've got a lot to talk about."

"I'll look forward to it."

Eagle hung up the phone feeling relieved. He had put his suspicions aside now, and he could find out where this relationship would lead. He felt he knew Barbara Kennerly now. Hannah Schlemmer was gone.

46

The phone rang as Wolf was sitting down to lunch. He had come to dread the telephone lately; there was too much bad news. He answered it anyway.

"Wolf, it's Hal Berger." He sounded excited.

"What's up, Hal?"

"It's back. The money's back."

"Which money?"

"Julia's money—what she stole."

"What do you mean, it's back?"

"It was wire-transferred back to her account; I hadn't closed it yet. The bank called this morning."

"How much?"

"Everything. Three million six hundred thousand and change."

Wolf went limp with relief. "I don't believe it."

"Aren't you pleased about this?"

"Pleased? I'm thrilled! I just don't believe it."

"Well, you can believe it. The only thing is, you can't get your hands on it yet."

"Why not?"

"As far as the bank is concerned, the money belongs in Julia's account, and they have a point. She deposited the money and gave instructions for its transfer. You don't come into it, the way they see it."

"So what do we do?"

"Julia's will is up for probate, and apart from a couple of small bequests to her sisters, you're the principal heir."

"Wait a minute, Hal; you're saying that I'm supposed to inherit the money to get it back? And pay inheritance tax, plus the tax and penalties for closing the retirement accounts early?" The adrenaline was pumping now. There was something he wanted to ask Hal, something about what he had said, but it would have to wait a minute.

"We can sort it out, I think. After all, we've filed a complaint with the police. Ordinarily, I think, they would hold the funds as evidence until Julia came to trial, but since Julia's deceased, there shouldn't be a problem with getting them released to you."

Wolf's telephone rang on the second line; he let the answering machine pick it up.

"What about the tax problems?"

"I've talked with your accountant, and he's going to ask for a meeting with the I.R.S.; he'll explain the circumstances and ask that the tax-free benefits of the retirement accounts be reinstated. If they buy it, it'll be as if nothing had happened, tax-wise."

"That sounds good. What if they don't buy it?"

"Then we'd have to sue, I guess; either that or eat the penalties."

"To tell you the truth, the penalties are starting to look good to me."

"Don't give up yet. Let's wait until your accountants talk with the I.R.S., and then we'll figure out how to proceed."

"All right."

"And don't worry; it's going to be all right."

"Well, I'm glad *something* is going to be all right."

He thanked Hal again and hung up, then let out a howl of triumph. "Not this time, Julia!" he yelled. "You didn't screw me this time!" He called Ed Eagle and told him the news.

"That's teriffic, Wolf. Norris said he'd worked out something with the Cayman banker, but not to say anything to you until everything was complete. You shouldn't have any problem with getting the police to release the funds. I'm not so sure about your I.R.S problem."

"In any case, I'm a hell of a lot better off than I was yesterday, Ed! Now I can afford you!"

Eagle laughed. "By the way, I had a call a few minutes ago from somebody named Spider who says he's a friend of yours."

"Spider was my cellmate in the pokey," Wolf said.

"My secretary took the message; he wouldn't leave a number—said he'd call back."

"I wonder what he wants."

"I'll let you know when I hear from him."

Wolf hung up and was trying to remember something Hal had said, something he'd wanted to ask him about, when he remembered the call that had come in during his earlier conversation. He went into the study and pressed the button on the answering machine.

"Hey, Wolf," a familiar voice said, "it's Spider, your old buddy from the Santa Fe slammer. I need to talk to you, and it's important. I'm on the road right now, but I'll be back late this afternoon. Meet me at the Gun Club out on Airport Road at six, will you? This is real important, buddy, and we don't want to talk about this on the phone." He hung up.

What the hell could Spider want? he wondered. Something told him he probably didn't want to know. Wolf shrugged it off; he wasn't about to show up at a biker bar. Spider probably wanted to be introduced to Madonna, something like that.

47

Wolf began to be worried about the Gun Club as soon as he drove into the parking lot. At least thirty motorcycles were bunched up under a floodlight near the front door, and all of them were Harleys; he was conscious that a black Porsche Cabriolet was out of place here. He nearly turned around and drove away.

Then he caught sight of the paint job on one motorcycle, and that changed his mind. Covering the gas tank was a carefully rendered illustration of a huge spider, which seemed to be hugging the tank. Wolf forced himself through the front door of the place.

He was immediately assaulted by rock music so loud that it knocked him back a step. The bar was dimly lit, and it occurred to him that he hadn't seen so many cowboy hats in one place since he had been on the set of a western at Universal. It was hard to get a clear look at anybody, and he couldn't spot any bikers. Then there was the flash of a strobe to his right and he could see into another room. A sign over the door said, simply, HELL.

Trying to seem confident, Wolf strode over and stood in the doorway, peering into the room, which was lit only by periodic flashes of light.

"What the fuck do you want?" a hoarse voice growled somewhere to his left.

Wolf peered in that direction and waited for the strobe to flash again.

"You lookin' to get your legs broke?" the voice asked again.

The strobe flashed, and Wolf could briefly see a squat, heavily built man dressed entirely in leather, leaning against a bar.

"I'm looking for Spider," Wolf said.

"What the fuck you want with Spider?"

Wolf decided a little aggression might get him further than open cowardice. "None of your fucking business. Just get Spider." On the other hand, he reflected, it could get his legs broken. He leveled his gaze at the man and waited to find out which it would be.

The biker glowered at him for about half a minute, then turned and disappeared into the gloom.

Wolf began to be aware that he was being stared at by half a dozen other people, none of whom he would want to sit next to at a dinner party. Then, as if he were the star of an elaborate magic act, Spider appeared before him in a blinding flash of light.

"Wolf!" the giant screamed. He enfolded Wolf

in a bear hug that lifted him off the floor. "Ol' buddy! Hey, guys, this here is Wolf!"

Suddenly everybody was smiling and nodding in Wolf's direction. It was as if he had entered a cage at the zoo and found the lions all to be kittens. There was an approving rumble from the group, and Wolf found himself participating in a number of odd handshakes, including a couple of high fives.

"This guy knows Madonna!" Spider crowed.

There was a stunned silence from the group, followed by a sound that seemed to Wolf like an expression of religious awe.

"Come on over here and sit down," Spider commanded, draping an arm around Wolf's shoulders and sweeping him across the room. They ended up in a booth with a striking girl who was wearing as much leather as anybody in the room. "This here's Crystal, my old lady," Spider said. "I told you about her in the slammer."

"Right," Wolf said. "How are you, Crystal?"

"Well-fucked," Crystal replied matter-of-factly. "Spider's been a bear ever since he got out."

"When did they let you go?" Wolf asked the biker.

"Couple days after you. When the guy came to, he decided he didn't want to press charges."

"Smart move on his part," Crystal said. "I'd have cut his balls off."

Spider roared with laughter. "She woulda, too."

Wolf didn't doubt it for a moment.

"Listen, Babe," Spider said to Crystal, "me and

Wolf's got to confer here for a little bit. You go bite somebody's ear off, okay?"

Spider got up, and Crystal hipped her way out of the booth. "See ya, Wolf," she said, flashing a broad smile that revealed a couple of gold teeth.

Spider got back into the booth. "You want a beer, Wolf?"

"Sure," Wolf said. His mouth was still dry after his entrance.

"Sally!" Spider roared toward the bar, "gimme a couple Dos Equis!"

Sally waddled over with the beers, finding her way by the light of the strobes. As she came, the music on the jukebox mercifully changed, and Kris Kristofferson started to sing "Help Me Make It Through the Night."

"Shit, I love that song," Spider said, swigging from the longneck bottle. "That one got me through a few nights."

"It's a good one," Wolf agreed, sipping gratefully from the beer bottle.

"Well, now," Spider said, leaning back and spreading his huge arms along the back of the booth, "how you been doin' since you got sprung?"

"Okay, I guess. I go to trial in a few days."

Spider nodded. "Yeah, and you got nothing to worry about with that Indian dude on your side. He's a heavy hitter."

"That's what they say." What the hell was he doing here? What did Spider want?

"You got something else to worry about, though," Spider said gravely. "Something your lawyer can't fix for you."

"What's that?" Wolf asked uneasily.

Spider leaned forward and spoke softly. "There's a contract out on you, Wolf."

Wolf wasn't quite sure he'd heard this correctly. "Say again, Spider?"

"Somebody wants you offed," Spider explained. "I heard about it."

Wolf leaned forward. "Tell me all about this, Spider; start at the beginning."

Spider leaned back again. "Well, y'know, after I got sprung, I needed some fresh air, y'know?"

Wolf nodded encouragingly.

"So me and Crystal and the dudes, we saddled up and headed north. Just blowin' along, y'know?"

Wolf nodded again.

"So, anyway, we're on the way back, and we stop off at Taos for a beer, and I run into this cat from another gang—a biker, y'know? And he starts telling me how somebody offered him this contract on this guy who's in the movies."

"Yeah, yeah," Wolf said, trying to hurry him along.

"Well," Spider said, refusing to be hurried, "I know somebody in the movies, since I met up with you, so I'm interested, and I say, 'Who is this guy they want you to hit?' "

"Go on."

"This dude says it's a guy in Santa Fe, and that interests me; and he says this address, in a place called Wilderness Gate. That ring a bell?"

"It sure does."

"I thought it would. Well, anyway, this is a job

for ten grand, half up front, and the dude is tempted. There's some bikers'll take a contract, y'know, but not this guy; he's never done nothing like that. I mean, he might off somebody in a fight, but he's not into cold-blooded killing."

"Who, ah . . . offered him this job?" Wolf asked.

"A lady, and a hot one, according to this dude," Spider said. "Dressed nice, long legs, nice tits."

"What color was her hair?"

"Blond; out of a bottle, he said, but a good bottle."

Wolf felt dizzy; he gripped the sides of the table to steady him. "Was there anything else about her? Anything else at all you can tell me?"

"Yeah, the top button of her shirt was undone, and she had a flower tattooed on one of her tits."

"I see," Wolf said, wishing the hell he did see. "Anything else?"

"Nah, that's about it," Spider replied. "She was loaded, though; had a lot of the green. Gave him a thousand."

"I thought you said he didn't take the job."

"He didn't. But she gave him a thousand to tell her somebody who would do it."

"Shit," Wolf said.

"Some spic in Santa Fe this dude knew, who did that kind of stuff. He called up this guy, and he said he'd do it, no problem, so he gave her his name, and she took off."

"When did this happen?" Wolf asked.

"This morning, 'bout ten o'clock."

"Where?"

"Up at Espanola, y'know, north of here about twenty miles. There's a bar up there where bikers hang out."

"Who was the guy she was going to see next?"

"He didn't say." Spider leaned forward. "But I'll tell you, Wolf, if I was you, I'd watch my ass."

Wolf nodded. He didn't seem able to speak.

"You got a piece, Wolf?"

"What?"

"A piece—a gun. I can get you something, if you want."

"Yeah, I've got one."

"If I was you, I wouldn't make a move without it," Spider said. "I mean, you could carry a knife, but if this guy's got a piece, that's not gonna do you no good, y'know?"

Wolf nodded. "You've got a point, Spider."

"You want me and some of the guys to, maybe, hang around your house, Wolf?"

Wolf had a bizarre mental picture of a biker behind every tree at Wilderness Gate. "Thanks, Spider, I appreciate the thought, but I don't think so."

"What're you gonna do, Wolf?"

"Well, for a start, Spider," Wolf said with feeling, "I'm going to watch my ass."

48

Ed Eagle was just starting to make fresh pasta when the phone rang. "Sorry, I'd better get this," he said to Barbara. He wiped his hands and picked up the receiver.

"Ed Eagle."

"Ed, this is Wolf."

Wolf sounded stressed. Eagle glanced at Barbara, who was examining a picture closely. "Hi, how are you?" he said, careful to keep his end of the conversation anonymous.

"Not good. You remember, I told you about my cellmate, the biker?"

"Sure, I remember."

"I just saw him; he says somebody has put out a contract on me."

Eagle inhaled sharply, and when he spoke, he was careful to keep his voice neutral. "And did you find what he had to say . . . credible?"

"I did. A woman turned up at a biker bar in Espanola about ten this morning and tried to hire a guy to kill me for ten thousand dollars. He refused the offer but recommended somebody else, a Latino in Santa Fe, who said he'd do the job."

"Was there a name for the person . . . placing the order?"

"No names, but he described her; she was a good-looking blond. Sound familiar?"

"It does." Eagle heaved a sigh of relief.

"Not only that, but she had a flower tattooed on her breast."

Oh, shit, Eagle thought. Then, unaccountably, he remembered something, something from Barbara's apartment.

"I see."

"So, what do we do?"

"What are you doing right now?"

"I'm sitting in my study with the drapes drawn and a gun in my hand."

"I think I had better send somebody over there."

"No, I don't want people slinking around here, protecting me. I'd rather do it myself."

"Under the circumstances, do you think that's wise?"

"I don't care about wise anymore. To tell you the truth, I think I'd really like to shoot somebody."

"Don't start thinking that way," Eagle said. "That's dangerous." He thought for a moment. "Do you mind if I come over there? We ought to discuss this."

"All right."

"I've got something to do first, then I'll be there as soon as I can."

"Fine."

"When I get there, I'll blow the car horn twice, just so you'll know it's me."

"Fine."

"And in the meantime, don't do anything rash."

"I'm not making any promises about that," Wolf replied.

"Pour yourself a stiff drink, and try to relax. I'll be there in less than an hour." Eagle hung up.

"Problems?" Barbara asked.

"You wouldn't believe," Eagle replied. "Come over here and sit down, Babs."

She crossed the room and sat on a barstool at the kitchen counter. "I think I like that—'Babs.'"

He placed a hand on her cheek. "I want to tell you some things and ask you some questions," he said.

"All right."

"First of all, I think I'm in love with you."

She smiled slowly. "Oh," she said weakly. "Well, before you go any further, I think I'd better tell you that I feel the same way about you."

"That's nice to hear," Eagle said. "Now that we've got that out of the way, I have to say some other things to you. If you start to get angry with me, just remember I love you."

"All right," she said. "But I don't think I could get angry right now."

"Good. First, a question: Where were you this morning?"

"At work. I spent the whole morning going over the computer printouts with Jim."

"And Jim would back you up on that?"

"Of course. What are you getting at?"

"Trust me for a minute. Remember back when I didn't trust you?"

"Mmmm, let's see, that was this morning, wasn't it?"

"That's right. Well, during the time I didn't trust you, I behaved badly."

"That's all right."

"You don't understand. I broke into your apartment and searched it."

"What?"

"On New Year's Eve. I left the party, drove back to your place, and turned it over real good."

"Oh," she said, nonplussed. "Did you find anything interesting?"

"Not really. Just a gun."

"A girl has to protect herself."

"It bothers me that you have a gun; I want you to give it to me."

Barbara shrugged. "Okay, if it'll make you feel better."

"It would make me feel a lot better."

"So the only interesting thing about me is my gun?"

Eagle placed a hand on her cheek and kissed her. "Not by a long shot. Oh, there was something else in the apartment."

"What was it?"

"It was tucked into a book called *Beautiful Girlhood*."

"Ah, a book to live by, that. It was my mother's."

"I thought it might be. There was a torn photograph inside."

She nodded. "Yes."

"Of two teenage girls."

Barbara looked away. "Yes. It was taken on Miriam's—Julia's fourteenth birthday. I tore Julia out of the middle."

"The other girl wasn't Julia? But she looked so much like you."

"It was my other sister, Leah."

"Another sister?"

She nodded. "Yes, named after my mother; she's a year younger than I am."

"You never told me you had a younger sister."

She shrugged. "It never came up. Is it important?"

Eagle was thinking hard now. "It may be. There's something I have to know about Leah."

"What's that?"

"Did Leah have a tattoo on her breast?"

Barbara smiled. "Yes. We all did that together— Julia, Leah, and I. It was kind of a lark, right after Julia graduated from high school."

"That's very interesting."

"Why?"

Eagle ignored the question. "Did Leah know Jimmy Grafton?"

"She met him a couple of times with me in New York. Jimmy wanted to get us both in bed together, an idea that I found repellent. What's going on, Ed? Why is this important?"

"Where is Leah now?"

"The last time I saw her she was living in New

York, but when I was released I called her, and the number had been disconnected."

"I think Leah may be in Santa Fe."

"*What?* That's crazy. Why would she be in Santa Fe? Anyway, she'd call me if she were here."

"She wouldn't know, would she?"

"I guess not, now that you mention it. Nobody knew I was coming here, and I couldn't find Leah to tell her."

"What is Leah like?"

"A lot like Julia," Barbara replied. "Julia was Leah's god; she worshiped the ground Julia walked on, wanted to be just like her. Unfortunately."

"Was Leah ever in any trouble?"

Barbara shook her head. "No, but she should have been. She was just lucky, never getting caught at things."

"Is she . . . bright?"

"Too bright for her own good," Barbara said. "*Cunning* might be a better word." She looked at Eagle. "Why do you think Leah might be in Santa Fe?"

"It's too complicated to go into right now. I have to leave, and I don't know if I'll be back tonight."

"Where are you going?"

"To Wolf Willett's, and I'll probably sleep there."

She arched an eyebrow. "I hope I don't have competition from Wolf Willett."

Eagle laughed, then kissed her. "Separate bedrooms, I promise. Why don't you fix yourself some dinner and crawl into my bed? There's always the chance I'll get back early."

She kissed him back. "You're worth the wait, but this business about Leah is worrying me."

"I wish I could explain now, but I have to go. Will you be all right?"

"Sure."

He kissed her again. "See you later."

"I'll count on it."

Eagle got a coat and started out of the house, then stopped. He walked back to his bedroom, opened a bedside drawer, and took out a .45 automatic pistol. He checked the clip, put the gun in his pocket, and left for Wolf's house.

At last, he thought as he drove from Tesuque toward Santa Fe, *this is beginning to make a weird kind of sense.*

49

Wolf sat in the dark, the pistol cradled between his knees, and thought. He was trying to recall his last conversation with Hal Berger, something in that phone call that had nagged at him, and he couldn't remember what.

A sound filtered through the walls of the house, and Wolf froze. What he had heard was the crunch of a car's tires on gravel. Now he heard a car door close. Was it Ed Eagle? No, Ed had said he would honk his horn.

Wolf leapt from his chair and ran through the darkened house toward the kitchen door, working the action of the pistol along the way. He huddled next to the door, pistol at the ready, safety off, and to his horror, he saw the door-knob turn. It was locked, thank God.

He jumped a foot as somebody began hammering on the door. "Wolf?" a voice called out.

"Who is it?" Wolf demanded.

"It's Ed Eagle. Open the door."

Wolf opened the door and stepped back.

"What's going on? Why are all the lights out?" Eagle asked.

"You said you were going to honk your horn when you arrived," Wolf said accusingly.

"I'm sorry, but when I saw the darkened house I didn't know what was going on, so I tried not to make any noise."

"You scared the shit out of me," Wolf said. He was trembling.

"Could you ease the hammer down on that pistol and put the safety on? I'd feel a lot better."

"Sorry," Wolf replied, doing as he was asked. "Come on into the study, and I'll give you a drink." He led the way into the room, switched on a dim lamp, and poured Eagle a large Scotch, then a bourbon for himself. "Sit down," he said, indicating the sofa. He took the wing chair next to it.

"Are you all right?" Eagle asked, sitting down and sipping his drink.

"Yes, I'm all right."

"I'm sorry I took so long to get here, but I had to stop by Bob Martinez's house."

"What for?"

"To report the threat on your life, of course. We can't just let that pass."

"Oh."

"I'm afraid it didn't do a hell of a lot of good. Martinez greeted the news with some skepticism. He did offer to put a guard on your house, but you'd already said you didn't want that."

"Is he going to do anything?"

"What can he do? All we've got to go on is the

Latino hit man. Martinez says there's no such thing as a contract killer in Santa Fe."

"He doesn't believe me, then?"

"Probably not. I think he believes it's some sort of ploy on our part."

"It's Julia's sister, isn't it? Barbara?"

"Yes and no."

"What kind of answer is that?"

"Yes, it's Julia's sister; no, it's not Barbara. I called Jim Arno on the way over here; he was working with her at the restaurant from nine until one. She couldn't have been in Espanola at ten."

"Then what do you mean, it's Julia's sister?"

"Well—"

"Wait a minute!"

"What is it?"

"There's another sister, isn't there?"

"How did you know that?"

"Julia's will. Hal Berger said she had made bequests to her *sisters*—in the plural. I've been trying to remember that all day."

"Yes, there's another sister, name of Leah. Barbara had lost track of her, but she has the tattoo— all three of them did—and she's got to be the answer."

"Maybe to a lot of things."

"I think you're right."

"Did you tell Martinez about her?" Wolf asked.

"No."

"Why not?"

"Because after the reception I got about the

hired killer story, I didn't think it would help to add a third sister to our story."

"I see your point."

"What do you want to do now?"

"About what?" Wolf asked.

"Well, there may be somebody stalking you. Are you just going to sit here with a loaded gun and wait for him?"

Wolf laughed. "I guess that was my plan." His eyebrows went up. "But I've got another idea." He picked up the phone and dialed information. "I don't know why I didn't think about this when I was with Spider earlier this evening." He got the number for the Gun Club, then called and asked for Spider. After a wait, the biker came on the line.

"Yeah, this is Spider."

"Spider, it's Wolf."

"Hey, man."

"Listen, do you think you could find the biker who told you about the hit man?"

"Well, he could still be in Taos. I could try a couple bars up there."

"I'd appreciate it if you'd do that, and if you get hold of him, find out who the guy was that he recommended; get as much information as you can about him."

"Well," Spider said, sounding doubtful.

"What's the problem?"

"Well, we got a kind of honor thing here."

"What are you talking about, Spider?"

"I mean, this dude took the lady's money, you know?"

"What?"

"Well, she trusted him, and he might take that serious."

"How about if I double the money? Then he'd have her thousand and two thousand more from me; would that help?"

"I dunno. Maybe."

"Well, I'd appreciate it if you'd find the guy and learn as much as you can."

"Okay, Wolf, I'll do that for an old cellmate."

"Call me back?"

"As soon as I find out something, one way or the other."

Wolf thanked him and hung up. "Spider's going to see what he can find out," he said to Eagle.

"Unorthodox, but it couldn't hurt," Eagle replied, sipping his Scotch.

The two men sat and chatted desultorily for the better part of an hour. Then the phone rang.

"Wolf, it's Spider."

"Hi, Spider, what did you find out?"

"Well, the dude'll take your offer, and he's named me to collect his money."

"Fine, I've got cash right now. You want me to bring it to you?"

"Not yet. He gave me a name and the place where the guy hangs out—a spic bar over on Agua Fria. I'll check it out first."

"Spider, maybe you'd better just give me the name now, and I'll get the police on it."

"Get serious, Wolf," Spider said sternly. "I'm not handing nobody to the cops. You just sit tight, and I'll look into this, maybe talk to the guy, and get back to you later."

"All right, Spider, whatever you say." He hung up the phone. "I don't believe this," he said to Eagle. "Now I'm hiring bikers to straighten out my life."

"Weirder things have happened," Eagle replied.

Wolf switched on the TV and found a movie on the Albuquerque/Santa Fe station. They settled down to wait for Spider's call.

50

The movie ended at eleven, and the news came on. Both Wolf and Ed Eagle were beginning to nod off.

"Good evening," the newscaster said. "In world news tonight, the Soviet Union has asked Western countries for massive supplies of food and medicines. . . ."

"Wolf," Eagle said, yawning, "I think I'd better stick around here tonight. You mind having an overnight guest?"

"Not at all, Ed. I'd be grateful for the company. I—" Wolf stopped, sat up, and stared at the television screen. Something had caught his ear.

". . . an incident at a Santa Fe bar earlier this evening was described as nothing less than a riot by police. We go now to Nick Evans, our Santa Fe reporter, who is at the scene."

The camera cut to a reporter bathed in a white light. Behind him, a building was on fire. "Just about ten minutes ago, our mobile unit picked up a police call to El Hombre, a bar on Agua Fria catering to a Hispanic clientele. We arrived on the scene just in time to witness a man flying through a plate-glass window. A fight had apparently broken out inside, and the presence of a large number of motorcycles in the parking lot indicated that a gang of bikers was involved. We watched from outside as two patrolmen entered the bar, then beat a hasty retreat and called for reinforcements. Units of the Santa Fe Police Department and the New Mexico State Police arrived shortly, and by that time the building was on fire and people were pouring outside, where they were met by riot-equipped officers.

"About a dozen bikers made it to their motorcycles and roared off down Agua Fria, pursued by police. Another eight bikers were arrested, along with as many Hispanic men who had been in the bar."

The camera cut to previously recorded tape and moved in on four policemen wrestling a man to the ground.

"It's Spider!" Wolf said.

Clearly the four were having trouble hanging on to him, and a moment later they were joined by two more cops. Together they got the biker handcuffed, on his feet, and into a paddy wagon.

"Holy shit," Eagle said.

The reporter continued. "All the arrestees were taken to Santa Fe County Detention Center for the night, and police say they will be arraigned tomorrow morning."

Eagle got up. "Come on," he said.

"Where are we going?"

"To the Santa Fe County Detention Center."

Things were quiet at the jail, and a solitary sergeant was on duty at the booking desk. "Evening, counselor," he said as Eagle approached the desk.

"Evening, Sergeant. I want to confer with a prisoner."

"At this time of night? These ain't regular visiting hours, Mr. Eagle."

"It's urgent," Eagle said. "I'd appreciate it if we could meet now."

"Who's this?" the sergeant asked, nodding at Wolf.

"My colleague, Mr. Willett. He's an attorney."

The sergeant sighed. "Okay, what's the prisoner's name?"

Eagle looked at Wolf, who shrugged. He turned back to the sergeant. "Spider," he said.

"Ah," said the sergeant, running a finger down a ledger. "Herman Albert Willis." He picked up a phone and spoke into it, then hung up. "Room number one, counselor."

Eagle led Wolf down a hallway and into a small room; Wolf recognized it as the one where he had been questioned by the police. They sat down, and a moment later Spider was ushered into the room. The left side of his face was swollen badly.

"Hey, Wolf," Spider said, sticking out a paw.

Wolf shook it. "Spider, are you all right? Do you need a doctor?"

"Nah," Spider said, taking a seat. "It ain't nothing. I caught a nightstick, that's all. The spics never laid a hand on me."

"Spider, this is Ed Eagle."

"Hey, Mr. Eagle!" Spider exclaimed, pumping the lawyer's hand. He looked back at Wolf. "What're you guys doing here?"

"We came to find out what happened," Eagle explained. "We saw something on television."

"Oh, yeah, they was there, all right."

"What happened, Spider?" Wolf asked.

"Oh, we went out there to talk to this guy, Chico, the one who's supposed to waste you."

"Did you find him there?" Eagle asked.

"Oh, sure, he was there. He didn't like it much that I knew about his contract, and he got some of his greasers on me. I whistled up some of my dudes, and it got crazy there for a while."

"Did you find out anything from Chico?" Eagle asked.

"Not much at the bar, but I found out some more when we got here."

"I don't understand," Wolf said.

"The cops put him in the next cell, so we had a chance to talk."

"Did you hurt the man?" Eagle asked.

"Oh, no, he was too far away to reach. I just let him know what was going to happen to him when he got out if he didn't talk to me."

"And what did he have to say?"

"He took the contract, all right. He was in that bar spending the money when I got there."

"What did he say about the woman who hired him?"

"Not much that my biker buddy hadn't already told me."

"Did she give him a name?"

"Jennifer, she said—but she wouldn't tell him her real name, would she?"

"I suppose not," Eagle agreed.

"He was going to do it, though," Spider said. "He was gonna go up to your house tonight, Wolf, after he got drunk enough."

"Jesus," Wolf said, massaging his temples.

"I wouldn't worry about him no more," Spider said. "One of the screws told me they was after him for an armed robbery last month, so he ain't going nowhere. Anyway, after our talk, we agreed that he'd be better off shortchanging the lady than making me mad. We're buddies now." Spider smiled broadly, revealing a missing tooth.

"So it looks like you're safe, Wolf," Eagle said.

Spider spoke up. "I wouldn't say that," he said.

"What do you mean, Spider?" Eagle asked.

"Well, there was something the lady said to Chico," Spider said. "He said she told him that if he couldn't get Wolf dead, well, she'd just have to do him herself."

"I think we've heard enough," Eagle said, rising. "Spider, I'll send somebody from my office down to the courthouse tomorrow morning to represent you at your arraignment."

"That's real nice of you, Mr. Eagle," Spider said, shaking the lawyer's hand again.

"I'll stand bail, if necessary," Wolf said.

"No, you won't," Eagle said sharply. "I'll take care of it; I don't want you associated with this business any further."

"Whatever you say, Ed."

They were driving back to Wolf's house. "I don't get it," Wolf said, shaking his head. "Why would Leah want me dead so much?"

"Well, for one thing, you've screwed her out of the three and a half million dollars Julia stole from you," Eagle replied. "It's obvious that she and Julia and Grafton were in this together, at least in the beginning, because she had the bank account code. She probably checked with the bank in Mexico City, and when the money didn't turn up there, she backtracked to the Caymans and found out that all of it had evaporated. That might have made her a little touchy."

"I see your point," Wolf said.

"She damn near got away with it," Eagle said. "If Russell Norris had arrived at the Cayman bank an hour later, the money would have been in Mexico, and you'd never have seen it again."

"What do you think she's going to do next?" Wolf asked.

"I would have thought that was obvious," Eagle said. "And when we get back to your house, I'm going to get onto Martinez again and see if we can get you some police protection."

"I won't argue with you this time," Wolf said.

Eagle was worriedly glancing in the rearview mirror.

"Ed," Wolf said, "is somebody following us?"

"I'm not sure," Eagle replied. "When we left the house, did you leave your gun there?"

"Yes," Wolf replied.

"Shit," Eagle said. "So did I."

51

As they drove up to his house, Wolf saw a strange car parked near the back door, a four-wheeler. He looked at the house; a shadow moved past the kitchen window. "Do you think we may have a problem, Ed?"

Eagle looked at the car, and his brow furrowed. "It's Barbara's Cherokee."

"Julia's sister?"

"Yes."

"Why would she be here?" he asked.

Eagle switched off his car. "Frankly, I don't know," Eagle said. "I left her at my place, and I thought she'd be in bed by now." He opened the car door. "We'd better find out."

Barbara was sitting at the kitchen table when they entered the house. She looked at Wolf. "Hello," she said.

"Wolf," Eagle said, "this is Barbara Kennerly."

Barbara held out her hand. "Hello, Wolf."

Wolf hesitated, then took it. "How do you do?" he said, rather too formally, but he was nervous.

"Let's go into the study." He led the way; he had left his pistol in the study, and he wanted to be near it. "Can I get you both a drink?" he asked. "I certainly need one." He looked around for the weapon; he was almost certain he had left it on the table next to the phone, but it was not there.

"Scotch for me," Eagle said, sitting down on the sofa.

Wolf poured a large single-malt over ice and handed it to the lawyer. "What can I get you, Barbara?" he asked.

"Vodka on the rocks, please." She sat down next to Eagle and placed her large handbag on the coffee table.

Wolf eyed the handbag nervously, then reached for the bottle of Smirnoff resting on the butler's tray with the other liquors.

"Do you have any Stolichnaya?" Barbara asked. "I'm sorry to be picky."

"I think I have some on ice," Wolf said. He opened the cupboard that contained the glasses and the small refrigerator, took a bottle of the Russian vodka from the freezer, poured the drink, then fixed himself a bourbon.

"Cheers," Eagle said, raising his glass.

The three of them drank, and Wolf sat down in a chair. "Well," he said, "I suppose we would have met sooner or later."

"I suppose," Barbara said.

There was an uncomfortable silence. Wolf noticed that Eagle seemed to be looking around for something. His gun, probably.

"Well, here we are," Eagle said inanely.

"Yes," Wolf said. He eyed the fireplace tools; the poker would make a nice weapon. Suddenly he wasn't nervous anymore. In fact, he felt quite happy to be here having a drink with these two nice people. He found himself starting to like Barbara, even if she was Julia's sister.

For no apparent reason, Eagle let out a laugh.

"What?" Barbara said.

"Nothing," Eagle replied. He took another pull at his drink.

Wolf remembered that he had wanted to know why Barbara was here, but it didn't seem to matter anymore.

"I didn't think you'd come home tonight," Barbara said to Eagle, as if she had read Wolf's mind, "so I went back to my place."

"Swell," Eagle said, then let out a high-pitched giggle.

Wolf began laughing, too.

"What's so funny?" Barbara asked.

Eagle giggled again. "I don't know."

Nobody seemed to have anything to say for a moment. Eagle finally broke the silence. "We've just been to the county jail to visit a biker," he said, giggling again.

Wolf joined him in laughter.

"What?" Barbara responded.

"I kid you not. Lovely guy, name of Spider. He'd just burned down a bar on Agua Fria." He burst out laughing.

"That doesn't sound like your kind of case, Ed," she said.

"Not normally," Eagle replied, "but Spider had been on a little mission for Wolf and me when he visited the bar."

Wolf tried very hard not to laugh at this.

"You've lost me," she said.

"I guess it's time to tell you about this," Eagle said, trying to control himself. "Spider and Wolf were cellmates for a night, when Wolf was arrested. He contacted Wolf today and said he'd heard a contract was out on Wolf's life." He put a hand over his mouth and tried to stop laughing.

Wolf did the same. He felt both tired and happy, but he couldn't think of a reason to be happy. After all, at least one of Julia's sisters wanted to kill him. He wondered which one.

"This business gets curiouser and curiouser," Barbara said. "Why would somebody want to kill Wolf?"

"I think the most important thing at this point is *who* would want to kill him," Eagle replied. He began giggling again.

"All right," she said, "who? And stop that!"

"From the description we got, it sounds like Leah."

Barbara stared at Eagle disbelievingly. "What are you talking about?" she demanded.

"I haven't quite got it all worked out yet, but I think Leah is a major presence in what has been going on here."

"But Leah is why I'm here," Barbara said.

"What are you talking about?" Wolf asked. He found the situation wildly funny.

"Well, when I got home tonight, the phone was ringing. It was somebody named Monica Collins."

Eagle looked at her. "Monica Collins called *you?*" He didn't laugh this time.

"Yes, I—"

"You know Monica Collins?"

"No, I'd never even heard of her."

"Why did she call you?"

"I'm trying to tell you, if you'd just stop interrupting me."

"I'm sorry; go ahead."

"She said Leah is in Santa Fe, and that Leah asked her to call me with a message."

"And what was the message?"

"Leah wanted me to meet her here."

Eagle burst out laughing again, and Wolf joined him. "Leah is coming *here?*" he finally managed to say.

"That was the message," Barbara replied, looking disgustedly at both of them. "And if you two don't stop this idiotic laughter, I'm leaving!"

"Look, Babs," Eagle said, trying to control himself, "I can't back this up—not yet, anyway—but I'd be willing to bet that one of two people killed Julia, Grafton, and Jack Tinney. Probably Mark Shea, too. One of my candidates is Monica C̶ but my favorite is your little sister, Leah."

voice was a lot like Barbara's, but it hind them. "That's not a bad

ned and looked toward

the door. A woman stood there holding what appeared to Wolf to be his pistol.

"Not a terrific guess," she said, "but not bad."

Wolf was the first to speak. His voice, when it came out, was cracked and hoarse and weak. "Julia," he said.

52

You mean Leah, don't you?" Eagle said, looking the tall woman up and down. He giggled.

"No," said Barbara, slumping back in her chair, "it's Julia."

"That was going to be my next guess," Eagle said.

"I don't know why you think this is funny!" Barbara nearly shouted. "She's got a gun!"

"I don't know, either," Eagle said. "It shouldn't be funny, but it is."

Wolf was no longer amused, but simply numb. He sat unmoving in the chair and stared at his wife. "Where the hell have you been?" he asked, as if she'd merely stayed out all night.

Monica Collins stepped into the room. "At my house, mostly," she said.

Keeping the gun out in front of her, Julia walked to Wolf's chair, took him by the arm, stood him up, and seated him next to Eagle on the sofa. Then she sat down in the chair. "Now," she said, looking at her watch, "you should just about be over the giggles. I think maybe Wolf already is."

"Pardon?" Eagle said. He seemed to be placidly accepting the presence of the gun.

"It's the effect of Mark's drug," she replied.

"What drug?" Wolf asked.

"The name is too long for me to handle," Julia said, crossing her legs, "but it very quickly instills a euphoria, followed by a kind of malleability. It's a hypnotic, you see. Mark found out about it in Mexico, and he used it with some of his patients. I don't think the A.M.A. would have approved, but it helped him hypnotize patients quickly." She looked at Barbara. "You don't seem too euphoric, Sis," she said, looking at Barbara's glass. "What are you drinking?"

"Vodka," Barbara replied. "I'm beginning to feel a little funny, too."

"You damn well should be. I spiked every bottle."

"So Leah was the one in bed with Grafton and Jack," Eagle said.

"Right, Mr. Eagle; you really do have a quick mind, don't you?"

"Not quick enough," Eagle said. He wasn't laughing anymore.

"What happened that night?" Wolf asked, not sure he wanted to know the answer. He wanted to run from the house, but he didn't seem able to marshal the energy.

"You don't remember any of it?" Julia asked.

"No," Wolf replied.

"Well, Wolf, you were the life of the party. Mark brought the drug over, and everybody had some, except Mark and me. Mark felt that, as a control, he shouldn't take it, and I just tossed my dose. Everybody else was flying, though."

"Please tell me what happened," Wolf said. His own voice seemed to him to be coming from somewhere else in the room.

"Well, with only a little nudging from me, both Grafton and Jack got interested in Leah, and they adjourned to a bedroom."

"What were Grafton and Leah doing here?" Barbara asked.

"Oh, Grafton—that little shit—and Leah turned up in L.A. not long after he'd broken jail; he'd looked up Leah in New York and snowed her into coming with him. They rang me up and invited me to lunch; Jimmy had this thing about wanting to write a movie, and he wanted to meet Wolf. I fixed that, and low and behold, Jimmy got his movie contract. But that wasn't enough for Jimmy Grafton. He started to hit on me and ask a lot of questions about what Wolf was worth."

"That sounds like Jimmy," Barbara said. "Nothing was ever enough for him."

"Right, sweetie," Julia said. "He was getting to be a real pain in the ass, but I played along with him."

"Where was Leah supposed to be in all this?" Barbara asked.

"In the lurch, I guess. I figured she deserved it, if she was stupid enough to be taken in by somebody like Jimmy Grafton."

"I was stupid enough to be taken in by Jimmy Grafton," Barbara said.

"Poor baby," Julia replied soothingly. "You sure were, and you had to pay for it. So it was Leah's turn. I'm sure she would have learned something from the experience."

"Whose idea was stealing the money?" Eagle asked.

"Mine," she replied, "but I let Jimmy think it was his. He got us passports, and we were all ready to go, he thought."

"You used my name," Barbara said.

"A whimsical touch," Julia said. Then she frowned. "How did you know about that?"

Barbara said nothing.

"When did you and the others come to Santa Fe?" Wolf asked.

"Right after you did. I chartered a Lear out of Van Nuys. We ran into Jack at the airport—he was just coming back from Puerto Vallarta, drunk, so I got him aboard, too. I couldn't let him get away after seeing me with Leah and Grafton, even if he was drunk."

"So what happened that night?" Eagle asked. "You keep changing the subject." His voice was very quiet now.

"Well, when the initial effects of the drug had passed, Mark left, the Three Mouseketeers hopped into bed, and I hypnotized Wolf. It was easy, just like Mark said it would be. That seemed a good time to finish the evening."

"Who finished it?" Wolf asked.

"Baby, I tried to get you to do it, but even

hypnotized, you couldn't handle it; you kept dropping that beautiful shotgun. It's like everything else; you want something done properly, you have to do it yourself. So I went down to the guest bedroom and started shooting. I got Jimmy first—he was the most dangerous—then Leah. Jack just stood up in bed with his back to the wall and stared at me, glassy-eyed, like a stuffed teddy bear, while I reloaded and put one into him. Then I put Wolf to bed, so he'd be there when Maria found the bodies the next morning. I wanted him alive to take the blame."

"Why, Julia, why?" Wolf asked pathetically.

"Had to be done," Julia said, "once Jimmy and Leah walked in and screwed everything up. You see, I was still wanted in New York for a little thing I got involved in there, and Leah knew it. That meant Jimmy Grafton knew it, too, so I had to get everybody together and finish it all at once. Then I was free to fly."

"So why didn't you fly?" Eagle asked. "You had the money; everybody was dead but Wolf."

"Things didn't go quite the way I'd planned," Julia said. "First, Wolf wakes up the next morning and, none the wiser, gets in his airplane and takes off for L.A. Then the local law identifies Jimmy and Leah as Wolf and me. *That* was one thing I hadn't planned on, but at least it made me dead, and that was wonderful."

"So *then* why didn't you run?" Barbara asked.

"I was worried about Mark," Julia replied. "He could put me on the scene that night. But Mark turned out to be surprisingly helpful—for a while, at least. When Wolf turned up at Mark's place—I was there that night—he hypnotized Wolf, and when he heard Wolf's version of events, he simply erased those thoughts from his memory. Mark was acting out of kindness, I think, but even though Wolf's story was pretty garbled, once Mark heard what he had to say under hypnosis, Mark became a danger to me. Not at first, but after a while, when he started to figure things out and get attacks of conscience. Then Mark had to go."

"You're breathtaking, Julia," Eagle said.

"Why, thank you, Mr. Eagle," Julia said, beaming at him.

"So why didn't you run after you killed Mark?"

"Well, I thought it would be a good idea if I stuck around until Wolf was tried. He'd be convicted, of course, and then I could travel wherever I wanted, secure in the knowledge that the police wouldn't be looking for anybody else. I moved in with Monica, and poor sweet Monica believed me when I told her that Wolf had killed everybody else and wanted to kill me. She was very helpful indeed."

"Julia," Monica said, her voice trembling, "how could you do that to me?"

"Oh, shut up, Monica," Julia replied. "I'll get to you in a minute." Monica was standing behind the sofa now.

"Amazing," Eagle said.

She looked at Eagle. "But you turned up, counselor," she said bitterly, "and I began to think that you might get Wolf off."

"Is that when you tried to hire somebody to kill Wolf?"

"No," Julia said, "that was dear old Monica's doing."

"I'm puzzled," Wolf said. "Does Monica have a flower tattoo like yours and Barbara's?"

"Yes, she does," Julia said. "For some months, now; Monica loves me so, but she is incredibly stupid."

"I'm sorry, Julia," Monica said. "I was only trying to help."

Julia turned and looked at the blond. "Monica, I told you to shut up." Julia raised Wolf's pistol and casually fired a shot into the woman's chest. Monica flew backward and disappeared behind the sofa.

Now it became very quiet in the room.

Eagle spoke first. "You're not planning to leave anybody alive here, are you, Julia?"

"That's right, Mr. Eagle, except for my little sister; she's coming with me. But there's something I want to know first. Where's the money? It isn't in the Cayman account, and they wouldn't tell me where it had gone."

"It's back where it belongs, Julia," Eagle said. "You waited too long to run."

Julia glared at the lawyer. "I guess you had something to do with that, huh?"

"It was my pleasure," Eagle said.

She turned to Wolf. "Listen to me, Wolf. You're very relaxed, and you want to go to sleep now. Very relaxed; just let your head fall. That's it, just go to sleep."

Wolf didn't try to fight it; sleep began to swim up at him. He fell down a deep well.

Eagle tried to move, but couldn't. Since Julia had shot Monica Collins, he had been very frightened, but he remained perfectly calm. It must be the effect of the drug, he thought. Still, his mind was clear.

Julia smiled. "Now Eagle goes. Then poor Wolf, terribly upset at what he's done, puts one in his brain. A neat murder-suicide, don't you think? And I don't even have to wait around for him to be tried. I think the authorities will buy it, since Wolf already has an undeserved reputation for blowing people away. I go public, explain to the police that I've been hiding because I was afraid Wolf would try to kill me, and suddenly I'm a rich widow. Wherever the money is, it's mine, and so are this house and the one in Bel Air and all the rights to Wolf's and Jack's films. Pretty neat, huh?"

Eagle waited with interest for Barbara's reply.

"I need a cigarette," Barbara said, reaching for her handbag. She rummaged around inside.

"After that," Julia said to Barbara, "it's you and me, babe. We can go anywhere we like." She stood up and pointed the pistol at Eagle.

"Julia," Barbara said.

Julia stopped and looked at her.

"Do you really think that I would sit here and watch you kill everybody, then just follow you off into the sunset? I wouldn't go to the toilet with you."

Eagle liked that answer.

"Well, sweetie," Julia said, swinging the gun around to point at Barbara, "I'm sorry you feel that way, but this is the only alternative."

"Wrong," Barbara said, her hand still in the pocketbook. The handbag exploded, and Julia flew backward into the big leather chair, which skidded a few feet, then came to rest against the paneling. The middle of her chest was a mess.

"Close work," Eagle said admiringly. "That little short-barreled thing is good for close work. I sure am glad I didn't take it away from you."

Barbara removed the smoking revolver from her handbag and placed it on the coffee table, then fell back in her chair, her hands over her face. "Please tell me there was nothing else I could do," she said.

Eagle still could not make his body move, but he couldn't take his eyes off Julia, either. Julia still held the pistol, and Eagle watched with rapt attention as she began to raise it again. "Barbara," he said.

"Ed, please give me a minute," she replied her face still in her hands. "I've just killed my sister."

"Not quite," Eagle replied. Julia had the pistol up now and pointed at Barbara. "Please shoot her again," Eagle said, with all the urgency he could muster.

Barbara took her hands away from her face as Julia fired. The chair next to Barbara's head exploded, and she jumped a foot.

Julia's pistol clattered onto the hearth. She looked at Eagle with something like hatred, then her eyes rolled back in her head.

"Never mind," Eagle said.

Barbara sat trembling in her chair for a moment. "Ed," she said finally, "you're stoned out of your mind, aren't you?"

"I believe I am," Eagle agreed. "Aren't you?"

"No." She sighed. "Julia said she spiked every bottle, but she didn't get to the Stolichnaya in the refrigerator."

"Oh," Eagle said.

Wolf woke up on the sofa in the study, feeling a little fuzzy, but refreshed. There was a murmur of voices in the house. He sat up and looked over the back of the sofa. There was a lump of some sort on the floor with a sheet over it. He got his feet on the floor, then tried to stand up, but he didn't make it the first time; he simply wobbled and sat down heavily again.

From the sitting position, he could see another lump in the chair next to him, again with a sheet covering it. There was a puddle of blood on the hearth next to the chair. The night began to come back to him.

"Wolf?" Eagle's voice came from the doorway.

Wolf turned and looked at him. "What happened?" he asked.

"What's the last thing you remember?"

Wolf thought. "I remember Julia. And we were laughing a lot. I can't remember why. I must have dreamed Julia."

Eagle came and sat down next to him. "It wasn't a dream," he said. "More of a nightmare."

Wolf nodded at the chair. "Is that Julia?"

"Yes," Eagle replied.

"Who's the other one?" Wolf asked.

"Monica Collins. She had been hiding Julia since the killings. She's the one who tried to have you killed."

Wolf nodded. He felt much as he had the morning after the first killings, but more lighthearted, somehow. "Why am I so happy?" he asked.

"The drug, partly," Eagle said. "I'm pretty happy myself; but I think it's more than that."

"It's over, isn't it?"

"It's over, Wolf."

Wolf began to cry.

Eagle put his arms around Wolf and held him.

It was very late before Eagle got back to his house with Barbara. At the front door, he picked her up and carried her across the threshold, then kissed her.

"Now what was *that* all about?" she asked, her arms around his neck.

"Fella does that in Santa Fe, girl has to marry him; that's Santa Fe Rules."

Barbara frowned. "Mama said she would come back to haunt me if I ever married a man who wasn't Jewish."

Eagle kissed her again. "Boy, have I got news for you," he said.

Epilogue

Jane Deering sat in the car and watched the entrance to the executive offices of Centurion Studios.

Sara squirmed in the backseat. "What's taking Wolf so long, Mom? He's been in there over an hour." Flaps was asleep, her head in the little girl's lap.

"It's business, honey; important business."

"What's it about?"

"It's about making a movie. Wolf has to convince some people that he can direct a movie."

"But Wolf makes movies all the time, doesn't he?"

"Yes, but he's always been the producer, remember? You know the difference between a producer and a director, don't you?"

"Sure. You think I'm dumb or something?"

"Well, this is the first time that Wolf has wanted to direct, and he has to get these people to give him the money to make the movie."

"Oh." Sara poked her mother in the back. "Here he comes," she said.

Jane looked up to see Wolf coming down the front steps. He wasn't smiling.

Wolf got into the car. "I'm sorry to keep you both waiting so long," he said. "I had a pretty tough meeting."

"What happened?" Jane demanded. "Are they going to finance the deal?"

"Maybe," Wolf said, "but there's an important condition."

"What is it? Is it something you can't live with?"

"Apparently they don't trust me to shoot this on my own; they're insisting I take on a partner."

"Well, is it somebody you hate?"

"No, I get to pick the partner."

"Then what's the problem?"

"You want to make this picture with me? You want to be my partner?"

Jane flung her arms around his neck. "Oh, you bet I do!" she yelled.

"Then there's no problem," Wolf said. "No problem at all."

Flaps lifted her head and grinned at everybody.

Acknowledgments

I would like to thank Brian Dennehy for suggesting the title of this book, and, for (sometimes inadvertently) assisting with the research, Steven and Barbara Bochco, Judy Tabb, Pitts Carr, Mark and Winanne Sutherland, Ted and Barbara Flicker, Bob and Pat Eggers, Doug Preston and Christine and Selene Gibbons, John Ehrlichman and Christie Peacock, Marcia Stamell, Ellen Windham, Landt and Lisl Dennis, Pat and Michael French, Ed Zuckerman, Bettina and Sandy Milliken, Sharon and Bob Woods, Jennifer Dennehy, and Melody Miller.

I am, once again, grateful to my editor, Ed Breslin, my publisher, Bill Shinker, my London publisher, Eddie Bell, and all their colleagues at HarperCollins for their hard work on this book.

I want to express my particular gratitude to my agent, Morton Janklow, his top associate, Anne Sibbald, and to all the people at Janklow & Nesbit for their continued enthusiasm and support over the past ten years.

Finally, I must apologize to the Irish veterinarian Wilf Woollett for once again mangling his name.

Author's Note

I am happy to hear from readers, but you should know that if you write to me in care of my publisher, three to six months will pass before I receive your letter, and when it finally arrives it will be one among many, and I will not be able to reply.

However, if you have access to the Internet, you may visit my website at *www.stuartwoods.com*, where there is a button for sending me e-mail. So far, I have been able to reply to all of my e-mail, and I will continue to try to do so.

If you send me an e-mail and do not receive a reply, it is because you are among an alarming number of people who have entered their e-mail address incorrectly in their mail software. I have many of my replies returned as undeliverable.

Remember: e-mail, reply; snail mail, no reply.

When you e-mail, please do not send attachments, as I *never* open these. They can take twenty minutes to download, and they often contain viruses.

Please do not place me on your mailing lists for

funny stories, prayers, political causes, charitable fund-raising, petitions, or sentimental claptrap. I get enough of that from people I already know. Generally speaking, when I get e-mail addressed to a large number of people, I immediately delete it without reading it.

Please do not send me your ideas for a book, as I have a policy of writing only what I myself invent. If you send me story ideas, I will immediately delete them without reading them. If you have a good idea for a book, write it yourself, but I will not be able to advise you on how to get it published. Buy a copy of *Writer's Market* at any bookstore; that will tell you how.

Anyone with a request concerning events or appearances may e-mail it to me or send it to: Publicity Department, Penguin Group (USA) Inc., 375 Hudson Street, New York, NY 10014.

Those ambitious folk who wish to buy film, dramatic or television rights to my books should contact Matthew Snyder, Creative Artists Agency, 2000 Avenue of the Stars, Los Angeles, CA 90067.

Those who wish to make offers for rights of a literary nature should contact Anne Sibbald, Janklow & Nesbit, 445 Park Avenue, New York, NY 10022. (Note: This is not an invitation for you to send her your manuscript or to solicit her to be your agent.)

If you want to know if I will be signing books in your city, please visit my website, *www.stuart woods.com*, where the tour schedule will be published a month or so in advance. If you wish me to do a book signing in your locality, ask your favorite bookseller to contact his Penguin representative or the Penguin publicity department with the request.

If you find typographical or editorial errors in my book and feel an irresistible urge to tell someone, please write to David Highfill at HarperCollins Publishers, 10 East 53rd Street, New York, NY 10022. Do not e-mail your discoveries to me, as I will already have learned about them from others.

A list of my published works appears in the front of this book and on my website. All the novels are still in print in paperback and can be found at or ordered from any bookstore. If you wish to obtain hardcover copies of earlier novels or of the two nonfiction books, a good used-book store or one of the online bookstores can help you find them. Otherwise, you will have to go to a great many garage sales.